5:30 BUS TO CLARKSVILLE

Polly Ward McVicker

PAGE PUBLISHING, INC.
New York, NY

First originally published by Page Publishing, Inc. 2014

ISBN 978-1-63417-164-9 (pbk)
ISBN 978-1-63417-165-6 (digital)

Printed in the United States of America

CHAPTER 1

I T WAS ONE OF THOSE RARE AUTUMN days that reminds one of the carefree days of summer. The sun was high in the sky, and the air was warmer than the date on the calendar indicated that it should be. Summer wasn't ready to step aside for autumn to arrive. So instead of the crisp, colorful days of fall, Indian summer appeared. There was a lazy warm sun in the sky, and it set the mood for those lucky enough to be outside to bask in the brief reappearance of summer.

A day like this at Ocean Beach was not wasted. Bicycles became visible on the boardwalk, ridden by vacationers who, only a few days ago, had huddled against the wind. Joggers moved steadily at their own paces, trying to recapture their strides achieved during the laborsome training of summer. A few skaters on Rollerblades weaved among those people who strolled leisurely in the warm sun. Even the cries of the seagulls did not interrupt the tranquil scene. It was only when the gulls vied for a scrap of food that the birds were noticed by those who were walking along the beachfront. Several summer vendors had opened their businesses, hoping to attract a few of the strolling customers. And…the smells of summer returned to add their presence to the scene…french fries with a vinegar topping, freshly popped caramel corn, hotdogs frying on the grill, and crab cakes bursting with flavor… the aromas added to the circus atmosphere. Parents sat on the boardwalk benches and watched as their small children played in the sand, trying to build the last sand castles of the year. Some teenagers had tied a piece of rope to the volleyball standards and had organized a pickup match. No one questioned why the kids weren't in school; it was too pretty outside to be sitting at a desk inside. A few guys were throwing a football around, trying to impress some girls who they hoped were watching their athletic efforts.

The beach had also attracted its share of sun seekers. There were about thirty different clusters of people lazing in the sand, watching the waves crash along the shore. Several plovers were at water's edge, watching to see what the water might bring them to eat. Even the gulls stood at attention, waiting for a handout from the beachgoers.

"Sami! Sami! Watch out for the lady!"

Four-year-old Samantha chased after the beach ball as it blew in the soft breeze. Her golden curls bounced as she raced after the ball. It had rolled in the direction of a young girl sitting quietly on a beach towel. She appeared to be lost in her thoughts and did not notice that a spritely, young cherub was racing toward her. Just as the ball approached the teenager, a gust of wind lifted it into the air. But it was too late for the spritely four-year-old to change directions. She fell before she collided with the girl, but sand flew everywhere, covering the girl and her towel with a light coating of the fine, gritty material.

"Are you all right?" The girl shook off the sand and stood up to help the little girl back to her feet.

"Samantha, come here!"

Sami walked slowly toward her father who sat on a blanket a few yards down the beach. Her head was bent slightly down, and her bottom lip began to quiver as she anticipated her father's anger.

"Look at you," her dad laughingly said as he brushed sand from the child's head. "You know better than to kick sand on people. You must be more careful. Come on. Let's go get the ball, and tell the girl you are sorry."

Sami's mood brightened immediately. She skipped across the sand as John, her father, went to retrieve the ball. The young girl on the towel was now sitting, dusting sand off her suitcases and shoes.

"Hi there."

"My daddy says to tell you I'm sorry. Did the ball hit you?"

"No. I don't think that it would have hurt much. The ball is so big and full of air. Did you find it?"

"I was chasing after the ball and *swoosh…*" Samantha waved her hands high in the air, pretending she was the ball dancing in the wind. "The ball flew away and I fell in the sand and the ball is gone and…*Oh!* You've got sand in your hair."

"That's OK. Did you get your ball?"

"My daddy went to get it. He can run fast. My name is Sami, and…*Oh!* You're the pancake lady!"

"The *who*?"

"Daddy! Daddy! It's the pancake lady!" Sami was calling to her dad as he approached with the elusive beach ball.

"It's the pancake lady. She brought us pancakes this morning for our breakfast. Did you make them? They were so good."

"My name is Debbie. And what is your name?"

"I'm Sami, and that is my dad."

John Webster had now joined the twosome. Sami had flopped down on the towel next to her new friend. John Webster recognized the girl as their waitress in the restaurant that morning.

"Samantha, introduce me to your new friend."

"Daddy! Daddy! It's Debbie, the pancake lady!"

"It's nice to meet you, Debbie. Samantha, you shouldn't be bothering this young lady. But I believe that you did serve us our breakfast this morning. Aren't you the waitress at the Green Frog?" John continued to refer to the girl as a young lady although she looked very young to him.

"Today was my last day." And then, as if to announce that the conversation was over, the girl lay back down on the towel, turned her back to John and his daughter, and dismissed the group with her actions.

Samantha and her father walked slowly across the sand as Debbie watched from her beach towel. She was furious with herself that she had given her correct name to the little girl but was pleased with herself that she had caught her mistake before she had given her full name to the older man. She had given her entire name to the restaurant when she applied for a job, but misspelled her last name to confuse any inquiries. She just needed to get away from here and have some time to contemplate her next move. She hoped that she had not aroused any suspicions and that after a few moments, the older man would forget all about the beach ball incident.

A young man, sitting on the beach a few yards away, laughed at the near collision between the little girl and the teenager. Was something stirring in his head? How did he get here, on this beach? Did he have a little girl? He looked at his hands, especially the ring on his finger. What did the initials ME represent? The ache in his head was deafening, and he put his head in his hands. Why did he have no memory of a trip to the beach? How long had he been here? Why couldn't he remember anything except this morning? What was his name? The young man was so immersed in his thoughts that he did not hear the young girl approach. Sami stood there for a few moments, just staring at the man who had been sleeping on the sand.

"Don't you feel good?" Sami almost whispered as she moved closer to the man. "My daddy says if you don't feel good, you should lie down and try to sleep. He says a good dream will fix anybody."

"Your daddy is right. A good dream will fix anybody. I was just sitting here watching the boats. I really liked boats when I was a little boy. Do you like boats?"

"Samantha, come here and leave the man alone. I'm sorry if she bothered you. She can be too friendly at times. Tell the man that you are sorry you interrupted his thoughts."

"She didn't interrupt anything. She's a very pretty little girl."

John Webster took his daughter's hand and slowly started across the sand.

Sami stopped and waved at the man as he sat down on the blanket. He stared blankly at the water and the passing boats. He had hoped that the man might have recognized him, or at least called him by name. How long could he stay here on the sand? As he attempted to stand up, a piece of paper dropped from his shirt pocket. It was a bus ticket for Clarksville. It lay in the sand before the man picked it up and examined it carefully. Did he know someone in Clarksville? Was this his home? Did he have family there? Where was Clarksville? Slowly, he collected his thoughts; he must stay here on the beach, and in a few hours, he would try to find the bus station. Perhaps if he exercised a bit, he would feel better. He stood up and weaved his way across the beach. It took all his energy to walk a few steps in the sand.

Jim Sterling quickly grabbed the man's arm and eased him down on his blanket. "I think you've had too much to drink. Why don't you sit here with me for a while? Did you sleep on the beach last night? You really have a lot of sand all over."

Putting up no resistance, the stranger looked up at his friend and cautiously surveyed his new friend. His pants appeared to be the bottom half of a uniform. And then he spied a gun tucked in a holster, strapped to the man's back. Although still a bit dizzy, the man decided to say as little as possible.

"Are you feeling better, buddy? I'm Jim Sterling. Can I take you somewhere or get you something?"

"No, just let me rest for a few moments. I'm going to catch a bus to…" He had to pause for a few moments to recall the place that was written on the ticket that he had found a few moments ago, "To Clarksville."

"I'm going to catch the five-thirty bus to Clarksville myself. Why don't we just sit here on the beach until time to go to the bus station? I don't know where it is, but we can find it together." But the young fellow who had staggered into his life was soundly sleeping on the blanket.

"Is your friend ill? Do you need some help with him?" Ben Somers approached the duo with a concerned look on his face.

"I've never met him before now. He just stumbled into this area. I thought that maybe he had been drinking, but I can't smell anything!"

"I don't see any bruises or contusions on him." Ben examined the sleeping fellow carefully, being very cautious not to wake him. "He really just looks exhausted. Maybe it's best if he just sleeps for a while."

"We're both going to Clarksville on the five-thirty bus, so I'll just let him sleep here until time to catch our ride. But thanks for your offer to help."

Ben reached into his pocket and pulled out a bus ticket. He closely examined the printing and saw that he too was scheduled to be on the five-thirty bus to Clarksville. "Looks like we're going to be traveling together. I'm on the same bus. I'll just sit here with you and wait. I'm Ben Somers." He offered his hand to his new friend.

"Jim Sterling." The two men shook hands and settled down on the blanket. "I'm glad you're going our way. I might need some help getting this gentleman to the bus."

Ben had noticed the outline of a gun in the holster, but he said nothing. The two men spent their time discussing passing boats, the gulls, the beautiful weather, etc. No one spoke of the gun.

Kate Connelly and Clint Rogers were also sitting on the beach waiting until time to board the bus. It was very easy to tell that these two were in love. They were sitting close together on the sand and holding hands. Periodically, Kate would whisper something into Clint's ear, or he would put his arm around her shoulder and give her a hug. But it was not a romantic scene. Kate was a beautiful girl who was struggling to hold back her tears. She turned her back on the rest of the beach and faced Clint.

"I won't give you up. You mean too much to me. But I know that Jay will do anything to protect his good name."

"Are you sure that the man you saw was a private detective?" he answered her, trying to reassure her that everything would be all right. "After all, it was just a man sitting in a car in front of the cottage."

"Yes, but I left out the back door."

"Did Erin see you leave? Did you leave her a note?"

"I think she saw us, but if by chance she didn't, she will see that my suitcase is gone when she checks the bedroom. I didn't want to wait around in case she came to the door."

"We'll be in Clarksville tonight and then it's on to Nebraska. No detective will find us unless we want to be found." Clint looked lovingly at Kate. "It will be so much easier after you've told your family and friends. It will be official. The wedding is called off, and we can start making plans."

"I don't think Jay will ever make it easier. He has talked about getting married since we were in high school, and he was furious when I went away to college. He has a very controlling personality; you know, local boy makes good and thinks that he can manipulate everything and everyone."

Before Clint could answer, his gaze went to the boardwalk. Walking down the ramp to the beach were two state policemen, accompanied by a uniformed officer from Ocean Beach. It was easy to detect that they were on the beach on official business. They stopped for a few moments to look at a picture that the local officer was carrying. Then the men began to scan the beach, looking for something or someone.

The carefree mood that had enveloped the beach quickly changed. The conversations became mute, and everyone sat very still. Debbie, the teenager, lay very still on her blanket, pretending to be asleep. She did not dare to look up to see if the officers were coming toward her. John Webster wrapped Samantha in a beach towel and held her close in front of him. The laughter and playfulness had ceased. Jim Sterling turned away from the men and proceeded to cover the sleeping stranger who lay next to him. Ben produced a paperback book from his pocket and buried his head in it, pretending to read. Clint and Kate left their towel and began to stroll down the beach, with intent on finding some seashells.

The state policeman looked at the picture and kept looking at those who were sitting on the sand. Although it was only a few minutes, it seemed like an eternity before the officers went up the ramp and back to the boardwalk.

One hour later, at exactly five-thirty, the bus left Ocean Beach for Clarksville with seven passengers aboard. Included on the passenger list were Kate Connelly, Clint Rogers, Debra Pierce, John and Samantha Webster, Ben Somers, Jim Sterling, and his sleepy friend who he called Joe Smith. All were on the five-thirty bus to Clarksville.

CHAPTER 2

Darkness soon descended as the bus rolled along the interstate highway. The passengers had settled down for the eight-hour trip; only a few whispers or murmurs broke the silence. Several passengers were sleeping, lulled by the monotonous turning of the wheels.

John Webster could finally relax as Samantha was sleeping soundly. She had been excited as the trip began, asking questions only a four-year-old can do. However, after the bus began to move, Samantha curled up in the seat beside her dad and was soon asleep. As the bus rolled on, John's thoughts drifted back to another bus trip, many years ago.

Sam Webster was a shrimp boat captain who eked out a living on the bayou of Louisiana. His wife had left him when their son John was seven years old, but his aunt Hattie was determined that young John would grow up to be a fine young man. She was a widow who closed up her home and moved in with the Websters and ran the household. Sam was up each day at four, on his boat by five, and would not be in port with his catch until three-thirty that afternoon. Aunt Hattie was in charge of young John!

"Johnny, where have you been? School has been over for two hours." Aunt Hattie felt responsible for John, and worried when he would disappear for hours. She liked to know where he was at all times.

"Oh, Aunt Hattie!" John's eyes were dancing with excitement. "We went down to the wharf and watched the boats. Then we jumped into the water and raced to the barge and back, and I won every race! Is Dad home yet? I've got to do my chores."

Aunt Hattie shook her head as the seventh grader rushed to change clothes. Although she worried about the boy, he was a good student and a very hard worker. Every free day he had, John would join his father on the boat and work side by side with him. Aunt Hattie knew how hard it was to depend on the shrimp boat for a living. Hurricanes could smash a boat into small pieces, or waves could swamp a boat and sink it, drowning everyone on board the vessel. There was also the threat of bacteria, growing in warm waters, could destroy the shrimp, and the men would have to look for their catch further from shore. Sometimes Sam Webster would be gone for several days before coming into port with his catch. It was not the life that she or Sam Webster wanted for young John, but they knew that he was happiest when he was on the boat, on the wharf, or in the water.

As much as he led a Tom Sawyer life in the summer, John's work ethic and curiosity made him an outstanding scholar at Swanee High School. He studied the laws of the shrimpers and his debate team captured state honors defending them on several issues. John also excelled in the pool. He was elected captain of the swim team and the Dolphins also became state champs.

Ironically, it was his love of the water that became John's ticket away from Louisiana. During his high school career, he had set national records in the free style as a member of the Swanee swim team. This achievement attracted the attention of Harvard's swim coach, Jason Brewer. So after graduation, and a summer of helping his dad on the shrimp boat, John Webster boarded the bus for Cambridge, Massachusetts, having been awarded a full scholarship for swimming.

"John! John!" screamed Coach Brewer. John was swimming laps in the pool as part of his daily workout. "There's a phone call for you. Take it in the weight room."

"Thanks, Coach." John pulled himself out of the pool and grabbed a towel. His year-and-a-half had gone by quickly; John felt very comfortable here. His swimming was going well, and his classes were challenging and stimulating. The transition from shrimper to Harvard had been smooth.

"Hey, John! Have you finally got a girl to call you?" One of John's teammates yelled teasingly from the pool. It was one of the reasons that John likes Harvard so much; there was a great camaraderie among the members of the swim team.

He was still laughing as he picked up the phone. He was curious as to who would be calling him.

"Hello."

"Hello, Johnny?"

John immediately recognized the voice of his Aunt Hattie. "Aunt Hattie? What's wrong?"

"He's gone, Johnny. He's gone."

"Aunt Hattie, calm down! I can't understand you. What's happened?"

"There was a storm in the gulf…your dad was ninety miles out… they found parts of the boat…he's gone."

Aunt Hattie was sobbing so hard that it was difficult to understand her.

"Aunt Hattie, I'll come home as soon as I can get a flight."

"There's nothing you can do here now. I'll call you when…when there is some news."

John hung up the phone and suddenly felt very alone. He pulled on his sweatshirt and walked slowly into the night. His ties to Louisiana were now severed. He had always known that if he had failed at Harvard, he could go back home and work the shrimp boat with his dad. Now all of that was gone.

John returned to Louisiana at the end of semester. There was a memorial service for his dad, and a lawyer told him what he already knew: there was no money. Aunt Hattie went to live with her daughter, and the house was put up for sale. John collected a few family items that he wished to keep and was on the bus for Harvard after one week. As darkness fell, John shed some tears for his youth. Now he was on a journey into his future.

The next two years seem to speed by, and John found himself preparing for graduation. He had distinguished himself in the classroom as well as in the pool. He had been accepted into Harvard Law School. He also had an invitation to the Olympic Trials this summer, where he hoped to parlay his United States record in the free style into a trip abroad to the Olympic Games.

But again, he felt alone. Aunt Hattie's health didn't permit her to come up to Cambridge to attend his graduation. She was all the family that he had, and she wouldn't be there. Since the death of his father, he had immersed himself in his studies and the swim team. It was when he was celebrating a victory in the pool, a new national swimming record, or preparing for graduation that he missed his family.

After he collected his cap and gown for the ceremony next week, John walked slowly toward his apartment. In his hand was an open letter from his Aunt Hattie. Suddenly, there was a collision that sent him sprawling on the sidewalk with a girl at his side. As he was attempting to get to his feet, he looked into the prettiest pair of blue eyes that he had ever seen. He became so enamored with those eyes that it took him a few moments to collect his thoughts.

"Are you OK?"

"I think so." She lay there on the sidewalk, taking a mental inventory of her cuts and bruises.

"I'm so sorry…this is my fault.… I was just reading a letter from home and wasn't looking where I was walking. Your knee is bleeding!" He immediately pulled out his handkerchief and held it to her knee.

"It's just a scrape," she said, but she winced as he held the handkerchief against the wound.

"The college infirmary is just on the next block. Let's let the doctor take a look at it." He carefully tied the handkerchief around her knee, and slowly lifted the girl to her feet. John put his arm around the girl and guided her toward the infirmary. Together they limped toward help.

"I'm John Webster…and I'm really sorry about this…I was so busy reading a letter from home that I wasn't paying attention." He again apologized for the incident.

"It must be a letter from a very special girl," she said laughingly.

Before he could answer, they found themselves at the steps of the infirmary. He carefully assisted her up the steps and into the doctor's office. The receptionist called for the doctor who took the young woman back into the examining room. John found himself standing near the door, listening for a name. He had dated many girls at Swanee High School and at Harvard and had enjoyed each association, but there was something different about this girl. After what seemed like endless hours (although it was only about thirty minutes), the doctor escorted the beautiful girl back into the waiting room.

"She's going to be just fine. It's nothing serious. I cleaned the abrasion and put a bandage on it. You might be a bit stiff in the morning, but that will soon disappear."

John thanked the doctor and shook his hand. He then took the girl's hand and walked with her down the steps.

"Please let me take you to dinner tonight. It will be my way to apologize for being such a clumsy oaf…Miss…"

"Janice, Janice Stevens. My friends call me Jan…and yes, I'd like to have dinner with you tonight. I'm staying at the Charles Hotel in Harvard Square. I'll see you about six-thirty, suite 402. Oh! Here's my car. Thanks for the assistance, and I'll see you tonight."

John walked back to his apartment, wondering what had happened to him today. He had been on many dates, but he had never anticipated any of them the way he was looking forward to this evening.

He was ten minutes early when he arrived at the Charles Hotel and took the elevator to the fifth floor. He nervously rang the bell and was greeted at the door by a white-haired distinguished gentleman.

"Good evening…I'm Joseph Stevens, Janice's father. You must be John. I understand that you and my daughter had a collision this afternoon.

"Yes, sir. It was completely my fault. My mind was on other things."

"Do you have business here in Cambridge?"

"I'm a student at Harvard, at least for two more weeks until I graduate. Then it's on to law school for three more years."

"A well-chosen profession! I'm a lawyer myself. Perhaps you have heard of our firm—Stevens, Stevens, and Associates, located in New York?"

"Yes, sir. It has an excellent reputation."

"It's one of the finest law firms in the country. We're very proud of our reputation."

"Daddy, are you talking business again?" Janice appeared from the bedroom and interrupted the two men. John thought he had never seen such a beautiful girl. She kissed her father on the cheek and started walking toward the doorway.

"It was good to meet you, sir. We shouldn't be too late," John said as he extended his hand.

"If I know my daughter, we'll be seeing quite a bit of you! I've never seen her so enthusiastic about a fellow that she just met," answered Joseph Stevens as he shook John's hand.

However, as soon as the couple had closed the door, Joseph Stevens went immediately to the phone and dialed. He paced the floor as he waited for the connection. "Henry, I want you to contact that private investigator that we used last year. Tell him to get a complete dossier on a Harvard student named John Webster…yes, John Webster…he is a senior at Harvard who says he's graduating in two weeks. Get back to me as soon as you have some information. It is a very important and confidential matter, for my eyes only."

For the next two years, John and Jan were inseparable. Jan was a junior at Radcliffe and the two studied nightly at the Harvard library. Upon her graduation, the couple became engaged, for John used the money from the sale of his house to purchase an engagement ring. Janice moved back to New York the following year after John graduated. However, she returned to Cambridge almost every weekend to be with him. The following June, John received his diploma from Harvard Law School with honors and soon passed the bar exam. It was then that

Joseph Stevens offered him a position at Stevens, Stevens, and Associates, much to the delight of his daughter. Janice was ecstatic that her husband and her father would be working together. John's happiness was dampened by the absence of Aunt Hattie, but his classmates were there for him.

A month later, the Websters returned from a honeymoon cruise that was a wedding gift from Mr. and Mrs. Stevens. John Webster had not been this happy for a long time. He was no longer alone.

John began his law career as a member of the prestigious law firm of Stevens, Stevens, and Associates of New York City. On his first day at work, he was summoned to the office of his father-in-law, Joseph Stevens. John had seen his office, met his secretary, and was eager to begin.

"John, we need to have a talk. There are several things that must be made perfectly clear now that you are here. I debated doing this earlier, but Mrs. Stevens and I decided this would be the perfect time! I want your undivided attention; do not interrupt me until I'm finished!"

John was puzzled by the tone of his father-in-law's voice.

"You have been given a job in this firm because you are my daughter's husband, and…because you were the top law student in your class. You will be given difficult cases…no favoritism…because you married my daughter. You will be scrutinized harder than any member of the firm has ever been. Mrs. Stevens and I weren't exactly pleased when our only daughter married a poor shrimper; we would not have selected you for a son-in-law. You'll have to prove yourself with Janice and her friends. And…of course, you'll have to prove yourself to Mrs. Stevens and me."

John sat there stunned, but he had heard enough. He had no idea that the Stevens felt this way. "Sir, you will have my resignation on your desk by noon…"

"And what will you tell Janice?"

For a moment, John felt trapped. Of course, Jan knew about his background and his life in Louisiana. However, it would break her heart if he left the firm. She had been so excited that her husband and her father would be working together.

"Mr. Stevens, you will not regret that you hired me to practice law with this firm. If you will excuse me, I have work to do," and John stormed out of the room. He was furious, but determined to prove himself to Jan and the Stevens family.

The next two years were a blur! His days were spent researching, writing briefs, and making presentations. Many days he was the last to leave the building as he thoroughly closed every loophole in each case that he was assigned. He gained a reputation as a highly competent and honest attorney. Many nights were spent with Janice at charity events and fundraisers or entertaining clients at small dinner parties at trendy restaurants or in their tastefully decorated apartment overlooking Central Park.

When Janice announced that she was pregnant, John was ecstatic! He had proven himself as a lawyer and he had a good marriage. It seemed that the tension between John and his in-laws had subsided. Nine months later, when Samantha was born, John's world was complete.

The birth of a granddaughter seemed to bring John even closer to the Stevens family. They adored Samantha and showered her with expensive gifts and love.

On the day of Samantha's third birthday, Joseph called John into his office.

"Is everything ready for the party?"

"Samantha had been talking about having a cake with candles for week. We'll see you about 6:00?"

"I want to discuss something with you, John. Mrs. Stevens and I don't like to think of Janice and Samantha spending another hot summer in New York City. So we went to a real estate agent who just happens to be an old family friend. She has found us a perfect cottage on the beach on Long Island. It's the ideal getaway for the summer and the commute is only one hour. We think the girls will enjoy spending summer there.

"Sir, that is very generous, but I can take care of my family."

"Nonsense! Janice is our only child, and Samantha is our only granddaughter. We want to do this for *them*."

Joseph Stevens's word stung John; it was obvious he was not included in the family group. "I'm sure they will love it. See you at six." John hurriedly left the office; he did not want to get into a confrontation with his father-in-law.

The summerhouse on the beach was gleefully accepted. Janice talked about walking on the beach with Sami, cookouts, and late evenings on the porch. Samantha, however, was more impressed with the cuddly, stuffed lobster, sent to her by her Aunt Hattie. John's anger over the gift subsided as he watched his girls dancing around the room. The thought of living near the water again pleased him too.

Several days later, John and Jan were having breakfast while Sami was still asleep.

"I'd like to drive out to the cottage today," Janice announced. "I need to check on a few things."

"Are you going to take Samantha with you?"

"No. Mother is taking her to the puppet show at Macy's. Big Bird will be there!"

"I heard her talking about Big Bird last night, but I thought she had just been watching Sesame Street. Will you be home for dinner?"

"I don't think so. I want to measure the rooms and the windows. The decorator is meeting me at four, and we will make a list of any changes. I want to pick out some curtains, look at fabric to cover the sofa, and shop for some porch furniture. Mother and Daddy will keep Sami, and I'll pick her up after dinner. We should be home by seven-thirty."

John left the breakfast table, grabbed his briefcase, and started out the door. "I'll send out for some supper and get caught up on some work at the office. Maybe we can all go out on the weekend to see the cottage and hear the changes you want to make."

Janice caught John before he opened the door. She threw her arms around him.

"John Webster, the luckiest day of my life was when I bumped into you on Harvard Square. I love you, John Webster."

"If I remember correctly, I knocked you down, and it was the luckiest day of my life. I love you, Jan Webster."

As he walked the short distance to the office, John mulled over in his mind how happy he was that he had such a great life. He adored Janice and Sami was the "light of his life." She was truly Daddy's little girl. He was not pleased with his relationship with the Stevens, but Janice did not realize the animosity felt by her parents. And…they were super doting grandparents. Life was good.

The morning sped by, and after lunch, he settled himself to thoroughly read an intricate brief.

"Mr. Webster, there are two men here who wish to speak to you."

"I told you I was going to be busy all afternoon…No interruptions!"

A uniformed policeman and a detective pushed past John's secretary and entered the room.

"Mr. Webster? Mr. John Webster?"

"Yes, I'm John Webster. What can I do for you, gentlemen?"

"I'm afraid we have some bad news. There's been an accident on the Sunrise Highway."

In a few seconds, John Webster's world collapsed. Janice's car had veered off the highway and hit a utility pole. She died instantly.

"There were no other cars involved and the weather conditions were good. We think she must have swerved to miss an animal and lost control of the car. You'll have to come down to the morgue to make a positive identification."

After the policemen left, John sat quietly, in complete disbelief of the news he had been given. His world had just stopped spinning! How do you tell a three-year-old that her mother will never be coming home? And…he had to walk down the hall and inform his father-in-law that his only child had perished in a car crash. Paralyzed by the news, he continued to replay the events over and over in his mind. Finally, he began the dreaded walk down the corridor to Joseph Stevens's office.

The funeral services were particularly heartfelt: a young woman who was very respected in the city, active in many charities, a devoted mother and wife was killed in a senseless accident. And of course, the only child of one of the city's prominent attorneys was a loss to the legal community.

After the services were over, and the condolences were acknowledged, John took a leave of absence from the firm and he and Samantha drove south to Louisiana. They spent hours walking along the beaches and the wharf. He rented a sailboat and they explored the gulf together. Janice had been here several times with John, and he wanted to show Sami several spots that were favorites of her mother. Of course, Aunt Hattie spoiled Sami with cookies and lemonade and regaled her with stories about her dad when he was a boy and other tales about the grandfather he never knew. It was a healing time for the Websters.

After a month, John and Sami returned to New York. Mrs. James, the Websters' housekeeper, was a widow who agreed to become a live-in nanny-housekeeper. Mrs. James would take Samantha to play school three afternoons a week and would otherwise be her caretaker and take her on planned outings. John was also going to limit his caseload and be home for dinner and family time each night. All the necessary arrangements had been made; he was ready to return to work.

"Good morning, Mr. Webster. Glad to have you back." His secretary cheerfully greeted him on his first day back at the office.

"Thanks, Mrs. Landon. It's good to be back to work. I'll be at my desk most of the morning looking over the pile of paperwork waiting for me. Hold all calls unless you consider them urgent!"

It was good to be busy again; he had less time to think of all he had lost. There were reminders everywhere of Janice…the paintings she had selected for his office, her college graduation picture, the Eiffel Tower souvenir from their honeymoon trip to Europe, and a family snapshot taken at the beach cottage. He paused for only a moment and then faced the mound of paperwork.

A few moments later, the door flew open and Joseph Stevens appeared! He seemed angry and slammed the door!

"John Webster! Where have you been? You said you wanted to get away for a few days, and you've been gone over a month! We've got a business to run here, and we can't do it if our associates aren't here!"

"You know I went home to Louisiana. I wanted to spend some time alone with Samantha. It's hard to explain to a three-year-old why her life will be different and that her mother isn't coming home. I spoke with Mrs. Stevens several times on the phone during the month."

"Well, I don't want my granddaughter associating with shrimper RIFFRAFF! It's bad enough that you named her after that no good sea-faring father of yours, but she will be raised in a proper manner here in New York. Mrs. Stevens and I will expect you and Samantha for dinner tonight at six-thirty."

"Sorry, sir, but Samantha and I will be having dinner with Mrs. James. And…Dad…er…Mr. Stevens, sir, Samantha is my daughter and I will decide where she goes and the people she associates with!" He was upset by the attitude that Joseph Stevens had displayed, but he remained calm.

"Now, was there anything else you wish to discuss?"

Joseph Stevens stormed out of the office, slamming the door behind him. His daughter had married beneath her station life, and now that she was gone, he was left with the mistake. John Webster should never underestimate his father-in-law! John Webster did not realize that *Joseph Stevens had just declared war!*

John eased himself into the chair. He was visibly shaken by the diatribe from his boss. If he had been single, he would've have packed up his personal items in his office, tendered his resignation, and walked away from Stevens, Stevens, and Associates. But he had to think of Samantha. Family had always been very important to him; he had special feelings for his childhood and growing up in Louisiana. To leave now would deny Samantha a set of adoring grandparents. He felt he had asserted himself with Mr. Stevens and made his wishes known. She was his daughter and he would determine her schedule.

It began two weeks later when John came home for dinner.

"Sami! Sami! I'm home."

"Good evening, Mr. Webster. Samantha isn't here."

"Where is she, Mrs. James?"

"Mrs. Stevens came this afternoon and took Samantha to the circus. She said she would have her home by nine. I told her Samantha's bedtime was eight o'clock, but she said you would understand."

"Mrs. James, I told you not to let Samantha leave this house without my permission."

"But Mrs. Stevens is her grandmother…" Mrs. James fought back the tears. "Mrs. Stevens will take good care of her; she loves her so much. She says that Samantha reminds her of her daughter, and she gets tears in her eyes when she mentions Mrs. Webster."

"Don't be upset, Mrs. James. Sami is safe with her grandmother. But I do want to be notified before she leaves again."

Mrs. Stevens was at the apartment promptly at nine, hugged Samantha good-bye, and ignored John. He did not see Mrs. Stevens for several months.

She unexpectedly appeared at his office one afternoon.

"John, I would like to take Samantha to Albany. My niece is getting married on Saturday, and the happy couple would like the entire family there. We should be home late on Sunday. Samantha has seen so little of this side of the family."

John hesitated, but he knew how much Sami liked to play dress-up, and how much she would enjoy a wedding with fancy dresses. Of course, he was not included as a member of the family. But he also knew how important her family was to Mrs. Stevens, and how much she would enjoy introducing her granddaughter.

"Mrs. Stevens, I'll call Mrs. James and have her pack Samantha's clothes for the trip. She even has a fancy pink dress that she can wear to the wedding." As he reached for the phone…

"Really, John, that won't be necessary. Mr. Stevens and I will buy her some appropriate clothes for the trip. Just call Mrs. James and tell her that I'm on my way to get my granddaughter."

Mrs. Stevens returned with Samantha two weeks later. John could not believe how much he missed her. He was told that after the wedding, the Stevens party had taken a trip to Canada, and then over to Niagara Falls. Mrs. Stevens called the apartment several times before John was home. She would tell Mrs. James the travel plans, but never left a phone number where they were staying. As Mr. Stevens later said to John, "Samantha was having such a good time, and we didn't think you would deprive her of a vacation."

John suddenly found himself inundated with work. He missed lunches to review cases and worked late into the night to finish his caseload. He met clients for dinner and often returned home after Samantha was in bed. John Webster's success rate with the firm was excellent, but he was totally exhausted.

"John, you look terrible!" Joseph Stevens commented as he walked into his son-in-law's office. "Give me an update on the Poltex contract."

"They have changed certain provisions in that contract numerous times. I faxed them the changes, and a few days later, I get more revisions."

"Why don't you take a few days, fly out to Los Angeles, and set up a meeting with them personally? You could probably finalize the details with a few face-to-face conferences! I don't have to tell you how important this contract is to the firm. It could open up many business opportunities on the West Coast. We have been trying to establish an office in the Los Angeles area for years. A successful conclusion to those proceedings could be the impetuous that we need!"

John's thought turned to Samantha. He saw very little of her these past few months. He had no personal life. He was constantly trying to prove to Joseph Stevens that he was an asset to the firm and not just the husband of the late daughter of the boss.

"I'll have to talk with Mrs. James and make arrangements for Samantha's kindergarten. And Sir, I really hate to leave Samantha…"

"Nonsense! When we sign this contract, you'll have more time to spend with her. It's been two years since Janice left us; you two should take another holiday."

"Well, I could possibly go for a few days…"

"Good Boy! Mrs. Stevens and I will stop and see Samantha while you're gone. Take a few extra days in Los Angeles to relax. You have earned it!"

"I'll call Mrs. James to see if she has any plans…"

"We've already taken care of that! Mrs. James will care for Samantha. We'll see that she is compensated well. We've booked you on a flight on Southwest Airlines out of La Guardia at seven-fifteen tomorrow morning. My driver will pick you up at five-thirty sharp!"

John resented that Stevens could control his life like this. Perhaps this trip would give him time to think about leaving the firm. He had talked with Aunt Hattie about moving back to Louisiana and establishing a law practice there. And…there was also the possibility of a transfer to consider. If Stevens, Stevens, and Associates opened a branch office on the West Coast, he could ask for a reassignment to

24

the Los Angeles firm and it would be a fresh start for the Websters. He would still be associated with Sami's grandparents, but he would have an entire country between them. It would also be a new setting for him, away from the constant reminders of his life with Janice.

The contract talks in Los Angeles took longer than expected. After seventeen days, the last of the disagreements had been ironed out, and the contract was finalized. John was very anxious to return home. Although he had called every day, he had only been able to talk to Samantha twice. Many nights, there was no answer at the apartment. It had been difficult to explain to her that he would be gone for a few days but Nana James, Pop Pop, and Gram would keep her busy. He also promised her a vacation, maybe to the Jersey Shore, when he returned. Samantha looked so much like her mother and had many of her mannerisms, but she had a love for the beach and the water that she shared with all the Websters. (The cottage on Long Island had been sold immediately after the funeral.)

John left the hotel early and took a cab to the airport. As he waited for his flight, he heard his name on the loud speaker.

"Paging John Webster! Paging John Webster! Please pick up the courtesy phone! Paging John Webster!"

John immediately thought that something was wrong with Samantha. He hurriedly rushed to the phone.

"John Webster here."

"John, this is Cliff Adams." John immediately recognized him as an executive secretary with the firm. "We need you in Seattle immediately! There's a ticket waiting for you at the North West counter. There's trouble with the Cetticorp contract. We'll fax you the contract and details as soon as you check into the Sheraton in Seattle, where we have reserved a suite for you. Good luck!"

Before John could answer, the phone went dead. He walked slowly to the northwest ticket counter and immediately had to board the plane. He desperately wanted to return to New York and Samantha. But…it was logical: if there was a problem in Seattle and the firm had a lawyer in Los Angeles, he would be sent to complete negotiations. For a few hours, John was pleased with the confidence that the firm had placed in him. He checked into the Sheraton, disappointed that he wasn't in New York, and realized that he would be awake most of the night, reviewing the contract.

After six days, contract talks were going smoothly, and John anticipated that he would be on his way home by the weekend. After a particularly long day, John returned to the hotel, exhausted. As he walked through the lobby, he was looking forward to a good night's rest.

However, under the door was a note from the concierge; he had a message to call Louisiana immediately! John knew that Aunt Hattie's health was poor, so he was pleasantly surprised when she answered the phone.

"Aunt Hattie, are you all right?"

"Johnny, a letter came for you. Someone is trying to take Samantha." She sobbed.

"Aunt Hattie, what are you talking about? Who is trying to take my daughter?"

"A letter came yesterday. The Stevenses have filed for custody of Samantha. The paper said that you are away from home too much and you are an unfit parent." She was sobbing so hard that it was difficult to understand her.

"Aunt Hattie, please calm down. You are going to make yourself sick. No one is going to take Sami from me. Did the letter give a court date?"

"It's on Friday…only two days from now. Will you be back in New York City for the hearing?"

"Of course! Aunt Hattie, you must calm down! I'm so glad you called me. Don't worry; things will be OK."

It was only after he hung up the phone that John realized what Joseph Stevens had orchestrated. He had never approved of a "Shrimper Lawyer" marrying his only daughter. When Janice died, the Stevens family had tried to monopolize Samantha by keeping him busy with important cases and business trips. It would appear that he had deserted Samantha to climb the corporate ladder. He must get home immediately!

But as sat in his hotel suite, he had a chance to organize his thoughts. Once he returned to New York, he would have no job and be in a court battle against one of the most powerful men in the city.

And…at least on paper, the accusations were correct. He had been out of the city and away from his daughter for over a month. He had spent long hours at the office and missed many meals and evenings with her. John sat for a long time on the edge of the bed to think. Mrs. James could truthfully testify in court that he was seldom home, at least for the last few months.

Carefully, John began to formulate a plan. No one in New York knew that he had talked to Aunt Hattie and knew of the impending court case. He needed time…

The following morning, he placed a call to Stevens, Stevens, and Associates, from the airport.

"Cliff, John Webster here. Tell the boss that contract talks are going smoothly and I should be back to work on Tuesday…Wednesday at the latest. Thanks." He hung up before there could be a response from New York. He then boarded a plane for New York City.

Upon arrival, he rented a car and drove to his apartment. Luckily Mrs. James was not there. He packed a suitcase for Sami and some clean clothes for himself and left Mrs. James a note, telling her that he and Samantha were going on a spontaneous vacation trip. He told her to take a few days off and he would contact her when they returned to New York. John then drove to the kindergarten where he immediately spotted his daughter on the playground. He spoke to her teacher (telling her the same story that he had told Mrs. James), and explained that Samantha would not be in school for a few weeks. John and Samantha were on the turnpike hours before anyone knew that he was back in New York City. He parked the rental car at the Newark Airport and hopped on a bus. Sami thought this was a big adventure and wondered if they were going to see Aunt Hattie. By nightfall, they were in a motel room in Ocean Beach.

Rain hitting the window of the bus immediately brought John Webster back to the present. He looked down at a sleeping Samantha, snuggled beside him, and used his jacket to cover her. He was now in control of his life with many decisions to make about *their* future.

And the bus rolled on…

CHAPTER 3

DEBBIE PIERCE SMILED TO HERSELF AS SHE saw the little girl asleep next to her father. At the beginning of the trip, Sami Webster had wandered up and down the bus aisle introducing herself and talking to everyone. She also introduced Lolly, a stuffed, red lobster doll that she hold close top her chest. As the bus drove her further from home, thoughts of her mother and father brought tears to Deborah Pierce's eyes. She couldn't imagine how worried they must be.

Dr. Robert Pierce could not believe his good fortune as he hung up the phone at the nurses' station. His residency in orthopedic surgery would be concluding in a few months and he and his wife Ellen had briefly discussed their future. But the phone call...he finished his rounds and raced down to the third floor where Ellen was a nurse in pediatrics. He spotted her as she walked from the nursery.

"Ellen! Ellen!" He grabbed her around the waist and twirled her around in front of a group of fellow nurses.

"Bob! Bob! What is it?" Ellen finally got her feet back on the floor and caught her breath.

"Ellen, I just got a phone call from Dr. Fredericks…*the Dr. Fredericks*!…Dr. Stanley Fredericks!" Bob was so excited he could hardly talk. "He tentatively offered me a position at his hospital. He wants to concentrate on his joint replacement surgery and has offered me the position of chief orthopedic surgeon. He wants us to come to Centerville at our earliest convenience to discuss the details. Dr. Fredericks said he had heard of some of the successes that I've had and wants to meet me. Can you believe it?" He once again picked up his wife and began to spin her around again as the nurses cheered.

It had been a difficult journey for Bob Pierce. His father died when he was very young and his mother had struggled to support her four boys. It was evident, however, at an early age, that Bob had a special gift. When his brother fell out of a tree and dislocated his shoulder, Bob patiently massaged his brother's shoulder until the arm was back in place. Often, his mother scolded him for splinting and bandaging the legs of the family dog. Because of a lack of money, Bob joined the army immediately after high school, much to the dismay of his science teachers.

However, after his tour of duty was over, Bob used the GI Bill to help him pay for college. Upon graduation, and due to his excellent work in chemistry and the lab, he was lured into the world of pharmaceuticals. The salary was excellent, but it wasn't fulfilling. So when he had saved enough money, and with the recommendations from his former instructors, (and a partial scholarship), Bob Pierce entered medical school. His work was outstanding, and soon he was interning at Johns Hopkins Hospital in orthopedic surgery.

It was while assisting during an operation on a three-year-old patient whose legs had been broken by an abusive boyfriend that Bob Pierce met a pediatric nurse named Ellen Warthen. Her compassion and special TLC of the little fellow captured his heart. They were married a few months later in a quiet ceremony in the Hopkins chapel.

Ellen Pierce had worked as a nurse and supported him as he continued his journey to become a surgeon.

Several months later, Bob and Ellen Pierce packed their meager possessions and drove toward a new life in Centerville.

Dr. Stanley Fredericks was fifty-five years old and a bachelor. He had dedicated his life to medicine, and although he had been involved with several women, he had never been married, except to medicine. He had succeeded in building a hospital in the small town of Centerville, and his outstanding reputation as an orthopedic surgeon had established him in the country's medical community. People came from all areas of the United States to be treated by Dr. Fredericks. His specialty was intricate joint replacement and repairing previously bungled joint surgeries.

The Pierces soon settled into their new life. Ellen Pierce redecorated their new home and soon was a member of all those clubs and organizations that were expected of a doctor's wife. Because of her love of her new life, she only agreed to work as a nurse in case of emergencies or when the hospital was short staffed. Dr. Pierce fell into a routine at the hospital and was extremely happy; his work was rewarding and challenging! He was often included in surgical conferences, and assisted in the operating room, gaining valuable techniques. Life was good!

Dr. Fredericks became like an older brother or favorite uncle to him. Many nights, Stan Fredericks joined the Pierces for dinner. Ellen became the official hostess at hospital functions and fundraisers with Bob and Stan Fredericks smiling with approval.

Eight years after, they moved to Centerville and one week before her fortieth birthday, Ellen Pierce confirmed that she was pregnant! And…nine months later…after completing an uneventful pregnancy, Deborah Fredericks Pierce was born. For the Pierces, life was complete.

Debbie soon became the sweetheart of Centerville General Hospital. She would come to the hospital with her mother and many days could be seen riding on the shoulders of Dr. Fredericks. He showered her with gifts and was like a second father to her. But it was her personality that made her such a darling at the hospital. While there, she would drift into a patient's room and soon entertain him with songs, dances, and a diatribe of childish poems. Illnesses, post operation surgery complaints, and body casts did not faze her. She was completely at ease in the hospital anywhere.

On Debbie's sixth birthday, Ellen had a small cookout for just a few of the hospital staff that had children near Debbie's age, and, of course, Dr. Fredericks, or "Uncle Fred" as Debbie now called him. She screamed with glee as she blew out the candles on her cake. She opened a pile of gifts and then Uncle Fred picked her up.

"You haven't opened my gift yet," he said as he carried her over to the fence. He opened the gate and led in a small brown and white pony. "Happy Birthday, Debbie," and he boosted her up in the saddle. Debbie just giggled and hugged the pony's neck. Dr. Fredericks held on to Debbie as he walked the pony around the yard. No one seemed to notice that, as the good doctor held her, his hand had dropped to the bottom of the saddle. Slowly, his had slipped under his hand her silk panties as he steadied her on the pony. Unknowing to those closest to him, *Dr. Stanley Fredericks had become obsessed with little Deborah Pierce.*

Whenever he had the opportunity, he would encourage Debbie to sit on his lap as he tried to touch or fondle her under her frilly dresses. He always had some candy or a treat for his goddaughter to lure her near him.

As she grew up, it was evident that Debbie was a very gifted child. She was an accomplished equestrian, winning competitions and shows with her pony, and later with the mare that Uncle Fred had given her. She was extremely athletic, excelling in the field of hockey, softball, and cheerleading. She played piano and was a participant in many musical recitals. A good student in school, Debbie often won scholastic awards. Of course, Dr. Fredericks attended these events with her parents and later would congratulate her with hugs, kisses, and "pats" on her body. He would put his arm around her shoulders and his hand would often rest over her breast.

During the summer, while she was in high school, Debbie was selected to participate on the traveling all-star softball team. To become a member of the group, she had to complete and pass a physical examination to be eligible to play and travel for the games.

"Daddy," Debbie said at the breakfast table the next morning, "When will you have time to fill out my softball form and give me a physical?"

"Why don't you stop at the hospital today after your riding lessons? I have a light schedule in surgery today. Come to the office; I'll be there."

"OK! I should be there about 4:00. I'll ask Jessie's mother to drive me there instead of home."

Later that day, Debbie slammed the door of the station wagon, thanked Mrs. Wagner, waved to her friend Jessie, and ran up the steps to the hospital. She jauntily walked down the hall, speaking to several nurses as she wended her way to her father's office. She opened the door, and Mrs. Jennings, her father's receptionist, greeted her.

"Hi, Debbie. This is a surprise. Are you here to see your father?"

"Yes, he's going to give me a physical examination today so I can play softball on the traveling team."

"You should call your mother to come and get you. Dr. Pierce has been called to the operating room for an emergency. Billy Simmons fell out of a tree and broke his leg in several places. I don't know when he'll be finished. I've cancelled all his afternoon appointments…here…you can use my phone."

But just as Debbie began to dial, Dr. Fredericks came into the office. The phone rang several times as Debbie tried to call her mother, but there was no answer. She eased the receiver down and turned to her godfather.

"I forgot that mother plays bridge on Tuesdays. She doesn't get home until 5:00. I'll just wait outside until Daddy's finished. Miss Jennings, will you make an appointment for me tomorrow? Maybe Daddy will have some free time then…"

Dr. Fredericks laughed. "Debbie, I have a few free minutes. I think this old doctor can still give a softball physical!" Laughingly, he put his arm around Debbie's shoulders and walked her down the hall to his office.

The office was empty as Dr. Fredericks turned on the light and reached for a paper gown. "Here, Debbie, put this on, and when you're finished, hop up on the examination table. I'll be in to check you over in a few moments. Where's the paper for me to complete?"

Debbie grabbed the paper gown and handed the physical form to the doctor as she walked by. She had an uneasy feeling that she couldn't explain. However, she went into the examination room, changed into the paper gown, and sat on the table.

Dr. Fredericks began the exam by checking Debbie's eyes, nose, ears, and throat. Then he took her blood pressure and reached for his stethoscope which was on the shelf. As he listened to her heart and lungs, his left hand crept to Debbie's maturing breast. He continued to listen through the stethoscope as he gently rubbed her breast.

"Everything sounds good," he said very professionally. Dr. Fredericks laid down his stethoscope and moved his hands to her stomach area. As he probed her stomach, his hands moved lower to her pubic area. A smile appeared on his face as he rubbed between her legs. Without thinking, he sharply thrust his fingers inside her. Debbie screamed as a pain shot through her lower abdomen. The scream startled Stan Fredericks, who had momentarily drifted into his own sick world. He quickly left the exam room, grabbed his coat, and raced out the office door. He ran to his car and drove out of the parking lot as his heart pounded and sweat poured down his face. He had made a mistake, and his reputation and his medical practice were now in jeopardy. How could he have been so careless?

Debbie sat on the table until the pain subsided. She was stunned at what had just happened to her. She slowly get dressed and looked for her physical form. When she didn't find it, she left the office and bumped into her father, who had completed the emergency surgery.

"Hi, Kitten…sorry about your appointment…Miss Jennings said that Uncle Fred gave you the examination. Are you ready to go home?"

Debbie quietly followed her father to the car, still trying to process what had just occurred in the doctor's office.

Later that evening, as Debbie got ready to take her shower, she noticed some blood stains on her underwear. She called for her mother and was sobbing when Ellen Pierce walked into the room.

"Debbie, what's wrong? Are you sick?" Mrs. Pierce sat on the bed and tried to console her daughter.

"He hurt me!"

"Who hurt you?"

"Uncle Fred!"

"Uncle Fred? Dr. Fredericks?"

"Oh, Mom, he touched me, and he rubbed me, and he put his hands where he shouldn't…and I'm bleeding…"

"When did this happen?"

"Daddy was operating, and I needed my softball physical. I called for you to come to the office to bring me home, but Uncle Fred said he could do my examination. He gave me a physical and it was awful…" She was crying so hard that it was difficult to understand her!

"Debbie! Debbie! Calm down! Tell me what happened!" She held her daughter tightly until the sobbing subsided.

Debbie choked back the tears and tried to calm down. She was shaking as she began to tell her story.

"After our riding lesson, Jessie's mother drove me to the hospital; Dad said he would do my softball physical today. He said that he had a light schedule…but there was an accident and he was in the operating room. So Uncle Fred said he would give me the physical…it was awful…he put his hands on me here," and she put her hands on her breast. Then he hurt me and I'm bleeding…" The tears began to roll down her cheeks again.

"Deborah, you are letting your imagination paint pictures again. Uncle Fred would never hurt you! He loves you very much. He loves us all; he made Daddy a partner in his medical practice. Because of him, we have a beautiful home, your horses, a great reputation…why, everything we have is because of Uncle Fred! He would never hurt you. When you get a physical, the doctor must examine your breasts. And Daddy and I talked to you about girls who spend hours riding horses will sometimes chafe and…"

"Mom, he hurt me!"

"I'm sure you were just nervous. Now take a hot bath and get into bed. Dad will talk to Uncle Fred tomorrow."

As Ellen Pierce walked out of the room, Debbie sat on the edge of the bed…*stunned.* Her mother did not believe her! She was going to do nothing! Tears stung as they fell from her eyes. Like her mother, her dad would do nothing! He worked with Uncle Fred. Debbie mimicked her mother's words. "Everything we have is because of Uncle Fred." Suddenly Debbie felt very dirty. She grabbed her robe and towel and walked toward the shower. And…at that moment…Deborah Pierce vowed that she would never again be alone with her Uncle Fred.

The following day, Dr. Fredericks entered the office of Bob Pierce.

"Hi, Bob. Is Debbie all right? She seemed very upset last night as I gave her a physical. She grabbed her clothes and ran out of my office. She didn't take her physical form. Miss Jennings had gone to copy some reports, so she wasn't there to stop her!"

"She's fine. She rode that horse you gave her for over three hours yesterday, and she was really tired. And you know her imagination…I want to apologize for her behavior. You've done so much for her; I can't imagine why she would run out!"

The two doctors laughed as Stan Fredericks put the completed physical on the doctor's desk. No one noticed the smile that came across his face. The Pierces did not believe the stories that Debbie had told them. And as the administrator of the hospital, Fred could terminate the contract with Bob Pierce at any time with a few unsubstantiated patient complaints. He now had an upper hand in his desire for Deborah Pierce.

"Bob," he called down the hall, "Let's get together soon for dinner. I don't get to see enough of that family of yours."

"Give Ellen a call when you have a free evening."

As time passed, Debbie succeeded in avoiding situations where she was alone with her Uncle Fred. He continued to be with the family, at parties, athletic events, concerts, and school functions as though the incident in the office had never occurred.

However, one day, as Debbie was going to her father's office, she entered an empty hospital elevator for the fourth floor. The elevator stopped at the second floor and Dr. Fredericks walked on. As the elevator ascended, Stan Fredericks push the STOP button and the elevator came to a halt between the third and fourth floors.

"You have been avoiding me." Dr. Fredericks leered at Debbie as he put his hand on her shoulder.

"Don't touch me! I hate it when you touch me!" She quickly brushed his hand off her shoulder.

Dr. Fredericks then put his hand over her shoulder and touched her breast. "I'll put my hands on you anywhere I please. It doesn't matter if you tell your father because he won't believe you. And…just remember, I can dismiss him from this hospital any time I wish."

Debbie again pushed his hand away and moved to hit the START button of the elevator, but Uncle Fred stepped in front of the panel. Perspiration gathered on his face as he became excited at the thought of being alone with her even for a few moments. He returned his hand to her breast and the smile once again appeared on his face.

Before he had a chance to speak, Debbie lunged away from his touch and pushed him against the EMERGENCY button! Immediately, a buzzer began to sound and the elevator started to move. As the door opened on the fourth floor, Debbie bolted from the elevator and ran to her father's office. Dr. Fredericks emerged from the elevator and walked to the nurses' station.

"Call maintenance and have them check this elevator. It just stopped between the third and fourth floors."

He casually walked down the hall to Robert Pierce's office and opened the door.

"Is Debbie feeling all right? We just had a scare in the elevator."

"She was really upset when she ran in here, but she has settled down now. What happened?" Miss Jennings was concerned for Debbie.

"The elevator became stuck between the third and fourth floors. Debbie became a bit claustrophobic. I'm glad she's OK now. Oh! Remind Bob not to forget the staff meeting today at 3:00."

Debbie cowered behind the door of her father's office. Tears were streaming down her face. She waited until she heard the door close before she ran from the office, down the stairs, and out into the street. She ran for two blocks and then finally realized she was away from the touches of Uncle Fred. She sobbed softly as she walked home, feeling trapped in a hopeless situation. But the tears soon subsided as her determination and fearlessness consumed her! She had one more year before she went to college. She would have to double her efforts to avoid being alone with her Uncle Fred again. She regained a jaunty spring in her steps and she skipped up the entrance to her home. *She had a plan!*

"Mother! Mother! Do we still have the pamphlet on the summer camp where we can take our horses?"

Ellen Pierce wiped her hands as her daughter brushed past her. "You told me only last week that you wanted to stay in town this summer and play softball. Have you changed your mind?"

"I'm going to call Jessie now…" She was talking about camp yesterday at lunch. Can you find the application?"

Debbie hurried up the stairs before her mother could see that she had been crying. Riding camp started two days after school was over; she would have only two free days. And…camp concluded just one week before school opened in the fall. A smile eased across her face; it would take some careful planning, but she avoid being alone with her godfather!

"Jessie," Debbie excitedly talked on the phone. "Do you still want to ride horses all summer? I've changed my mind! I'm sure mom will take us up there…Oh, Jess…I'm so excited…ask your mother and call me back!"

Debbie hung up the phone and lay down on her bed. She had stopped shaking as he lay there and thought of the events of the day. It was a waste of time to tell her parents the truth. If she had proof and her mother and father believed her, it would be the end of her Father's career here in Centerville. Dr. Fredericks would cancel her father's contract with the hospital after revealing some false accusations from patients. Without hospital privileges, her dad would have no medical practice and the family would have to move. Debbie knew that it would be her responsibility to avoid ever being alone with Uncle Fred. She must never relax her vigilance and allow herself to be unaccompanied with him. But she knew she had to be the perfect daughter when the family gathered and Dr. Fredericks was included.

Debbie spent the summer in Virginia with her friend Jessie. The girls had a carefree summer of swimming, riding horses, jumping, and showing them, hiking, and all those other things that teenage girls do when they are away from their parents for an entire summer.

And then it was September. Debbie threw herself into her school activities and her classes. This was her senior year; she would make the most of it. As she was returning home from cheerleading practice, several days before her seventeenth birthday, Debbie's mind was drifting away to the college applications she had completed. Many of her friends were going to the state university, but she had applied to several Ivy League Schools and she also applied to two schools on the West Coast. There would be *No Surprise Visits* from anyone.

"Hi, Mom! Hi, Dad! Sorry I'm late. We have a tough game on Friday night and we practiced a few new cheers…what are you two smiling about?"

Dr. Pierce immediately erased the smile from his face. "You're late for supper. Go wash your hands, and put the pup outside."

Debbie hurried to the back door. As she opened it to let Digger out for a run, her eyes were quickly drawn to a new red Porsche sitting in the driveway with a huge gold bow on the top.

"Happy Birthday, Darling. Now you don't have to be late for supper again." A smile was now on Dr. Pierce's face.

Debbie rushed to hug her mom and dad and then out the back door. She was so excited that she ran around the car several times. Finally, she calmed down, opened the door, and eased behind the steering wheel of her car. She moved her hand over the seats and smiled. She had always feared that Dr. Fredericks would appear at school after practice to take her home. Now she had her own car and would never again check the street for her godfather's car. She would shower, change clothes, and wait until her friends were ready. Then they could all walk to their cars together!

But fate was to turn her back on Debbie Pierce. As she sat in French class, there was a knock on the door and the school secretary stepped into the room.

"There's an urgent telephone call for Deborah Pierce. Is she in this class?" Debbie rose from her seat. "Please follow me."

Debbie left the classroom concerned. She had never received a phone call at school.

"Debbie, this is Mom…Dad and I are fine. I just got a call from the Pennsylvania State Police that your grandmother has been in an auto accident. She has been taken to the hospital in Pittsburgh. Your dad's in surgery, and I couldn't reach him. I'm going to drive over to Pittsburgh to attend to your grandmother. Tell Dad I'll call him tonight. Sorry to worry you with such news. I love you, Honey."

"I love you, Mom. Drive carefully, and tell Grams that I hope she feels better soon. I'll tell Dad all about it at dinner."

Debbie eased the phone down on the receiver and walked slowly back to class. Just one more class, and then she had cheerleading practice for about two hours. She hoped to get home before her father.

Advanced chemistry seemed to drag by at a snail's pace; Debbie's mind wandered to the summers she had spent with her Grams. She looked forward to several hours of physical activity. Maybe it would get her mind off the phone call.

Cheering practice was difficult. Several of the stunts went badly and they practiced them over and over again. As the squad readied themselves to try the rolling pyramid cheer one more time, the trainer appeared in the gym.

"Coach Roberts! Coach Roberts! Someone's trashed the locker room!"

"What are you talking about?" Coach Roberts tried to calm the upset fellow. "Slow down! What's wrong?"

"Someone trashed the locker room…Clothes are thrown everywhere…My wallet is gone!"

The cheerleaders rushed to the locker room and were dismayed at the sight. Clothes were ripped and scattered about the room. Purses were dumped in the floor, with mirrors cracked, and pictures were shredded into tiny pieces.

Debbie walked slowly to her locker. Her new coat was gone and her slacks had holes cut into them. Her sweater was tied into knots, but she ignored those things as she searched for her wallet. She finally found it, dumped in the shower room. Her wallet and personal items were there, but missing were her money, credit card, and most importantly, her car keys.

"Girls! Girls! Let's quit for the day." Coach Roberts announced to the cheering squad. "Collect all of your belongings that you can find. Help each other sort through this mess to get your personal items.

Then, make a list of items that are missing or destroyed and bring your list to me in the morning. I'll take the list to Principal Lockhern."

Debbie walked to the exit door and was glad to see that her car was still in the parking lot.

"Coach Roberts, may I use your phone? My car keys are gone and I'll get my dad to bring my other set!"

Coach Roberts nodded and handed Debbie her phone. Debbie dialed her father's office, and Miss Jennings answered the phone.

"Miss Jennings, is my daddy still there?"

"Debbie? Is that you? Your dad is still in the operating room, but he should be finished soon."

"I've lost my car keys. Will you ask daddy to bring me the extra set? I'm going to stay here at school until he gets here. I don't want whoever might have my keys to come and get my car."

"I'll tell him as soon as he's finished."

As Miss Jennings hung up the phone, she glanced at the clock. It was five-fifteen…fifteen minutes past office hours. She put on her jacket, got her purse, and wrote a note for Dr. Pierce. Knowing he would return to the office for his coat, Miss Jennings taped Debbie's note to the door of Dr. Pierce's office. After she left the office, she strolled down the hall; as she was leaving the building, she spoke to Dr. Fredericks coming into the hospital.

Debbie said good-bye to most of her friends. Coach Roberts came out of the locker room.

"I called Mr. Lockhern and he wants to see me immediately. Just make sure that the door is closed tightly when you leave."

It was dark when Debbie finally saw a set of headlights pull into the parking lot. She grabbed her gym bag, opened the door, and rushed out into the night. She hurried back to check that the door was closed securely, and then ran to the car. It was only when she was within ten feet of the car did she realize that it was *not* her father's car. It was Uncle Fred!

Debbie looked for somewhere to run, but she had locked the door of the gym when she closed it. Dr. Fredericks was out of the car in a flash, and grabbed her by the arm. He pulled her toward the car, opened the door, and dragged her inside.

"There's no need to scream. No one will hear you now!"

"Uncle Fred, please let me go…I won't say anything to anyone… Please let me out!"

Dr. Fredericks drove the car from the parking lot to the highway. As he sped along, he said nothing.

"Why are you doing this? Daddy is your friend…Please take me home! I promise I won't tell anyone!"

"Unless you want your father fired and disgraced, you won't say anything to anyone."

He continued to drive in silence until he came to a deserted baseball field. He drove into the park and stopped the car behind the dugout.

"Debbie, I want to be alone with you because I love you. Don't you understand that?"

Dr. Fredericks leaned toward Debbie and put his hand on her shoulder. As he smiled a sick smile at her, his hand moved down the front of her blouse to her breast.

Debbie pushed his hand away from her and pressed against the door as hard as she could. The movement seemed to infuriate Fredericks. He grabbed Debbie's arm, pulled her toward him, and slapped her across the face as hard as he could. Debbie's body slumped forward; she did not move!

Debbie's failure to respond further incensed Fredericks. He grabbed her lifeless body and slapped her several more times, but got no response. He pulled off her jacket and tugged at her sweat pants. Perspiration dripped from his face when he finally released the limp figure. He struggled to remove his coat, but Debbie's body was slumped against him. Fredericks was now in a sexual frenzy! He pushed Debbie away from him, opened the car door, and stepped out to remove his jacket.

The lifeless body seemed too explode with energy! Debbie unlocked the door and quickly opened it. With a burst of strength, she hopped out of the car and dashed into the night. Fredericks screamed, jump into the car, and immediately turned on the car headlights. Debbie Pierce was nowhere to be seen. He slowly drove around the ball field, cursing at the missed opportunity. After several minutes of circling the field, Fredericks finally drove away.

Debbie remained huddled on the floor of the dugout for what seemed like an eternity to her. Although she heard the car leave, she was too frightened to move. She had never been so scared as she was now! After about a half an hour, she slowly got to her feet and walked out of the ball park, remaining in the shadows. The walk home was over two miles; each time Debbie saw headlights, she would hide behind bushes or parked cars.

Robert Pierce was concerned when he arrived home to an empty house. There was no Ellen or no Debbie. He called the school, but there was no answer. Finally, at 7:45, he heard someone coming up the front steps. As he opened the door, Debbie stumbled into his arms sobbing.

"Oh, Daddy! Where were you? Why didn't you come to get me or bring me the keys?"

Dr. Pierce was shocked at the sight of his daughter. Her clothes were disheveled, and there was a large bruise on her face. She was crying uncontrollably! He took her in his arms and walked her over to a chair. He then took her by her shoulders and sat her down. Using a cold, wet cloth, he wiped her face. As he comforted her, the tears subsided.

"What happened, Honey? Are you OK? Where's your mother?"

Before she could speak, Debbie thought of Uncle Fred's threat and the story that she had concocted on the long walk home.

First she told him of her grandmother's accident and that her mother was in Pittsburgh. Mother had told her that she would call them tonight. Then she launched into her situation.

"Someone came into the locker room and ransacked it while we were practicing our cheers. My car keys and money were stolen and my clothes were torn and trashed. I called the hospital and Miss Jennings said she would tell you to come to the school and bring my extra set of keys. I watched from the gym and hoped that no one would take my new car while I was waiting. Everyone left, and when I saw some headlights, I thought it was you. When I closed the gym door, it locked and I couldn't get back into the building. I thought it was you, but as I got close to the car. I saw it was a stranger. I really got scared! I dropped my books and they scattered everywhere. I think the car followed me for a few blocks. I was so scared that I ran all the way home."

"I didn't see Miss Jennings. I was late getting out of surgery and Miss Jennings was gone. I guess I missed the note! What happened to your face?"

"I fell when we did the rolling pyramid! Nothing has gone right for me today." Debbie began to cry again as her dad put his arms around her. The scene was interrupted when the phone rang.

Debbie could hear her dad explain to her mother the problems of the day. She felt so dirty; she just wanted to take a hot shower and go to bed. She hated to lie to her parents, but what choice did she have? Her dad soon appeared in her room.

"That was your mother on the phone. Grams has a broken ankle, a few cracked ribs, and a concussion. She'll be in the hospital for a few days to closely observe her. Your grandmother isn't that young anymore. It's just a precaution. Your mother is going to stay in Pittsburgh until she is discharged; she hopes to find someone to stay with her when she goes home. So (using his best Humphrey Bogart imitation), it's just you and me, kid. Go get cleaned up and we'll go get your car and some pizza."

One of the most horrible experiences in Debbie Pierce's short life was finally over.

Later that night, after supper at the Pizza Pub, rescuing her car and books, and completing her homework, Debbie was snuggled safely in her bed.

She had relaxed her defenses today and had been careless. Uncle Fred had seized the opportunity to come after her. She rubbed her bruised face. Tears rolled down her cheeks as she once again vowed that she would *never* be alone again with her Godfather. *Never! Never! Never!*

And her plan worked perfectly. Her eighteenth birthday was to be a quiet, family affair, but Debbie begged her mother to include her school friends. Dr. Fredericks felt overwhelmed with cheerleaders, football players, and chorus members. He really wanted to be alone with Debbie and give her the diamond bracelet that he had bought for her, but the *damn* teenagers wouldn't leave the house! Christmas proved just as difficult. Although he was invited to spend Christmas Day at the Pierce's home, Dr. Fredericks made a point of stopping at the house unannounced, especially when he knew that Dr. and Mrs. Pierce were at the hospital function. Usually, no one was at home, and on few occasions when Debbie was there, she was always surrounded by her friends. They were making cookies, designing posters for a basketball game, or wrapping gifts. Debbie could see Uncle Fred seething as he made polite conversation, discussed his bogus reason for being there, and then making excuses to leave. In March, Debbie received confirmation that she was invited to bring her horse to Virginia and tour with the Olympic Equestrian team. If she could avoid her Uncle Fred until summer, she would be in Virginia with her horse until time to come home and pack for Stanford and leave for California. She felt that her dirty secret and her father's position at the hospital would be safe.

It seemed that once again, her plan worked perfectly. Debbie carefully avoided going to the hospital alone or being at home without her parents during the entire spring semester. After graduating with honors, she and her friends hopped from one graduation party to the next. The following day, she and her horse were on the train for Virginia. As the train left the station, Debbie had tears in her eyes. They were tears of relief that the charade was finally over.

On August 20, Ellen and Bob Pierce met the train from Virginia. Debbie had just ten days to pack and to get to California for her freshman year of college.

"I'm not going to ask if you enjoyed the summer…Your letters and the smile on your face tell us that you had a terrific experience."

"Dad, it was super! Mac says he wants me back next summer. I learned so many neat things about riding. He says that if I keep practicing and progressing, I could be invited to the equestrian Olympic trials next July. And…he has arranged for a stable in California so I can continue riding while at school. He says he will call you with the details."

"Debbie, we had a change of plans. Daddy and I have been invited to John Hopkins Hospital to conduct a seminar on the importance of surgeons in small hospitals. It is an attempt to formulate a plan with a general surgeon at a hospital and a network of specialist ready to step in if needed. The plan also stresses the importance of operating room nurse to be available. If we accept the invitation, we have to leave for Baltimore on Friday."

"What do you mean?…if we accept"

"Of course, you'll accept! What an honor!"

"We'll ship most of your belongings to California on Saturday. Uncle Fred has volunteered to accompany you to Stanford. He has taken off for a few days and will fly out with you. He has gotten hotel rooms for you two, and can stay in California until you get settled. Daddy and I will fly out in three weeks for parents' weekend."

Debbie tried to hide the fear that slowly crept throughout her body.

"Mom! Dad! That's great! You'll be telling that Big City Hospital the challenges of doctoring at a small hospital."

"We hope that we can encourage surgeons to go to small hospital with a great support system around them. We have really had a good life here, and a small town is a great place for families with children. Right, kiddo?" Dr. Pierce smiled enthusiastically.

"You two will *knock 'em dead*!"' Again the car exploded with laughter.

"We'll pack all your clothes and send them by UPS. Uncle Fred has the plane tickets and the hotel reservations. You can fly out on Saturday and go to the hotel and relax. Check in time at the dorm is two on Sunday. Monday morning is registration, but you already have your classes. You just need to verify them. Your Uncle Fred will stay until you are settled in, probably until Tuesday or Wednesday. Your dad and I are hoping that next semester you can have your car there. We are really upset that we can't go with you, we feel that this symposium is really important. Uncle Fred seemed so glad that we asked him to help out and go with you. You know Debbie, Stan Fredericks has been so good to us…he is like a family member. Daddy owes much of his career to him."

Debbie sat quietly in the back seat. She was glad that it was now dark outside and her parents could not see the look on her face. She had heard this speech before…How Dr. Fredericks had bolstered dad's career and how indebted the Pierces were to him. It was now important that Debbie formulate a plan. She knew what she had to do! She would not be alone with him, no matter where!

The next few days were a hive of activity. Clothes were sorted, boxes packed, and then UPS picked up the cartons. Details were completed to ship her horse to California; it was decided the horse would arrive after one month, giving Debbie some time to settle into a routine at school. On Friday, Ellen and Bob Pierce were delivered to the airport for their trip to Baltimore.

Also, on Friday, Debbie Pierce repacked a suitcase and drove her sports car to the bus terminal. After studying the departure schedule, she purchased a ticket to Ocean Beach. It was ironic that she would be only several hundred miles from Baltimore and her parents instead of on the West Coast. She only wished she could devise a plan to get to college as scheduled, but she could not think of any way without Stan Fredericks learning of her plan. She left no note for her parents, knowing that her nemesis would find it and follow her. A few hours later, she had a job as a waitress in the Pancake House, sharing an apartment with several other servers at the restaurant.

"Are you asleep?" Samantha Webster had sat down beside Debbie and interrupted her reverie. "Daddy says we might have a rainbow after the rain stops. Have you ever seen a rainbow?"

And the bus rolled on…

CHAPTER 4

JIM STERLING SMILED AS THE LITTLE GIRL walked up and down the aisle of the bus, stopping and chatting with each passenger. Slowly, she worked her way to the empty seat next to him.

"Are you going to see your grandma?" Samantha seated herself beside her newest friend. "Daddy says after we have a vacation, we can go and see Aunt Hattie. She's my grandma. She has a boat and...a PUPPY! Do you have a puppy?"

Jim smiled and before he could answer, the little girl bounced out the seat and continued to move up and down the aisle. He stared out the window of the bus as it rolled up the interstate. The rain dashed against the window, and he thought about an earlier time, many years ago. There was also a small puppy...

"Jimmy! Jimmy! Have you seen your brother Marty? Jimmy! Jimmy! Where are you?" Carolyn Sterling closed the screen door as she stepped out on the back porch. She scanned the backyard looking for the boys.

"Where are those boys?" Carolyn muttered to herself as she wiped her hands on her apron. Once again, she scanned the backyard. "Marty has a piano lesson in an hour and he should be here," she mumbled. As she started to call again, the front door slammed and the two boys ran into the kitchen.

"Where have you been?" Carolyn Sterling was very upset. She grabbed Jimmy by the arm and shook him hard.

"You are supposed to look after your little brother. Look at him! He's filthy, and his piano teacher will be here in a few minutes. Marty, go upstairs and wash up. Miss Hannah will be here soon to give you a lesson and you are a mess."

Jimmy put his hands in his pockets and held back the tears. It wasn't his fault that Marty wouldn't come home from the pond. He begged Marty to leave, but he had wanted to stay and dig worms for the fishermen. He also told Jimmy that he had found a dead puppy, and he wanted to bury him before he went home. Jimmy thought it was odd that someone would kill a puppy and just leave it there. It was also odd that the puppy's body was still warm. Marty would dig worms, get money from the fishermen, and then bury the pup. He knew their mom would be mad, but he couldn't get Marty to leave until he made some money and buried the pup. It was difficult for the youngster to understand why his mother was so harsh with him when she never punished his little brother. He could not hold back the tears as he threw himself across his bed. His sobs were drowned out by the sounds of the piano.

A few days later, Marty ran up to Jimmy at lunch recess at school.

"Jimmy! Jimmy! You gotta help me! Some boys are going to beat me up!"

"What? Why are some guys going to beat you up?"

"I don't know…Here they come!"

Marty made a dash for the front door of the school as the two older boys approached.

"Hey, guys! Why don't you leave my little brother alone? He's a lot smaller than you. Why don't you pick on someone your own size?"

"He stole a dollar from me. I had four quarters on my desk."

"I did not," yelled Marty from the school's steps.

"Leave him alone…" But before he could finish his statement, one of the older boys hit Jimmy in the eye with his fist. The blow came as a surprise and knocked Jimmy to the ground. As soon as he lay prone, the second boy kicked him in the stomach. He tried to get to his feet, but a fist caught him on the lip and blood spurted everywhere.

Rage overcame Jimmy; he got to his feet and started swinging. He caught the shorter boy in the stomach and he dropped to the ground, winded. Jimmy kept pounding the other boy until the teacher finally pulled them apart.

"James Sterling, stop this instant! Get inside to the principal's office, NOW!"

Jimmy calmed down and slowly walked toward the school as Miss Pitchard checked the other boys for injuries. He knew he was in trouble.

Later that day, the two brothers walked home. Jimmy's eye was black, and there was a bruise on his cheek. His lip was swollen, and his clothes were dirty with blood and mud splattered on them.

"I didn't know those guys were going to hit you…"

"What were they so mad about?" Jimmy asked, expecting an explanation for the melee.

"Well, I found fifty cents on the top of Ralph's desk and he said I stole it." Slowly, he pulled two quarters from his pocket. "Here…Do you want one?"

When Jimmy didn't answer, Marty dropped both coins in his pocket. The boys had just entered the front door when their mother appeared.

"Jimmy! Get in here! The principal telephoned a few moments ago and said that you were fighting on the playground. Look at you! You are a mess! Your clothes are ruined!"

She grabbed his arm and squeezed it so hard that he let out a sharp cry.

"Get up to your room. Your father will come up and talk to you when he gets home from work. I don't know why you can't be a good boy like your brother."

Jimmy hesitated a moment, waiting for Marty to explain the incident that had occurred, and started the fight. Marty sat quietly in the kitchen, eating his after school snack. Jimmy knew then that Marty was going to say nothing, so he quietly walked up to his room. He finally realized that he would never be as good as Marty was, in his parent's eyes. Marty was their *baby* and their *favorite*. He resolved to avoid his brother and his friends while in school.

Several years later, Jim was awakened in the middle of the night.

"Jimmy! Wake up! You've got to help me. I'm in trouble!"

Jim sat up in bed, rubbed his eyes, and tried to clear his mind.

"Be quiet. You'll wake up Mom and Dad. What time is it?"

"Jimmy, the guys dared me to steal a car…and the cops chased us for miles…we hit a parked car and kept going…the police stopped at the wreck car and we drove away!"

"Where is the car now?"

"I parked it down the street."

"That was a foolish thing to do! Why did you bring the car here?" Marty just sat in silence. "Go to bed, NOW! Don't say anything to anyone."

Jim quietly left the house and walked down the street to the stolen car. The front fender was badly dented. He got into the car, started it, and drove a few blocks down the street without turning on the lights. It took him over an hour to drive it several miles away from his home. He then carefully searched the car for any traces of Marty and his friends. Next, he wiped off the steering wheel before abandoning the car and began a two-mile run home. He barely got back into his bed before his mother was calling him to get up for school.

Jim dragged himself into the kitchen. He was exhausted and his heart was still pounding. Marty was nowhere to be seen.

"Where's Marty?"

"He isn't going to school today. He isn't feeling well. Hurry up, or you will be late!"

Jim rushed to school, anxious to listen for rumors of a car accident. The topic of discussion at the lunch table was that there had been an incident that had occurred last night. It seems that Tami Crockett, one of the school's cheerleaders, was returning home from a babysitting job when her car was sideswiped by a hit-and-run driver. She was rushed to the hospital where doctors were trying to save her badly mangled foot. The car had been found, but no one seemed to know who had been driving. Marty's friends ate very quietly at their table.

When Jim got home, he walked slowly up the stairs to Marty's room. Marty was sitting on the bed, with the stereo blaring.

"How are you feeling?" Jim asked sarcastically.

"I feel a lot better. I was really tired."

"You lied to me. You said you hit a parked car. Do you know that Tami Crockett might lose her foot? You are in BIG trouble!"

"And so are you, big brother…You drove the car away…If I get caught…Well, you'll be in hot water, too! And Mom and Dad won't be happy that you didn't take care of me."

Jim walked slowly from the room. He realized what a mess he had gotten himself into because of trying to prevent his parents from being hurt by Marty's behavior. How could he have been so stupid! And Marty was right. If their parents learned the details of the accident, they would be heartbroken. Somehow, Carolyn Sterling would twist the facts and blame him.

A mutual understanding now existed between the two boys. They were openly friendly when at home around their parents, but outside their home, they seldom spoke to each other. The remainder of Jim's senior year was uneventful until the end of the semester exams.

Jim had two hours before his Government exam, so he went to school, put his jacket in his locker, and want to the library for a final review of his notes. Soon he was joined by his friend Todd.

"Mr. Keaton is really mad!"

"What is his problem? Did someone get 100% on his exam? He prides himself on those exams being the toughest in the school."

"Someone stole the Algebra exam! Mr. Keaton is furious. He says he is going to search everyone who was scheduled to take the test. And he is going to search all the lockers of the math students. If he finds anything, he is going to call the police and charge the thief with robbery. Whoever has that exam had better ditch it fast!"

"I wish someone would steal the Government exam before I take it," laughed Jim. "Who would be desperate enough to steal a high school exam, knowing the consequences?"

Jim's exam was difficult, but he had studied the previous night and thought he had done well. He collected his jacket from his locker and walked to his car where Todd was waiting for him. This was Jim's last exam and he and Todd had planned to go to the Army Recruiting Office to enlist. It has always been Jim's plan to join the army and become a member of the military police. After his tour was over, he then intended to apply to the State Police to become a trooper. His career plans would be set in motion today. Fifteen minutes later, he and Todd were standing in front of the recruiting office.

"Let's get something to eat before we sign up. It will be our last meal as civilians," Todd chuckled. He and Jim crossed the street and walked into the local diner.

"You are always hungry," laughed Jim. "You had better be careful; the army won't take you because you eat too much. They can't afford to feed you!"

The boys ordered burgers, fries, and sodas and continued their gleeful banter. It was only when they were ready to leave that the mood changed. The waitress cleared the dishes and presented the boys with their checks. Jim reached into his jackets for some money.

"What's this?" Slowly Jim pulled several folded sheets of paper from his pocket. An uneasy feeling crept over him before he opened the papers. Todd looked on in disbelief as Jim stared at the stolen Algebra exam.

"How did these get into my coat?"

"Did you take them? Why in the *hell* did you take algebra exams? You took algebra two years ago!" Todd was really surprised that his friend would do something so foolish as to steal some exams from a class that he had taken several years ago.

"I didn't take these," but Jim knew who had stolen the exams. Marty had gone to a party last night and had gotten home very late. He had gone to school before Jim had gotten up, telling their mother that he was going to meet a group of classmates to cram for the math exam.

"Someone must have stuffed them in your locker before old Keaton could search for them. Why don't you go to the bathroom, tear them into little pieces, and flush them down the toilet? You don't want anyone to know that you have them."

Jim mechanically walked to the men's room, tore the exams into small pieces, and flushed the evidence down the commode. The two boys paid their bills and walked solemnly out of the diner and across the street to the resulting office where they enlisted in the army. The gleeful mood of the day had turned somber. The day that held the promise of the beginning of his career plans had almost ended in a disaster. If he had been caught with the stolen papers, he would have been expelled from school...no graduation....no *army*...no *military police*...no state trooper training...a criminal record.

Jim drove home, glad that he had a friend like Todd. He knew that the day's events would never be mentioned again. After he arrived there, he went immediately to Marty's room. Luckily, their parents were not at home. He sat down on the bed and waited for about 15 minutes when Marty entered the room.

"Hi, Big Brother. What are you doing here?"

"Did you steal those algebra exams and put them in my locker?" Jim fought hard to control his temper.

Marty looked straight at Jim and showed no remorse.

"I knew no one would search you. You didn't have to take the exam. Do you have the exam with you? I need to memorize some of the answers!"

"Do you realize that if I had been caught with those exams, I wouldn't have graduated?"

"Yeah...Yeah...Yeah...Big Deal! Do you have the exam? I want to take a look at it...You know...I need to get an idea of what to study!"

Jim walked across the room and grabbed Marty by the shirt. He tried to keep his voice calm and his temper in check.

"Marty, in two weeks, I'll be leaving for basic training at Fort Jackson, in South Carolina. Until that time, stay away from me. I'm not mentioning this to Mom and Dad, but I don't want any trouble from you. Just keep away from me."

"Go ahead and tell them. They won't believe you. Mom thinks you pick on me because you are older and bigger than me. Now, where's the test?"

Jim left the room, shaking his head! Marty was right. Mom and Dad always made excuses for Marty's escapades. He had always known that Marty was the *baby* of the family, and according to them, he could do no wrong. This attitude hurt him; yet, he loved his parents very much and would do nothing to hurt them.

The next two weeks were a whirlwind. Jim took his favorite girl to the senior prom. Graduation practices were disrupted only to paint the class logo on the water tower as was the tradition of all senior classes. The next week, graduation was held in the football stadium, where Jim won a good Citizenship Award. The post graduation parties lasted until dawn. Jim had a few days to say good-bye to his friends and family before leaving for Fort Jackson.

Basic training was difficult, but Jim Sterling was determined to complete the eight weeks with distinction. The letters from home hinted that Marty was still having problems, but there were always explanations and excuses for all the incidents. Jim tried to put the news from home in the back of his mind. He knew that he had to excel if he was to go to school for the military police. When the eight weeks were over, James Sterling was proud of the *Expert* classification he had achieved for marksmanship. He also had orders to report to Fort Leavenworth, Kansas, to begin his training for the military police. When he went home after basic training, Jim and Marty continued to observe a friendly truce. They were polite, but spent very little time together.

On his last day at home, Jim came downstairs to find his mother sitting at the kitchen table, crying, with her head in her hands.

"Ma, are you OK? Why are you crying?"

"It's Marty. He didn't come home last night. I've called all the hospitals and the police to see if anyone had reported an accident, but no one has seen him. Dad has gone out to look for him. He has been such a confused young man lately."

"What do you mean, Ma?" Jim asked as he poured himself a cup of coffee.

"It's the crowd that he hangs around with after school. Most of the boys have quit school. They don't have jobs. I've smelled alcohol on Marty when he comes home late. The principal called and we had to go to school because your brother reeked of beer. He left school at noon with that crowd of no good friends, and they had beer in the car. He was suspended from school for one week. He says he won't do it again."

"Ma, you have to be stricter with Marty."

"I know, but he's our baby and he doesn't mean to get into trouble. It just happens. He was never like you, Jim. You were the oldest and you were always an independent, confident, and responsible child. You knew from junior high school that you wanted to be a policeman. Marty is sixteen years old, and his goal in his life is to have fun. When you lived here, Marty was never in trouble. You were such a good influence on him."

Jim smiled as he thought of the many times that Marty had been in trouble when they were both living at home. It was difficult to believe that his folks knew nothing of Marty's escapades. It was now amusing to him that his mother had somehow twisted the problem with Marty to be his fault. If he had still been living at home, Marty would not be in trouble; at least they would know nothing about it. Before he could respond to his mother, the back door opened and his dad appeared.

"I've looked everywhere. I even went to the high school to see if he was there. I checked his first period class, and the teacher told me he hadn't been in class for several weeks. The principal stopped me in the hall and asked for Marty and I told him that Marty had a severe case of pneumonia and was being cared for at home. (Once again his parents had made an excuse for their youngest son.) Then I drove to the police station. There was apparently a string of robberies at convenience stores last night and it was difficult to find anyone to talk to about a missing boy. I finally saw a desk sergeant and he knew of no accidents."

Carolyn Sterling began to cry. "Suppose the boys had an accident and are hurt? They could be wrecked in a ditch or in a car that has turned upside down in a field."

Mr. Sterling walked over to his wife and put his hands on her shoulders.

"Dad, give me the car keys. I'll see if I can find him."

Jim first went to the mall where he quickly walked from one end to the other and back. He knew when he was in school that kids would skip school and hang out at the mall. He then drove to the homes of Marty's friends, but he saw no activity anywhere. Next, Jim stopped at a pay phone to contact the police again, but no accidents had been reported. As he was slowly driving down Main Street, he noticed Darryl Riggin's car parked in front of Dover's Bar and Grill. He remembered that Darryl had been with Marty the night they had stolen the car and had an accident. Jim parked the car on a side street and walked into the restaurant.

It took a few moments for Jim's eyes to adjust to the darkness of the room. It was the usual bar and grill with paneled walls, a bar with ten stools, and a dining area in the black. Four men were sitting at the bar, drinking beer. Jim looked around and was about to leave when he heard a burst of laughter coming from the dining room. As he walked into the area, he saw Marty, Darryl, and two other guys sitting at a round table drinking beer.

"Hi, Big Brother!" Marty called to Jim and waved at him to come over to the table. "Why don't you come over and have a beer with us?"

"It's a little early for me to have a beer. Marty, can I talk to you for a moment? Privately?"

"Anything you want to say to me, you can say in front of my friends. We have no secrets!" Marty took a drink of his beer and laughed.

Jim walked over to the table, bent down, and whispered into his brother's ear. "If you don't leave immediately with me, I'll tell the bartender that you and your friends are seventeen years old, and then he'll throw the group of you out of here and embarrass you and your friends. You can stay and finish your beer or leave quietly with me. It's your choice."

"I've got to go guys. It's been a *hell of a night*. Darryl, I'll see you later to pick up my…uh…uh…things."

The two boys walked out of the bar and into the sunlight. Marty could tell that his big brother was upset. It took Jim a few minutes to get his emotions under control. Marty was still a self-centered *brat*.

"Do you have any idea how you have upset Mom and Dad? They are so worried. Where were you last night? Ma's so concerned that she called the police to see if you were…"

Marty interrupted Jim before he could finish his sentence.

"Why in the hell did Ma call the police? What did she tell them? Are they looking for me? Why can't she mind her own business?"

Jim stopped on the street and looked straight into Marty's eyes. His face was pale and his hands were shaking.

"Marty, you are seventeen years old and still live at home. Where were you last night? Were you involved in those robberies?"

"We were just riding around, drinking a few beers, and having some fun. We finished all the beer and no one had any money. Tom had his winter coat with his ski mask in the pocket. He said he knew how to get some money; he took Darryl's brother's pistol from the glove compartment and robbed Smitty's Convenience Store over on Green Street. I was so scared…I just sat in the car. But after he got back in the car and we drove away, Tom dared each one of us to rob a store. It was like a game! Everyone had to rob a store and the one who got the most money had to buy the beer. I won! I got $223 and I was buying the beer until you came into Dovers. It was just a game. No one got hurt."

Jim was furious. What kind of friends did Marty associate with in school and in his spare time? What was Darryl doing with his brother's pistol in the glove compartment of the car? Was it really his brother's pistol? They got into the car and drove down Main Street to the city park. He stopped the car near a pay phone. The boys sat quietly for a few minutes as Jim collected his thoughts. He finally was calm to speak.

"I want you to call Ma and tell her you guys went over to Jackson to the movies. Tell her you had a flat tire on that long deserted stretch of road and no one would stop to help you that late at night. Tell her I found you asleep in the car. As soon as we get the tire fixed, we'll be home. Go ahead! Call her!"

Marty meekly obeyed his big brother. He called his mother and repeated the story as Jim had told him. Then Jim got on the phone to assure his mother that Marty was not hurt. They would be home as soon as the tire was fixed, and they took it back to the car. He then hung up the phone and turned to his brother.

"Let's go get a cup of coffee, eat some breakfast, and have a talk."

"Yeah, we need to kill some time while the supposedly flat tire is being changed," Marty laughed.

The boys got back into the car and Jim drove to the local diner. They went inside, ordered two cups of coffee and some breakfast, and moved from the counter to a booth for more privacy. For a few moments, no one spoke.

"I don't know why you're so upset. Nobody got hurt and no one knows that it was *us*. Ma believed your story, and Dad will believe anything Ma tells him." Marty chuckled at his last statement.

Jim fought hard to control his temper.

"Do you ever think of what might have happened? Suppose the owner had a gun? You don't even know how to shoot the gun you were carrying. You could have been killed, and just as bad, you might have killed someone. How do you think Ma and Dad would feel then?"

"Big Deal! No one got hurt!"

"Marty, I leave tomorrow for Fort Leavenworth, Kansas. You have a year and a half of school and then you can move out of the house, leave this town, and do anything you want to do. Don't mess up your future by robbing some mini-mart for a few beers. Think, Marty, Think! Now, finish your breakfast, go to the bathroom and get cleaned up. Then, let's go home."

Jim left early the next morning for Kansas.

His specialized training for the military police was difficult, but this is what Jim had wanted for most of his life. He was also encouraged to take several criminology classes at the local community college. His life was back on his planned career path.

As happy as he was with the unfolding of his life, the letters from his mother were very upsetting. Marty had quit school; his mother didn't understand how the school officials could put Marty out of school after he was found drunk in the bathroom. It was only after she went to school did she discover that Marty had constantly been in trouble and had forged her signature on many of the communications sent to the Sterlings. Mrs. Sterling said that Marty couldn't settle down because he missed his brother. But Jim knew that his poor behavior had started long before he joined the army and left home. Another letter informed him that Marty refused to go to the alternative high school at night. (He said that school was for losers.) He thought it might interfere with a job he might get. No job was mentioned in future letters. His mother did tell Jim that they had bought Marty a car so he could go job hunting. Near end of his training, a letter from home mentioned that Marty had made several appearances in traffic court. As his mother said, "Boys will be *boys!*"

When his orders came for Jim to go to Vilseck, Germany, he decided not to go home although he had a few days before leaving. He wanted to keep some distance between him and his brother.

Jim Sterling fell in love with Germany. He did not let the disappointment in his mother's letter that he did not come home spoil his first impression of his new post. He was able to see the country, tour through Europe, and gain a great deal of experience in law enforcement. Most of the problems that a military policeman had to confront came from drunken soldiers, a few who were AWOL, and some over zealous drivers. He became a silent bystander at seminars and conferences sponsored by the local police. He was also surprised how quickly he learned the German language.

The news from home was unsettling, but Jim realized that Marty no longer had him as a crutch to help him out of a jam. He hoped that Marty might eventually grow up and act responsibly. The last few of his mother's letters had failed to mention any trouble involving his little brother. Jim wondered if Marty had matured or if he was not too smart to get caught. He was glad for the family when mother wrote that Marty had moved to Pittsburgh. She failed to say if he had a job.

His discharge from the army was a time of mixed emotions for Jim. He had distinguished himself in the army; he had even debated reenlisting and making a career in the armed forces. However, his dream to be a state trooper was stronger. As soon as he was back in the states and separated from army, he took the first train back to New Jersey where he immediately applied to become a member of the state police.

Training was intense, but after his stint in the military police, Jim did not find it too difficult. He was an excellent marksman and he welcomed the challenge of the law class. He notified his parents when he was due to graduate from the academy, but no one attended the exercises. Jim sent his address to his folks when he received his first assignment in the Wildwood/Atlantic City area off the New Jersey Turnpike.

Trooper Sterling's first assignment was to patrol the Garden State Parkway with a seasoned officer. It was basic, routine duty for a probation trooper on his first assignment. He gave out traffic citations, made DWI arrests, checked for runaways, etc. Being a rookie, Jim worked most holidays, but he always talked to his parents on the phone on a weekly basis. Marty's name was seldom mentioned.

"All Right! Listen up!" The captain called to order the weekly briefing of the troopers of the barracks.

"There is a stolen car ring operating out of Pennsylvania. The cars are traveling on the turnpike and then on to Maryland or to Western Pennsylvania. Many of them are shipped overseas out of the Port of Baltimore. Out sources tell us that if the cars reach Pittsburg, they appear to be sold to chop shops. We are talking about BMW s, sports cars, etc. High on the list are foreign cars. The parts are worth a fortune in Central America. The operation seems to be too sophisticated for a bunch of teenagers, so treat anyone you stop as potentially dangerous! That's all for today; let's get to work!"

"Some guys will do anything to keep from working at a steady job," Jim commented to his partner, Chester "Chic'" McMahan. "It's easier to steal a car than to punch a time clock." The twosome got into the patrol car and drove out on the parkway.

A few weeks later, while working the midnight-to-eight shift, their patrol car got an emergency call.

"Attention all units! Attention all units! Trooper down! Trooper down! Anyone in the vicinity of Atlantic City Parkway near Hammonton proceed immediately! All Units! Trooper down! Proceed with caution!"

Jim and Chick turned on their flashing light and raced toward the scene. This was the worse possible alert that a squad car could get. One of their fellow troopers was in trouble. It was dark and no one could tell if the gunman or gunmen were still in the area. Jim felt his heart begin to race a bit faster. The car sped up the turnpike through the night.

It took only twelve minutes to get to the crime scene, although to the two troopers, it seemed like an eternity. A second patrol car was already there. The picture before them was one of horror…

One of the troopers was face down on the highway, bleeding from the back of his head. The door of the patrol car was open with the radio still blaring! Behind the wheel of the car was Trooper Hal Evans, dead after a spray of bullets hit him several times. The windows of the patrol car were blown into a thousand pieces, scattered over the highway. A trooper was running from his car with a blanket while his partner was screaming into the two-way radio for an ambulance. Chick slammed on the breaks as Jim jumped from the car. He raced to the bleeding trooper, removing his jacket as he ran. He rolled over the bleeding trooper and held his jacket over the wound. He looked into the eyes of a dying man…

Blood gurgled from the head of the man.

"Sterling…Sterling…Ster…" and the body went limp. Jim began CPR immediately, but the wounds were too extensive. The ambulance arrived a few moments later, but there was nothing the EMTs could do but put the two dead men in the ambulance.

The troopers blocked off the area looking for any clue as to what had transpired. There was a radio message that the two dead troopers had stopped a Mercedes and had asked for a license tag check. Of course, no Mercedes was at the scene and the tag check revealed that the car was stolen. It was a dead-end investigation.

Hundreds of troopers from across the nation attended the funerals of the two slain men. The solemnity of the occasion overshadowed the sense of frustration felt by the lawmen. The only clue that the troopers had was the call from the two slain men, alerting the barracks that they were stopping a Mercedes for speeding and wanted a license tag check.

The crowd walked slowly from the grave site. The service was especially difficult for Jim. Hal Evans had been in his class at the academy. He also had nightmares since the man died in his arms. He relived the moment over and over in his head.

"Tough way to lose a friend."

"Yeah…" The man's voice interrupted Jim's thoughts. "I only met him once at the barracks. No one deserves to die like that."

"I thought that you two were good friend. I heard he was calling your name when he died."

"He must have seen my name badge." But the man's statement kept running through Jim's mind. Why was the dying trooper's final words were *his* name? Did he recognize Jim Sterling after a brief meeting in a crowded interrogation room? Perhaps the man said something other than his name. Everything happened so fast. "Did I miss something?" Jim poured over these facts for many weeks.

During the next few months, the investigation into the deaths of the two troopers intensified. Every bit of information or rumor was analyzed for any clue it might give the lawmen. The entire barracks donated their free time to helping the investigators follow any lead. But the information led them no closer to discovering who had murdered their friends.

Jim's career continued to spiral upward. He was given a commendation for his efforts at the scene of the shooting. He and Chick returned to regular duty, patrolling the parkway, making routine stops.

A message to call his mother brought a sense of dread. Had something happened to his dad? Was Marty up to his old tricks? Jim waited until he was off duty, in his own apartment, before he dialed the number.

"Hello."

"Ma, it's me, Jim. I got your message to give you a call. Are you and Dad OK?"

"Jimmy, we're so worried. Marty was going to the dentist and was late. So he drove a little bit fast…" Jim could hear his mother begin to cry.

"Ma, slow down…I can't understand you."

"The police stopped him for going too fast and they said the car he was driving was stolen. Marty didn't know the car was stolen…He's not a bad boy…"

"Ma! Ma! Where is Marty now? Did he call you?"

"He's in jail in Monroeville, Pennsylvania. Oh…he told me, Jimmy, but I was so upset that I didn't write it down. Jimmy, I think that the police always pick on Marty. It seems like he is always blamed for everything. Your dad is so worried." Mrs. Sterling was now crying uncontrollably.

"Ma, tell Pop that I'll make a few phone calls to see what I can find out. I'll give you a call as soon as I know anything. Now…try not to worry."

Jim hung up the phone and thought of all the trouble that Marty had been involved in as a kid. His parents always had an excuse for his troubles. Since he hadn't heard from Marty for several years, he assumed that his brother had grown into a responsible adult. But as he picked up the phone to try to locate Marty, the sense of dread returned to him.

It was the third call to Monroeville Police that Jim finally located his brother.

The dispatcher would give him no information on the phone except that Marty was being held there. He called his barracks, took a few days off, and began the long drive across the state of Pennsylvania to Monroeville.

"Sergeant, I'm Jim Sterling of the New Jersey State Police. (He had purposely worn his uniform. Local policemen usually cooperated with a uniformed policeman from another area.) I'd like to talk to someone about a man you have in your lock up, Martin Sterling."

"Is he a relative of yours?"

"My brother."

"Just a moment…I'll call my captain."

After a few minutes, Jim was ushered into the office of Captain Duncan.

"Please sit down. I'm Captain Duncan. How can I help you?"

"Jim Sterling, New Jersey State Police." He immediately showed his identification card and his badge. He eased into the chair in front of the desk.

"I'd like some information on a fellow you have in the lockup. His name is Martin Sterling. He's my brother."

"We stopped Mr. Sterling in the Pennsylvania Turnpike, going forty miles over the speed limit. When the officer checked for license and registration, he was told to proceed with caution because the car had been reported stolen a few days ago. We immediately arrested Mr. Sterling and we are holding him on possession of a stolen vehicle."

"Has he contacted a lawyer?"

"Yes, and we've called our special investigative unit, working on the stolen car ring that has been operating in the area. We also have some new information that links this car thievery gang to the murder of your two troopers."

"And you think that Marty, er…Mr. Sterling…is part of this?"

"He will not give us any information, but his actions certainly seem to fall into the pattern. He was driving a stolen BMW, traveling on the turnpike near Pittsburgh with no bill of sale for the automobile, and could give no reason for speeding, or any destination!"

"Has he said anything?"

"Not a thing! He used his phone call to phone his parents. But a strange thing happened! Marvin Jones, an attorney in our area who has handled some really disreputable clients, came here yesterday and talked to Sterling. He only stayed a few minutes and then he left. He said he would be back, but I've not seen him today. Of course, he knows his rights, but he refused a court appointed attorney."

"Is there any evidence that links him to the auto theft ring?"

"Only circumstantial…but when Marvin Jones appeared, without a call…the task force wants to talk to him…"

"Can I see him?"

"As a policeman or a brother?"

"As a brother."

"Remember, if he tells you anything, you have no immunity and we could call you to testify. And you knew those two policemen who were gunned down on the highway!"

"As a brother," Jim repeated.

Jim was led to a holding cell at the back of the barracks.

"Hi, Big Brother." Marty seemed glad to see his brother. He had the same air of confidence about him as he did the last time Jim had seen him.

"You really got yourself into some big trouble this time. What were you doing in that car?"

"Boy, you really look sharp in that uniform? Has Mom and Dad seen you dressed in the official garb?"

"Marty, this is serious. What were you doing in that car?"

"I was playing cards with a group of guys in Parkersburg, West Virginia, when I remembered that I had a dentist appointment the next morning in Pittsburg. One of the guys loaned me his car. I guess I was in a hurry. Hey! No *big deal*! Why is everyone making a federal case out of it?"

"The car was stolen."

"I didn't know that. The guy just threw the keys across the table and told me to take his car."

"Then this can easily be cleared up. Just give me the name of the man who loaned you the car…"

"I don't know his name."

"Give me the name of anyone else at the card game. Maybe someone can identify the owner of the car."

"I don't know anyone's name. I heard about the game at a gas station. Besides, I don't want to get anyone else in trouble."

"Well, give me the name of the dentist you were going to see."

For the first time, Marty was speechless. He sat quietly on the edge of his bunk. It was then that Jim realized the police account of the traffic stop might be accurate. He quietly turned around and walked out of the cell.

"Give Mom and Dad a call when you get home. Tell them that I'm OK and I'll call them soon. And don't you worry about me, your *Little Brother*. I've got a good lawyer and I'll be out of here in a few days."

The drive back to New Jersey seemed endless. Jim had very mixed emoticons as he traveled down the same route that Marty had been driving when he was arrested. It was also a route that two of his fellow patrolmen could have travelled many times. Could his own brother be involved in the murder of those troopers? He didn't want to consider the consequences of such a scenario. It would devastate his mother and father. He began to reminisce about the petty incidents in which

Marty had been involved. He had studied cases where kids had grad-uated from petty crimes to more serious offenses. But Marty? Marty? Marty was his kid brother. Marty couldn't have killed anyone. And he must remember that he was assuming some details that were not facts at all. Marty might have stolen a car, but his little brother could never murder anyone!

He fell into bed exhausted, not bothering to call his parents. When he did not get a phone call from them, he guessed that Marty was out of jail and had contacted them. He never mentioned his trip to Pittsburgh or the facts that had emerged about his brother. No need to stir up an investigation until he had some proof!

Several weeks later, there was a special briefing of those troopers that patrolled the parkway near Atlantic City.

"A few weeks ago, we apprehended a suspect in the stolen car ring. The task force decided, after questioning the suspect, that we would release him, but put a surveillance team on to keep an eye on him and his movements. Sources have informed us that there is a convoy of stolen cars coming up the Garden State Parkway during the next few days. This is a tip from an unknown source and the movements of our suspect. We are putting all those troopers who patrol that area on high alert. We will constantly update you on any stolen car reports that we receive. There is a strong indication that these car thieves might be involved in the murder of our fellow troopers, so be very, very careful. Those people have nothing to lose! They will do everything they can not to be apprehended. Again, BE VERY CAREFUL!"

Because of the time that had passed, Jim never thought of his brother Marty or his possible involvement with this group. Instead, his thoughts drifted to the slain trooper, and the look in his eyes as he was dying.

The following few days produced no arrests in the auto theft case. On the sixth day, events occurred that would change James Sterling's life forever.

On Friday, Chick and Jim started a week on the twelve to eight o'clock shift. It had been a quite night but at 2:30 AM, Chick answered a radio call. Two stolen cars had been identified by their tag numbers.

Traffic was light, but minutes later, a Porsche sped by. Chick checked the hot sheet…

"We're in business, partner. That Porsche is hot! Call into the station for back up!"

Before Jim had a chance to phone the barracks, a second stolen car, a BMW, passed where the police car had pulled off the road.

"Attention! Attention! We're in pursuit of two hot cars near Route 559! Turn off near Ocean City. Send back up immediately!"

Jim was racing down Route 559 in pursuit of the two cars. His siren was screaming as the light flashed. They were soon joined by several other patrol cars that had been in the area. The five cars overtook the BMW after a few miles. Thankfully, the car pulled to the side of the road. Jim pulled his squad car at an angle as Chick jumped out with his gun drawn. The door slowly opened on the BMW and a man appeared with his hands in the air. Chick rushed forward and put the man in handcuffs. It took several anxious moments before the passenger side door opened and a woman emerged from the car with her hands in the air. As Jim held his gun on the suspect, Chick took a second pair of handcuffs and shackled the woman as she screamed curses at them.

As the troopers attempted to get the suspects in the back of the squad car, another Porsche streaked by! Someone started shooting at the crowd from the window. Chick was hit in the leg and one of the suspects was killed instantly. Jim, who was still sitting in his squad car, on the radio, immediately shifted gears and raced after the speeding Porsche. He had seen Chick go down and had no idea his condition. But he knew several other troopers were at the scene and would call for an ambulance. His patrol car was racing down the parkway and gradually gaining on the stolen Porsche that was in front of him. The Porsche showed no sign of stopping, but instead seemed to go faster. When he finally pulled the speeding squad car next to the Porsche, Jim drew his gun.

He then stared into the eyes of the driver of the stolen car. He was staring into the eyes of his brother, Marty Sterling!

The shock of seeing Marty driving the stolen car caused Jim to ease up on the gas pedal and Marty sped away. He just could not comprehend that his brother, Marty Sterling, could be involved stealing cars! A cold chill came over Jim. If his brother was involved in stealing cars, he was also involved in several murders! The thought caused him to drive his squad car on the shoulder of the road and stop. He found he was shaking so hard that he could not drive.

It was then that Jim realized the dilemma that he had. As a good state trooper, he must tell the truth and implicate his brother. He could identify possible murder suspects! His brother had shot his partner and possibly shot two state troopers. And then he thought of the dying trooper. He wasn't calling James Sterling; he was identifying the man who had shot him…Martin Sterling! He had sworn to uphold the laws of the state of New Jersey against any criminal…the oath never said that a trooper could give a pass to relatives.

But if he turned in his own brother, his family would be destroyed. His parents would be devastated. He had always been responsible for his little brother, and he had failed.

James Sterling did not return to the crime scene; he drove his patrol car to his apartment instead. He quickly changed clothes, packed a small suitcase and drove the squad car to the barracks, parking it in the back lot. Then he walked to the bus station and bought a ticket to Ocean Beach. It sounded like a nice place to go for a couple of days for him to collect his thoughts and decide what the right thing to do was.

His reverie was interrupted when Samantha hopped up into his lap. "Does your grandma have a puppy? Daddy says when we get to Grandma's that I can get a puppy! And Daddy says we can take him on Grandma's boat with us! Do doggies like to eat shrimp?" Jim smiled.

And the bus rolled on…

CHAPTER 5

KATE SMILED AS THE LITTLE GIRL CHATTED endlessly with the fellow across the aisle. Darkness had brought a hush to the bus as it sped along the highway. Only the sound of the rain dashing against the windows broke the solemn mood of the group of travelers. Even the child seemed to lower her voice, drawn into the ambiance of the moment. Most of the passengers on the bus had turned off the reading lights and were dozing in their seats. Only an occasional cough or giggle broke the silence.

Kate glanced over at her friend who was asleep on the seat beside her. It seemed impossible that she had known Clint for only a few weeks. The peaceful expression on his face did not reflect the turmoil that was waiting for them in Nebraska. She rested her head on his shoulder as her thoughts moved to her home and the problems facing them when they arrived. Had it been only eight weeks since she graduated from the University of Nebraska? Could anyone ever have imagined the turn events that would change her life forever? What explanation could she possibly give her parents? How has her life become such a mixed-up mess? Such a crazy, wonderful, mixed-up mess?

The monotonous droning of the tires prompted Kate to snuggle closer to Clint and reflect on the past few weeks.

"How is your exam schedule?"

Kate shook her head, and smiled at her roommate. Her schedule for the next three weeks was hectic.

"I have two exams on Tuesday, one on Wednesday, and a final exam on Friday. My parents and Jay are arriving on Sunday for the graduation festivities. There's practice on Monday and the final ceremony is Wednesday. Then I've got to completely pack four years of acquired college furniture, books, clothes, and all the other things I've accumulated while a student here. Dad and Jay are coming in two cars to help me carry home all this 'stuff.' Thank goodness I spent my entire Christmas vacation and Spring Break on wedding plans. I'm going to go home and CRASH!"

"CRASH?"

"Do absolutely nothing! I just want to relax for the next three months before my wedding. I never realized how hard it would be change a major course of study after my sophomore year. Jay told me that I should major in Art History. He said that he couldn't imagine me working with poor people all my life. My schedule this last semester was horrid! It will take me months to get the University of Nebraska out of my mind. Then, in September, I'll walk down the aisle and become Mrs. Jay Coleman!"

Erin laughed at her roommate. They had shared the joys and disappointments of college life after arriving on campus four years ago. She had celebrated with Kate when she became engaged to Jay and would soon be travelling to Omaha to be maid of honor in her best friend's wedding.

"Do you know what you need? OCEAN BEACH! Why don't you come home with me to Ocean Beach and relax for a few weeks before the wedding? I don't have to be in New York to start my job until the middle of September. I'm going to spend one last summer there. You have been telling me for four years that you like to see the ocean. Send all your things home with your parents, and come home with me. I can promise you the sun, swimming, lazy walks on the beach, bicycling, and great seafood dinners. Then we can drive to Omaha together."

"Erin, that sounds great! But there is so much to do. I'm sure that Jay has a schedule to follow to get everything done for the wedding. You know how organized he is!"

But Erin would not listen to her roommate.

"Don't give me an answer now. Think about it and you can give me a decision on Friday, if we survive our final exams."

Kate laughed at Erin. It was easy to understand why the two girls had become such good friends Erin seemed to sense when something was bothering Kate or when she was worried or upset. It was Kate who was a settling influence on the effervescent Erin.

"Can you imagine what Jay would say if I decided to go home with you instead of returning to Omaha? He would have a *cow*!"

"If you lived near the ocean, he could have a *fish*!"

Both girls giggled as Kate picked up her books and walked rapidly to the library. She wanted to review the notes she had taken all semester before her first final and then study the paintings of the classical artists. But Kate found it difficult to concentrate. Her mind kept returning to the spirited conversation with Erin. She had wanted to accept the yearly invitation to come to the beach (Erin had invited her several times), but her summers were spent with Jay and working at the museum in Omaha. Maybe it would be relaxing to go home with Erin for a few days. She got up from her seat, went to the stacks, and pulled *Beaches of the Atlantic* from the shelf. She opened it quickly as if she was sneaking some X-rated book, and spent the next hour not studying her notes, but gazing at pictures of sandy beaches. She began daydreaming about lazy days in the sun. Her reverie was interrupted when several girls began packing up their books and one of the books dropped to the floor.

Kate immediately closed the book and looked around the library. She was very embarrassed! What was she thinking? How could she even consider going to the ocean? Jay would expect her to come home and assume her responsibilities concerning the wedding. She had always done what Jay wanted her to do! She had been Jay's girl since the tenth grade. They had become engaged at the end of her sophomore year when he had graduated from college. It was Jay who encouraged her to change her major to Art History; she had started college as a sociology major. He returned to Omaha and soon went to work for a prominent accounting firm. She had spent most of her holidays this year planning her wedding. Why was she now thinking about the beach? But…if she did decide to go, most of her wedding plans were complete. She gathered her books and slowly walked back to the dorm to meet Erin for dinner. However, the beach visit was still very conspicuously present in her thoughts.

The week became a blur of activity. Kate crammed for her two exams on Tuesday, identified seventy-five paintings for her Art History final on Wednesday, and dragged herself into her Economics final on Friday, totally exhausted. After the test, Kate returned to her room and sat down among piles of boxes and clothing. Her energy was drained! Her parents, and Jay were arriving on Sunday. She needed to get busy and pack up her belongings. But Kate just sat there, listening to the radio. Suddenly, she jumped up off the edge of the bed and opened a suitcase. The Beach Boys were singing one of their hits. "Surfer Girl" was blaring on the radio, and Kate made a decision. She had never seen the ocean, and this was her opportunity to experience it with her friend. She would clean out her room, send the boxes to Omaha with her parents, and go to Ocean Beach with Erin. She finalized her decision by dropping her bathing suit into the suitcase. She had never done anything so irrational in her life! What would Jay say? This was so unlike her!

It took some serious explaining to convince her parents that a trip to Erin's home would be a necessary *time out* before the excitement and hubbub of the wedding. At first, Jay was livid, but he condescendingly agreed to the trip. After she explained her last semester and how hard she had to work after changing her course of study, Jay could see how harried she had become since Easter. However, he also emphasized that after they were married, there would be no time for "silly" vacations to the East Coast.

So when the graduation exercises were finished, Kate loaded four years of accumulated college necessities into Jay's and her parent's car for the return trip to Omaha. She was surprised at the feeling of relief that overcame her as she waved good-bye to her loved ones. An hour later, Kate and Erin were on the train to the East Coast and Ocean Beach!

"You were up early this morning," Erin called to her friend as she came in the kitchen door.

"I wanted to see the sun rise over the ocean…It was so beautiful! Did you know there are people swimming and walking along the beach? It's only eight o'clock in the morning!"

"Most of those people are looking for shells. The tide washes them in, or it uncovers them as the water washes over the sand. We can go to the beach and gather shells, if you want to."

"Are they free?"

"Yes, they're free. I need to wash the University of Nebraska out of your head. You have lived in that state too long. I've got to get you in a bathing suit and barefooted. You are drenched and have shoes on! You need to let the sand get between your toes and cool off in the waves! Now, get dressed in some dry clothes. I'll introduce you to Ocean Beach on the seat of bicycle. You Mid-West girls know how to ride a bike, don't you?"

"It's been a few years, but I think I can remember how to pedal a bike!"

Kate playfully threw a towel at Erin. She hurriedly put on a pair of dry shorts and a T-shirt and followed Erin outside.

"I'll race you to the bikes," and Kate rushed and hopped on a bicycle. The two girls peddled from the house to the boardwalk and joined the other vacationers there. Joggers were running at various speeds and skate boarders were weaving around the morning strollers. Kate felt a certain carefree frame of mind as she peddled down the boardwalk. She had not felt this good in years. But suddenly, she felt guilty. How could she feel this way with Jay in Nebraska? Why didn't she miss him?

"Hey, Slowpoke! Let's stop at the Flying Fish Diner for a stack of pancakes. They're the best on the boardwalk."

Kate hit the brakes and jumped off her bicycle as it slowed. She had not ridden a bike in years; Jay thought it was childish.

"Who ever heard of eating pancakes at a place called the Flying Fish? But I'm so hungry that I could literally eat a flying fish!"

The remainder of the morning was a whirl of activity. The girls giggled like teenagers as they ate hotcakes; they jumped back on their bikes and raced down the boardwalk, calling to each other and weaving between joggers. Erin was pointing out some of the more interesting businesses and eateries. As they rode, the wind tossed Kate's hair as she peddled to stay close to Erin. It had been a long time since she had been on a bike or felt so good!

By twelve o'clock, the girls were in their bathing suits, basking in the sun on the beach. Kate had found a trashy novel and had begun to read as friends of Erin stopped by to talk.

Kate turned around to see Erin stand up and hug an extremely handsome guy with the bluest eyes she had ever seen.

"Kate, do you remember me talking about a pesky kid who lived down the street and who almost drown me while trying to teach me to surf?" A grin came across Erin's face. "The pest's name is Clint Rodgers. This is the only person in Ocean Beach to call me Scottie. Clint, this is my college roommate, Kate Connally. She's here for some *rest and relaxation.*"

Before Kate could stand up, Clint dropped to the sand next to her. He had the bluest eyes that seemed to penetrate into her thoughts. Dressed only in a pair of cut-off blue jeans, his skin was bronze from the sun. His hair had been bleached almost white. As Kate opened her mouth to speak, Erin ran her fingers through Clint's hair.

"If you don't get out of the sun, your hair will be white! What are you doing here? I thought Mom told me you were working in Boston."

"I've taken a six-month leave of absence from the firm. Dad had some heart problems and recently had bypass surgery. There were some complications, and Dad is finally feeling better, but he wasn't able to open the store this spring. So I thought I'd take some time off and run the shop until Dad is better. It feels like old times, managing a surf shop. Josh Duncan comes in and helps on the weekends. And I have to admit, I'm really enjoying it. After studying four years to be an architect and securing a job with Walls and McGrath, one of the top firms in New England, I actually enjoy waxing a surfboard and selling Boogie Boards! Someone told me that, 'Once you get sand between your toes, you will always come back to the beach.' Guess that applies to me. I'm having more fun. Does this make me a Beach Bum?"

Clint paused a moment as he looked directly at Kate. "And what brings you two beauties to the beach?"

"We're just hanging out here for a few weeks. Then we're off to the Midwest, Nebraska to be exact for a wedding. I don't start work at the UN until September 15, and two friends invited me to share their apartment with them in the city, so I don't have to find accommodations. After this summer, no more carefree time on the beach for me."

"Scottie, my friend, I can't imagine you sitting for six hours a day translating documents or leading tours to tourists that are from South of the Border! And what about you, dear? What are your plans?"

"Clint, this is my college roommate, Kate Connelly. This is her first time at Ocean Beach."

"Well, Katie Connelly, what are your plans?"

Kate smiled. No one had called her "Katie" since she was a little girl.

"Well, the reason we are going to Nebraska is for my wedding. My life is pretty well planned—marriage, a honeymoon at the Grand Canyon, and then back to Omaha where I'll be the Assistant Curator at the local museum in the city. After listening to you two guys, my life sounds so dull."

"Well, let's liven it up a bit. Why don't I pick you two up tonight for an evening at the Burger Barn? Katie, it's the coldest beer and the best burgers in Ocean Beach…and the band isn't bad either. What do you say, Scottie? Some of the old gang are back in town and will be there. I won't take *no* for an answer; I'll pick you two up at seven-thirty!"

Clint turned around and walked toward the boardwalk, throwing a wave over his shoulder. Kate's eyes followed him as he strolled across the sand. Erin had decided to go for a swim and Kate picked up her book. But she could not concentrate on the words. The memory of those blue eyes and sun-bleached hair would not let her direct her attention to the pages. She had never known such a person. In

Omaha, she had no male friends except Jay. And she had only two girls that she had maintained any contact with after high school. When she was home from college, she spent most of her time with Jay and *his* friends. Sometimes, a girl would call, and they would meet for lunch. She had no idea where her high school friends were…only an occasional wedding invitation or a birth announcement. It seemed that she had stumbled into a friendly, informal way of life…and in this carefree existence, there were a blue-eyed blond named Clint.

As the girls were getting dressed, the phone rang.

"Kate, it's for you."

Kate rushed to the phone, trying to imagine who would know she was at Ocean Beach. Was something wrong with her parents?

"Hello."

"Well, have you gotten this *silly* teenage beach bunny vacation out of your mind?"

"Oh…Hello, Jay."

"When in the *hell* are you coming home?"

"Is something wrong?"

"My friends don't understand this little vacation that you've decided to take." Kate could hear the anger in his voice. "We're getting married in September and you decide to go the shore? Several wives of my business associates wanted to host teas and lunches for us, and you're not here! What in the *hell* am I suppose to tell them?"

"Jay, calm down." Kate looked to see if anyone was close enough to hear her conversation. "I attended three bridal showers during spring break. No one mentioned any lunches or teas! Jay, I need this time to unwind and relax after a hectic graduation schedule. All the plans are finalized—flowers, photographer, church singer, and the reception. If there is a last minute snafu, I'll take care of it when I get home."

"I'll be glad when you leave the damn ocean and get back to your responsibilities. I don't like this at all! After we're married, these little escapades will cease! You belong in Omaha at the museum and with me!"

"Good bye, Jay." Kate eased the phone down. She refused to argue with Jay over the telephone. How dare he talk to her like that! She knew her responsibilities for the wedding and at the museum. She had never shirked her duties! And Jay's statement that she "belonged to him" really irritated her. She always thought that marriage was a partnership, not signing a paper to be a possession. Jay had never spoken to her like this before now, but she had never defied him before! Her reverie was interrupted by a towel thrown in her face. Erin had gotten her revenge from this morning.

"How is lover boy?" she asked teasingly.

"Jay's OK. He wants me to come home…immediately."

"And I want you to get dressed…Nothing fancy, just ocean beach clothes. Put on a pair of shorts and a shirt! If you don't get moving, you'll get the towel thrown in your face again! Clint will come in here, see you in your bathrobe, and throw you over his shoulder. Get dressed!"

Promptly at 7:30, a pickup truck was outside the house, horn blaring. Erin was pleased at how relaxed Kate seemed after the phone call. She had gotten some color on her face and had developed a bounce in her step. Erin and Kate squeezed into the front seat and the threesome sped away to the Burger Barn. Kate had put the phone call out of her mind; the music from the Barn could be heard several blocks away.

It was a beautiful night. Groups of people had spilled out on the sidewalk in front of the Burger Barn, laughing and enjoying the company of old friends. Clint found a parking place and whisked the girls into the hall. Immediately, the girls were mobbed by Erin's friends. Kate's somber mood, due to the insulting phone call, lifted at once as she was swept away to the dance floor.

Twenty minutes later, Kate collapsed in a booth. She was perspiring and her face was framed in wet ringlets. She ordered a beer and attempted to cool down.

"Mind if I join you?" Clint eased into the booth opposite Kate with two mugs of beer in hiss hand. "I'm your waiter for tonight," and he handed her a mug of the cold beer.

"Thanks, I needed this," she panted.

"What do you think of Erin's friends? I'll bet they're different from the Midwest crowd. This group was good friends in high school, scattered their many ways for college and work, but always seems to get together in Ocean Beach several times during this summer. Next year,

Erin will come home from New York to join this 'Zany' crowd for a weekend. Look at her. She's flitting around here like a firefly. And...I believe you're feeling better. Is that a smile I see? Could it be that the beach has weaved its magic on you? Is this crowd a bad influence on you? Yes, I definitely see a smile on your face."

"I haven't had this much fun in years!" and without thinking, she started telling Clint about her phone call from Jay, her thoughts on her future life, especially the fact the she would belong to someone, and her future life in Omaha. She now had doubts about her upcoming marriage. She had assumed that she wanted Jay and her orderly life in Omaha, but now, after two days at Ocean Beach, she had questions and many doubts.

"Wow! I hope we haven't spoiled the wedding plans!" he laughed.

They both sat very quietly for a few moments.

"Let's dance." Clint guided her to the dance floor for the band's rendition of *Ebb Tide*. He held her close and realized that the feelings that had come over him this afternoon on the beach, as he looked into her eyes, was not going to vanish. He found himself wishing that the song would not end. She seemed to fit perfectly into his arms. He felt like a schoolboy as he held her and smelled her freshly washed hair. After the song ended, he walked her back to the booth and neither of them spoke. They continued to dance and talk quietly for the remainder of the evening, oblivious to the crowd that had gathered. Clint took Erin and Kate home with promises to meet them on the beach soon.

Kate lay awake for several hours, thinking about the events of the day. It was Clint's face that kept appearing in her dreams, not the face of Jay Coleman. She had never felt this way. Her emotions were completely devoid of reason. She could still feel Clint's arm around her as they danced. He was so easy to talk to and those eyes seemed to penetrate to her soul. Jay had never seemed interested in her ideas or her feelings. She turned her engagement ring on her finger; it seemed to burn into her skin. She was going back to Nebraska at the end of the summer and become Mrs. Jay Coleman. It was all planned; her life was mapped out for her several years ago. But throughout the night, it was Clint who appeared in her thought and dreams!

A few days later, sitting on the beach, Kate found herself looking at the pages of her book, but not being able to concentrate on its contents. She had not seen Clint for several days; she had avoided him by keeping busy with Erin. Each noise brought her attention to the beach, hoping it was Clint. Soon he appeared, carrying a surfboard under each arm.

"Scottie, my pal, it's time to see what you can still do on a surfboard! Katie, did you know that I taught Scottie to surf when she was ten years old? Come on, Erin, let's show Katie how we can ride the waves…And yes, I almost caused her to drown during the lessons!"

Erin grabbed a surfboard and raced Clint into the water. Kate had never seen this side of Erin's personality. Ocean Beach had an effect on her too.

Kate realized how silly her feelings for Clint were as she watched her "Roomie and the hunk" riding the waves. Erin and Clint were good friends, and because she was visiting Erin, Clint had been exceptionally nice to her. She felt like a silly schoolgirl with a school-girl crush on a new fellow. She was engaged to marry Jay, and because he had hurt her with his terse phone call, she had allowed her emotions to stray. A phone call would be made to Omaha tonight to assure Jay how much she cared for him. And…Kate vowed that she would avoid being alone with Clint.

Clint and Erin were laughing as they approached the blanket. They surrounded Kate and shook their wet hair, spraying her with cold water.

"Come on, Katie, it's your turn!" Clint clutched one ankle as Erin pulled on the other. Together they pulled Kate into the surf, laughing as the water rushed over her. Sputtering with salt water in her mouth, Kate managed to grab Erin's leg and pull her down in the surf. Then they both tugged at Clint's legs, sending him crashing into the water. Shrieks of laughter could be heard all around the beach. The three young adults had suddenly become "The Three Amigos of Summer." They rolled and tumbled in the water for over an hour.

Exhaustedly, they lay on the beach, basking in the sun. It seemed as though everyone was too tired to speak. Kate had not felt so contented for a long time. She even put her return phone call to Jay out of her thoughts.

Erin broke the silence. "I've got some food in my backpack, which I left on my bike. I'll be back in a few minutes." She grabbed her shoes and ran for the boardwalk to get the food.

"Are you sure you don't want to go with her?" There was a sharp tone in Clint's voice.

Kate sat up on the beach towel and looked at him quizzingly. "I don't think she needs any help…Is something wrong?"

"Not with me, there isn't! But you have been avoiding me for the last few days. I never get a chance to talk to you. It seems that you are always busy with Erin and never have time to talk. You're going to find out that I'm a hard guy to ignore. Then I thought that maybe you didn't like us boys here at the beach." He grinned as he took her hand.

Kate felt a tingling sensation as Clint held her hand. She did not understand this feeling that came over her. But before she could assure him that they were still friends, Erin ran back to the blanket with her backpack. Kate withdrew her hand and lowered her head to prevent Erin hadn't seen the contact between she and Clint.

"I've got pretzels, cheese puffs, chips, and some sodas. How is that for a junk food lunch?"

Immediately, the party atmosphere returned. Erin threw a cheese puff and hit Kate on the mouth. Clint shook a soda can, popped the top, and sprayed the two girls. They both laughed as Kate put a pretzel rod in her mouth and gave her impression of a girl having an "after sex cigarette."

At two o' clock, Clint left the girls to return to his business. Erin and Kate lay quietly in the sun for a few moments before anyone spoke.

"Tell me about Clint…"

"There's not much to tell. We grew up together. He's a few years older than us, but at a place like Ocean Beach, age doesn't seem important. There were twelve or fifteen of us who would help our parents in their businesses and then we would bum around the beach together after dinner. We were buddies, inseparable for a time. Then, one by one, the gang left Ocean Beach for college or other pursuits. But we remained friends, and it's a celebration whenever we get together. Clint,

Molly, and Ed were the first to leave. I guess the ironic thing about the group is that no one has come back to Ocean Beach to work and live here. But when we get together, it's like we are kids again, sixteen years old, enjoying life at the beach! You must have good friends that you meet when you go home to Omaha…you know…good high school friends."

Kate ignored the comment about good friends in Omaha.

"How about Clint? Is he just a good friend?"

"Clint Rodgers moved to Ocean Beach when I was five years old. His mother had died and his dad thought it would be good to move to a new location. Mr. Rodgers opened a carpentry shop and was soon fixing water skis and surfboards. He adapted to beach life really fast. He's the best surfer in our group. I guess Clint inherited his love of carpentry and building. After high school, he won a full scholarship to Boston University and graduated top architect in his class. We thought he would come back to Ocean Beach and design beach homes, but he took a job with a top firm in Boston, and we rarely see him anymore. I didn't think he would be here this summer."

"Does he have a steady girl?"

Erin threw her head back and laughed aloud. "Every girl in Ocean Beach would like to be Clint's steady girl and I'm sure there are many more in Boston. I don't think Clint's ever had serious feelings for a girl, but now I'm not so sure. I saw the way he was looking at you when I came back on the beach with the food. I was ready to rush home and call Jay," Erin said teasing with a giggle.

Kate's face began to turn red. She sat motionless for a while. Clint had thought she was mad at him. Had she missed something this afternoon? Then she quickly turned to face Erin.

"What a silly thing to say! After four years of rooming together in college and hearing about Jay constantly, you know I am going to marry him. In three months, I'll be Mrs. Jay Coleman.

"Well, I'm just telling you what I saw. We're all gathering at the Burger Barn again tonight. Chrissy is home from Europe, so the gang will all be there. Clint will be there; watch him carefully. I think he likes you."

Kate took a long shower and sat for a while on the edge of the bed. She remembered the night they had danced at the Burger Barn, and she could still feel his arms around her. Then she pushed those images out of her mind and thought of Jay. But Clint reappeared! Why was he so terse with her today? He knew that she was just here for a few weeks, visiting Erin, and would soon leave for her wedding. "Jay would think I'm so silly to worry about Clint's attitude. Jay would say I'm being silly to think about Clint at all! Why am I having these conflicting thoughts?" As she dressed for the evening, Kate took a good look at herself in the mirror. Her skin was a golden brown after weeks in the sun, and it seemed to glow. Her hair had blond highlights and she pulled it back in a bouncy ponytail with curls around her face. The denim shorts and shirt she put on complimented the blue in her eyes. This was not the same person who left the University of Nebraska. At that time, she had her life planned and all the pieces were in place. There would be graduation, vacation, final plans, wedding, honeymoon, and curator. But the girl in the mirror was not sure of the plans now. She was...

"Kate! Are you almost ready? We're going to be late. Clint's outside, sounding the horn!" Erin's voice interrupted Kate's daydream. "Come on, Slowpoke; we don't want the burgers to get cold."

Kate smoothed her hair, grabbed her wallet, and ran down the steps. Clint was waiting in the pickup truck with Erin beside him. Kate scrambled into the front seat and the truck sped down the road. As they drove, Kate tried to imagine Jay in a pair of cutoff shorts, riding around Omaha in a pickup truck. Erin chattered away about Chrissy and her junior year abroad in France. She had studied art at the Sorbonne, and had not been to Ocean Beach for over a year.

"Tell me, Scottie, do you think Frenchy missed us?"

"Do you two have a pet name for all of your friends?" Kate asked inquisitively.

"Katie, me darling, only the people *we* like." Clint's Irish imitation was thick and amusing. Their conversation on the beach was forgotten. The three friends laughed and chatted as the truck rambled on toward the Burger Barn.

It took only a few minutes for the Barn to become alive with conversation and music. Chrissy regaled the group with stories of her year in France, most of them having no connection with her studies. Kate thought about her art classes and how she would love to go to Paris. Omaha, Nebraska, and the public museum seemed like such a long way from the art museums of France. As Chrissy continued her stories of her exploits on the banks of the Seine River, Kate wandered off to the bar, grabbed a beer, and sat down at a table, lost in her own thoughts.

"A penny for your thoughts?" Clint was standing next to the table with a beer and a basket of peanuts. "Or maybe I should say, 'A peanut for your thoughts,'" as he laughingly sat down.

Kate started giggling as her mood immediately lightened. Perhaps it was the jocularity of the crowd or the beer, but a change came over her. She grabbed the peanuts, put them on the table, and took Clint's hand to lead him out on the dance floor.

"Come on, Mr. Rodgers, let's see your best dance moves."

"Katie, darling, we make a handsome couple out here on the dance floor. Do try to keep up with me!"

The two danced and laughed until the perspiration dripped from them. Then the band changed tempo and started the old favorite, *Harbor Lights*. Clint gathered Kate into his arms. She felt a warm glow throughout her entire body as she melted against him. It has been said that strange things can happen while you are dancing. Any thoughts of Omaha, Jay, a wedding or a museum vanished as they glided about the room. She felt his muscular body commanding her around the dance floor. The masculine scent from his shaving lotion became intoxicating.

"Let's get out of here! I need some air!"

Clint kept Kate's hand in his as he moved through the crowd toward the door. She followed him as if in a trance.

The cool night air did little to break the mood of the evening. Before she could speak, Clint put his arms around Kate, drew her close, and began to kiss her. She did not pull back from him, but instead answered his embrace very enthusiastically. They stood locked in each other's arms for several minutes; not a word was spoken.

"Clint, I…"

"Don't say anything. I've wanted to do this since I met you on the beach the first day you were here." His lips moved over hers and the passion between them grew. The two of them were lost in the moment.

It was Kate who pulled away from Clint. She stepped back from him as she tried to clear her head.

"Clint, this is crazy! I shouldn't be here. I'm going to be married in a few weeks."

Clint started to walk toward her, but Kate continued to back away.

"Please don't," she said, unsure of her emotions.

"Let's take a walk on the beach and talk." Once again, Clint took her hand and together they walked through the parking lot to the beach. Kate followed, unable to control her actions. There was a light breeze and a crescent moon was high in the sky. They walked silently, holding hands, both people hoping the moment would not end. Clint suddenly stopped, took off his shoes, and smiled at Kate.

"You'd better take off your shoes. No one in Ocean Beach walks in the sand with his shoes on!" Clint's jovial mood had returned.

As if mechanical, Kate kicked off her shoes and continued walking. Finally, she broke the silence.

"I don't know what has happened to me. One month ago, my life was organized and well planned. I graduated from college and had my wedding details in place. My bridesmaids have their gowns and the reception is at the Shrine Club. Three hundred invitations have been sent. We have our reservations for our trip to the Grand Canyon. My job at the museum will be waiting for me when I get home. We even have our apartment furnished. And then I came to Ocean Beach, and my world has turned upside down. I've spent carefree, fun-filled days at the beach, I've raced on a bicycle like a teenager, and I've danced until I was exhausted. I've also met a group of people who don't plan and organize their lives, but they *live them*, to the fullest. And I met you, Clint Rodgers, and you have made me question all of my future plans and Jay Coleman being in my future. Do I love him? If I do, would I be walking on the beach, on a moonlit, summer night, holding hands with a guy who I hope will kiss me again?"

Before she could continue, Clint was holding her tightly, kissing her hair, her face, and finally her sensuous mouth. It was one of those perfect moments—a moonlit night, waves crashing on the shore, and two young people falling in love. Time seemed to stand still as Clint and Kate stood there folded into each other's arms.

"I've surfed through life dating lots of girls." Clint began jovially. "I was even on Boston's Most Eligible Bachelor's List! And Katie Connelly comes to Ocean Beach. She's a serious college graduate who is engaged to be married. She looks at life like a kid, and enjoys every moment. Suddenly, I can't get her face out of my dreams. I found myself making excuses to meet her for breakfast or for a swim. My feelings were hurt when I felt that Miss Connelly was avoiding me. So I used my humor and wit to try to get Miss Connelly to like me, or perhaps to build a wall that no one would realize how much I would be hurting when Miss Connelly returned to Nebraska to marry her Mr. Coleman. But I had to keep seeing her, and she was usually surrounded by mutual friends. And the persistence of Clint Rodgers has achieved success. Kate, I can't explain how I feel; just know standing here with you feels good, and I'd like to continue this for a long time."

The two continued to walk along the beach, holding hands, absorbed in their own thoughts and in each other. It was one-thirty in the morning when the two young people started back to the Burger Barn. Time was meaningless; they were together and they were happy. It was 3:00 AM when they strolled across the parking lot. They rode back to Erin's home in silence.

When they arrived at Erin's, Clint began to open the door.

"Clint. Don't get out. I'll be all right. I just need some time to think."

"About me, I hope," he laughed as he drove away

The next morning, Kate was up early, having spent a very restless night.

"Got in a bit late last night, didn't you?" Erin said jokingly. "When the Barn closed and I didn't see you anywhere, I thought you were old enough to find your way here. And the gang did notice that Clint's truck was still in the parking lot."

"Erin, I'm so mixed up…Maybe coming to Ocean Beach wasn't such a good idea." Kate then blurted out the events of the previous evening. When she was finished, she was sobbing uncontrollably. Erin walked across the kitchen and put her arm around her friend.

"Maybe coming to Ocean Beach was the smartest thing that you've ever done." Erin's joking mood was gone. "I don't know what to tell you about Clint. I've never seen him like this. I do know you have four weeks before we are to go to Nebraska for a wedding. Listen to your heart. Don't make a mistake that will have consequences for the rest of your life. Plans can be cancelled, if you are not sure."

The remainder of the day passed quickly. Kate and Erin rode their bikes to the beach where Kate attempted to read. She found herself staring at the pages of the book; she could not concentrate as her thoughts were on Clint. The girls grabbed a sandwich for lunch and decided on a movie for the evening. They stopped for an ice cream cone after the show and rode their bikes home in silence. Erin's mother had left a note that Jay had called. Erin smiled as Kate dropped the paper in the wastebasket.

Clint called early the following day.

"Katie, darling, I'm taking the sailboat out for the day. How about meeting me at the pier at nine-thirty for a day of sailing? You can invite Scottie along too, if it will make you feel safer. I'll bring some food; you bring your bathing suit and some suntan lotion." Then, in his joking way, Clint said, "Or you can skip the bathing suit and swim nude. Is it a date? Oops…wrong word…Would you like to go sailing?"

"Sounds like fun. I'll ask Erin and meet you at nine-thirty!"

Erin was meeting Chrissy and some of the other girls for lunch on the Boardwalk, so Kate pedaled her bicycle to the marina alone. She eagerly anticipated a day with Clint, and she hoped that Erin was not making excuses so they could be alone. It was upsetting to her that she could not remember being so excited to see Jay. She had not returned the phone call, telling herself that she wanted to clarify her feelings for her future husband.

Being from Nebraska, Kate had never been sailing. Clint guided the boat out of the marina into the ocean. He taught Kate some of the easier maneuvers of the boat and soon they were gliding over the waves. The mood was jovial and no mention was made of the previous moonlight stroll on the beach. For lunch, Clint had brought some cheese, lunch meat, apples, crackers, and a cooler of sodas. After sailing for a few hours, the snack food tasted like a banquet. They cleaned up the lunch, and then the couple relaxed on deck.

"How long have you been sailing?"

"My dad taught me soon after we moved to Ocean Beach. Then I got a kayak in the third grade and just graduated to larger boats as I got older. Several years later, Dad bought this boat and we've shared a lot of good times on her. When I went away to college, Dad stored the boat, but he always had it in the water and ready to sail when I came home for the summer. Jeb, Rick, and I sailed her to the Florida Keys after my junior year of school. I like my job in Boston, and I think I would like it even better when I get a sailboat moored in the Boston Harbor. If you live in Ocean Beach, you must have a boat, and learn how to sail. If you live in Nebraska, I guess you must have a cornfield," he said laughingly, "or a cow?"

They sailed along the ocean in silence for a while. Then they anchored the boat, changed into their bathing suits, and took a dip to cool off. Later, as they dried off on the deck, they swapped outrageous college stories.

Kate was a bit melancholy when they sailed back into the marina at sunset. She hated to see such a perfect day come to a close.

"Grab a mop, Mate, and let's swab the deck!" The somber mood was gone as they scrubbed the boat, periodically throwing water on each other.

Kate thanked Clint for an outstanding day on the water and got on her bike. She was thoroughly drenched! As she began to pedal, Clint yelled to her.

"See what you would miss if you return to Nebraska, land of cornfields."

The next two weeks were a blaze of activity. If the girls went to the beach, Clint managed to take a break from the surf shop and join them. He taught Kate how to maneuver a jet ski, took her parasailing, and took her sailing several more times. Kate met Clint outside the surf shop at closing time, and they spent most evenings together. Erin never questioned her friend; instead she continuously teased her.

Returning back to Erin's house after a day at the beach, Kate realized that it was her final week of vacation. As she opened the backdoor, she recognized Jay's voice on the answering machine. Her faced turned scarlet with embarrassment as Erin played the message.

"Kate! Where in the *hell* are *you*? If you are not back here by Friday, I'm hiring a private detective to go to Ocean Beach and bring you home!"

Kate ran into the bedroom with tears streaming down her face. She was so ashamed and hurt by the viciousness in Jay's voice. After a few minutes, Erin quietly came into the bedroom and sat on the bed, next to her friend.

"Oh, Erin, what am I going to do? I can't go back to Nebraska and marry Jay. I know now that I don't love him. It's like marrying an old pal although I don't think old friends would talk to each other in such a tone of voice. After all these years, it is what is expected of me. And since I've been here, I've seen a different side of Jay's personality. He is very demanding and controlling! He doesn't consider my feelings or desires. He wants to control my life, not share it! I'm not sure that there is any such thing as an ideal relationship or marriage, but Jay thinks he can orchestrate a scenario that can produce perfection. I realize now that I shut off a part of my life by devoting all my energies to Jay and not meeting new people at college. When I see your relationships with your friends, I realize I ignored my friends for Jay! When I get back to Omaha, I want to reconnect with these people. I'm not sure I can ever cultivate the relationships you have with your pals but I want to try. I know I have a lot of explaining to do to everyone. I'm not sure my mother and father will understand, but I know they love me and want me to be happy. I realize that when I'm with Clint, I'm happy and feel alive and free to express myself. It's a feeling that I've never had with Jay…I've always tried to live up to his expectations, and disregarded my own dreams."

"How does Clint feel about you?" It was a question that Erin hadn't said since Kate had met Clint and spent so much time with him.

She had never questioned Kate's relationship with Jay or her friendship with Clint. She knew her roommate was a level-headed girl and would make good choices.

"I don't know. We haven't talked about the future. We have just enjoyed each other's company. I know I care a great deal about him, but I've only known him for six weeks. He makes me laugh and feel special. I can't imagine leaving Ocean Beach and never seeing him again. We don't worry about hosting dinner parties or making business contacts or attending teas. We just enjoy the moment."

"Are you meeting him tonight?"

"He has to work until eight o'clock tonight. I'm meeting him at the shop and we're going to the Burger Barn for a late supper."

"I think you and Clint should have a serious talk."

"Erin, you have known Clint longer that I have. You know he has always had girlfriends and has never gotten serious about any of them. What am I going to say?"

"Tell him about the message from Jay and see where the conversation goes. Our bus tickets are for September 10, in a few more days. You've got to make a decision!"

Kate showered and walked slowly to the Surf Shop. Deep in thought, she arrived a bit late. The shop was closed, so Kate walked to the outside steps leading upstairs to Clint's apartment.

She knocked on the door and got no answer. As she opened the door, she called to him. The sound of the shower was drowning out her calls, so she came in and walked into the living room. There were pictures of all phases of Clint's life—the surfer, the high school football player, the college graduate, and pictures of several buildings that he had designed. There was also one of Clint and his dad taken in front of the surf shop. Kate was intently looking at the photographs and did not hear Clint enter the room.

"This is a dream I've had for a couple of weeks. I'll come home from a day's work, take a shower, and find Katie waiting for me."

He was still damp from his shower, dressed only in a robe as he slowly walked toward her with desire in his eyes. They were in each other's arms in a moment. All of the joking and teasing of the previous weeks would disappear with the first kiss. Each wanted something from the other; Clint scooped Kate up in his arms and slowly moved into the bedroom. Their eyes were locked on each other and there were no pretests or questions.

No one said a word as Clint lowered Kate on the bed. She reached her arms up and encircled his neck, gently pulling him down next to her. He soon found her sensuous mouth and showered her with passionate kisses.

"Clint…I"

"*Shh*…Don't talk!"

His hands moved from her face, down the T–shirt she was wearing and over her heaving breast. She arched her back to meet his caress as her hands searched under his robe. Soon Clint's hands went under her shirt and her bra; he lifted her shirt and his hungry mouth found her taut nipples. She slowly sat up in bed and pull her bra and T-shirt over her head. Her ample breasts moved up and down as her breathing increased. He was overcome with desire as he pulled her shorts and panties down over her legs. He tossed his robe aside and lay down beside her as their naked bodies meshed together. After weeks of sexual tension, they succumbed to their desire for one another. Kate was very near sexual delirium as Clint masterfully made love to her. Never had she experienced such passion and tenderness. Clint raised her sexuality and made her feel beautiful and wanted.

They lay for a long time, wrapped in each other's arms. Just as he started to get up, she leaned over and brushed her mouth lightly over his.

"It's taken me a while to figure out my life," she said.

But before she could continue, Clint had his mouth on hers, his tongue probing.

"Oh, Clint, make love to me again!"

The heat had returned to the couple as Clint began to kiss Kate's body. He heard her gasp, and then begin to moan as he made love to her again. Later, they lay quietly, exhausted and spent.

After a while, they dressed and drove to the Burger Barn. Kate then relayed Jay's message. After making love to Clint, she could talk about it without crying. Before she could express her feelings, Clint began to speak.

"Are you going back to Nebraska? Are you going to marry Jay?"

"Clint, I have to go back to Omaha. I have created a situation that is going to hurt a lot of people. And *no*, I am not going to marry Jay Coleman. But I have to cancel the wedding and reception hall, return gifts that have been received, and try to make my mom and dad understand my decision. I don't think I can ever make Jay understand that an embarrassing moment now is better than a lifetime disaster! The bus tickets are for September 10, but there is no need for Erin to go now; there will be no wedding. This is something I have to do."

"I'd like to go with you. I hope I was part of your decision. Mr. Jay Coleman doesn't dare show me a bad attitude. Besides, if I go with you, I know you'll come back to Ocean Beach…with me. Katie, I don't know what will happen between the two of us, but I know I've never felt about a girl the way I feel about you. After Labor Day, business slows down in the surf shop until the fall tournaments begin in late September. Dad is feeling better now and he can take over the shop until I get back. Do you think a week will be long enough?"

The truck came to a stop in the parking lot as Kate began to hug Clint.

"Are you asleep?" Little Samantha had moved across the aisle and was tugging on Kate's knee.

"I'm going to see my grandma. She has a puppy." She looked at Clint in the adjoining seat and whispered, "Is he asleep?

And the bus rolled on…

CHAPTER 6

THE RAIN CONTINUED TO PELT THE WINDOWS of the bus as it rolled through the countryside along Interstate 70. The bus had made a dinner stop at Park -N- Dine in Hancock, Maryland. Three passengers were added to the band of travelers. An elderly couple and a young fellow, possessing only a backpack, joined the group. Jim Sterling ate with Ben Somers and then purchased a sandwich and some chips for his nameless friend. Kate and Clint sat with Sami, her father, and Debbie. Of course, Sami chatted throughout the entire meal about her plans when they reached her grandma in Louisiana. After about an hour, everyone was back on the bus, settled in their seats, and ready to resume their journey to Clarksville. The trip lasted only a few miles before an interruption. Several of the passengers stirred as the bus slowed down for a roadblock. A policeman was waving a flashlight in the drenching rain. He walked up to the bus and boarded it to speak to the driver.

"You can't continue on Route 68. We've got a rock slide over the west bound side of the road, throwing some large rocks over to the other side. No traffic can get through this mess. We've got a state road's crew coming in to remove the rocks, but it's going to take a couple of hours. You can detour on Old Route 40 to Flintstone and then get back on Route 68."

The trooper stepped back to the ground as the bus driver began to maneuver the bus onto Route 40. The sudden movement of the bus woke up the remaining passengers, who inquired about the delay. Jim Sterling was startled as the bus made the sharp turn. He looked at his new friend, who was also awake. The man's eyes still looked empty as he stared at the little girl who was standing near him, chattering away. She was clutching the side of the seat, trying to keep her balance as the bus bumped along the detour.

"Do you want a piece of candy? You didn't eat supper with us. Are you hungry?"

"Samantha! Samantha! Come back here and leave the passengers alone!"

The bumpy road had caused John Webster to stir from his nap. It took him a moment to realize where he was, where they were going, and that he and his daughter were safe. Sami ambled back to her seat and picked up her "goodie bag," searching for a piece of candy. She did not realize that the man in the aisle seat was still staring at her.

Mike Elliott's mind was as blank as the emptiness in his eyes. He had no thoughts as to why he was on this bus or why he was going to Clarksville, but there was something about that little girl that stirred some feelings inside him...

Mike Elliott had always wanted to be a doctor. As a youngster, Mike was constantly bandaging his sister's doll or putting a splint on any pet in the neighborhood. He was the boy who got a junior doctor kit for Christmas when he was six years old, and when he was ten, he received a chemistry set for his birthday. After mastering First Aid and CPR, taught by the Red Cross, Mike got a job as an orderly at the local hospital. Every free moment that he had, Mike watched a procedure in the operating room or assisted a nurse in one of the rooms. The care and treatment of patients seemed almost second nature to him.

No one was surprised when Mike Elliott stated his intentions to become a doctor. His grades in high school easily earned him a scholarship and acceptance to the University of Maryland in the pre-med program.

It was possibly the happiest four years of Mike's life. He loved his classes and his professors challenged him to do his best. During the summer, Mike resumed his work at the hospital, and, in the fall, he added more responsibility to his schedule when he became a trainer for the Terps, the University of Maryland football team. It was a grueling schedule, but Mike loved every moment of it. He enjoyed taping ankles, wrists and ribs, but he really liked diagnosing injuries and helping the players recover. Of course, he never voiced his diagnosis, but he smiled to himself when his diagnosis agreed with the team doctor.

"Mike, you're up early. I thought you'd sleep late this morning, now that you have some free time." It was six-thirty in the morning, during Easter break, when George Elliott found his son sitting at the kitchen table drinking a cup of coffee.

"Dad, I got accepted into medical school at the University of Chicago."

"Son, that was your first choice of medical schools. Congratulations!"

"I guess I was so busy studying, and, yes, enjoying these past few years that I forgot about money."

"You know your mother and I will help you all that we can."

"I know that, Dad, but you and Mom already helped to pay for the four years at the University. I know the scholarship only paid for the bare necessities, and you paid the rest!"

"And we're so proud of you. Your mother and I have talked about this and on Monday, we're going down to the bank and we're going to take out a mortgage on the house."

"Dad, I can't let you do that!"

"Your mother and I want to do this. You can pay us back when you open your medical practice."

"Dad, suppose something would happen that you couldn't work or Mom would get sick. You could slip on an icy sidewalk or have an accident. I don't want you to ever lose this house…OUR home. I was talking to some officers from the army. They have a program that will pay for my medical school and perhaps some specialized training. In exchange for my medical training, I will become a commissioned officer in the army and serve a few years as a doctor in the military. Of course, the army can send me anywhere I am needed, and it will be at least another few years before I can start my own medical practice. But I can gain valuable experience on all types of injuries. I want to talk to some more people about the program especially any doctor who had used this funding to go to school. It really sounds like a good plan for me."

"I've never heard of a program like that, but I'm a mailman. I wouldn't know about these things. But don't rush into anything until you really check out all the facts. You know your mother and I want to help you."

Mike got up from the table and walked over to his dad. He put both hands on his father's shoulders.

"Don't you think you and Mom have done enough?"

"We can mortgage the house and get some money for your tuition and…"

"Well, you're right! You haven't done enough!" Mike began to laugh. "You haven't fixed your famous western omelet for me since I've been home." Mike was really laughing now as he tossed an onion at his dad and opened the refrigerator to get out some ham, eggs, and peppers. "I'll set up the toaster, and we'll get this breakfast on the table."

The two men laughed and joked throughout the breakfast, which was a delicious omelet. It was just like a thousand other Sunday mornings with Mike and his dad, enjoying their time together.

Mike made inquiries about the army's program and talked to several physicians who had trained this way. Most of the surgeons had served in hospitals in the states. One doctor was stationed in Germany. It seemed to be a good option for him. He had no wife, no children, or even a steady girlfriend. What he had was a burning desire to become a doctor and the army's plan seemed the simplest solution. So two weeks after Easter break, Mike Elliott became a member of the United States Army.

The following years were more intense than anything he had experience. He was fascinated by the wonders of the human body. It could be ravaged by injury or disease, but it had the recuperative power to heal and recover with the proper care. As he rotated through several medical specialties, he found that each one had a unique appeal, making his choice extremely difficult. His love for all types of medicine caused Mike to make a decision that would affect his career. He would continue his work as a general practitioner and postpone any decision about specialty training until his military service was over.

Graduation was a day of mixed emotions. The grueling curriculum was finally behind him, and it was now time to move on with the knowledge he had acquired. His parents made the trip to Chicago and were beaming with pride as he was commissioned in the United States Army, and was awarded high honors for his medical studies. Following graduation, Mike was stationed to Fort Sam Houston, in San Antonio, for indoctrination and military training.

It was after 1:00 AM when the phone began to ring.

"Hello."

"Dad, it's me, Mike."

"Mike, is anything wrong? It's after midnight."

"Dad, I've got my orders. I'm going to Vietnam." There was a long pause, deadly silence.

"When are you leaving?"

"In three weeks. I won't get home to see you and Mom before I leave."

"What's your assignment?"

"I'm assigned to an Army Field Hospital. I'll be near the fighting, but not in it. But I think I'll be able to help a lot of wounded guys if I'm there."

There was another prolonged silence before his father reacted to the news. It was one of the few times that Mike was sorry he had only a sister and no other male siblings. Many of his family's hopes, dreams, and love had been entrusted with their only son.

"Well, Mike, we had hoped you would be stationed stateside, but we knew that this could be a possibility. I'm not going to wake your mother. Let me talk to her in the morning and tell her the situation. You know how she worries."

Mike smiled; since he had played football in high school, it had been his dad who worried about him getting hurt. But it was his mother who was concerned that he would catch every infectious disease while he worked at the hospital.

"Thanks, Dad. I'll call before I leave. I'll talk to Mom then. Tell her not to worry."

The next three weeks were difficult. Ed Casey, Thomas Rossi, and Mike Elliott were fresh out of medical school, each with a debt to pay to the United States Government. Ed Casey was a jolly Irishman who had a wife and two curly haired little girls. He had gone to Stanford Medical School specializing in orthopedics. Where Mike vacationed at the Atlantic Beaches, Ed grew up in Malibu, surfing in the Pacific Ocean. He married his college sweetheart, who with the girls, was now staying in Malibu with his parents. Thom Rossi grew up in New York City, graduating from New York University and completing his training in various city hospitals. He specialized in thoracic surgery; and like Mike, he was single. Regardless of their backgrounds, the three men quickly became good friends. After endless meetings and training, the threesome would sit at the local pub swapping cadaver stories from medical school.

"Have you been to your mailbox today?" Casey lifted the pitcher and refilled everyone's glass with beer. He was the joker of the group. "I found a letter from Big Brother!"

"And what does our Big Brother say?"

"He says in four days, we'll be residents of Saigon, on the Modern American Plan."

A hush fell over the group before Thom began to speak.

"Have you guys seen the news reports about Vietnam? It looks horrible."

Mike chimed in. "It reminds me of the old World War II movies about the Philippines…Jungle fighting…Hot…Hand to hand combat."

"And the field hospitals look primitive."

"Well, we are trained in shrapnel, phosphorus burns, Triage…" Mike started a list…"It's like taking another class in med school."

"Yeah, War Wounds 101," added Ed Casey, laughing.

"You know what really bothers me? I was in town a few days ago and stopped into a drugstore for some gum. The clerk and some of the shoppers were talking about a rally in front of the Alamo, a rally against the war. There was a guy in there who started to argue with them. It sounded like he had been in Vietnam. They ridiculed him for serving his country. I just stood by and listened. I guess that I was so busy with finals and my work in the hospital that I failed to realize the controversy that the war is causing in this country. It appears that a large percentage of the citizens in the United States feel we shouldn't be sending troops to Southeast Asia."

Suddenly, the conversation had turned serious.

"I don't think we can take sides," Thom climbed in. "Besides, we don't have any choice. But those people aren't demonstrating against us. We're going to save lives, not kill people. I didn't hear anyone say the rally was against doctors." Dr. Casey tried to regain the lighthearted mood.

"Are you trying to say that we sold our souls to the devil for medical careers?"

"I'm certainly not going into town and announce that I'm training to go to Saigon!" Thom laughed and lifted his glass.

"A toast! To the three Musketeers! May they serve their country well!"

"What a toast!" Mike said smiling. "This is San Antonio, Texas. I think we're the Three Tall Texans! Except for the fact that none of us are from Texas!"

Two days later, the newly commissioned doctors were on a flight to Saigon.

Nothing could have prepared the young men for their assignment. The city was in complete chaos. Hundreds of children lined the sidewalks, begging for money or any food that the Americans would give them. Prostitutes shopped themselves, grabbing the soldiers on their arms and stating their prices. Vietnamese soldiers wandered the area with bloody bandages on their wounds. Oxen were pulling carts through the streets, defecating and adding to the raw sewage that flowed into the sewers. Men stoned on drugs wandered glassy-eyed through the crowds. Groups of refugees with no food or shelter filled the streets, carrying all their possessions on their backs. Music also filled the streets from the raucous smoke-filled bars. Periodic gunfire could be heard at a distance and planes shattered the atmosphere as they passed overhead.

It was Casey, the clown of the group, who broke the silence.

"Well, Dorothy, or Mike, or Thom, I don't think we're in Kansas anymore."

Thom and Mike did not answer. They just stared in awe at the horrendous conditions they were witnessing. The three young men had all done volunteer work in the poor sections of various cities in the United States, but nothing could compare to the scene that was before them.

"Part of me wants to get out of this car and help these people." Mike's sentence was interrupted by the sound of a low flying fighter plane. "And the other part of me wants to get back on the plane and go home."

"I don't think our Uncle Sam would like it if we went home. After all, he invited us to his Garden of Eden, and he wouldn't like it if we refused his invitation." Casey tried to add some levity to the situation. "Let's get out of here and check in for our assignments."

It was chaotic in the next few days for the three men in unfamiliar surroundings. Mike was assigned to an Army Field Hospital outside of De Nang. It was a medical unit, about ten miles from the fighting. This would be the first stop after a medic had pulled a wounded soldier from the jungles. Helicopters and ambulances would bring the wounded back to the field hospital. There, a group of five doctors, including Mike, and other support staff would treat the wounded, sending many of the lesser wounded back to their units after a few days of recovery. The more seriously wounded would be treated and sent to Saigon for further surgeries and then on to Germany or back to the United States. Thom was assigned to the hospital ship, anchored in the harbor at Saigon, and Casey was at another field hospital hear Hue.

Upon arrival, Mike had a few minutes to become familiar with the camp. The five doctors assigned there lived in a tent near the hospital. Two doctors were on duty in the hospital tent at all times. All five doctors would be called to the hospital at any time, all hours of the day or night, if wounded arrived.

Mike had unpacked his duffel bag when a corpsman pulled up the tent flap to inform the doctors that a group of wounded soldiers were expected by helicopter in ten minutes. Mike's hands were shaking as he took a deep breath and walked into the sunlight. The camp was buzzing with activity; people were rushing everywhere.

The helicopter landed on the pad with several wounded soldiers inside.

"Doc! Doc! Help my Buddy…he's hurt real bad…"

Mike was the first physician to reach the helicopter. He jumped aboard, but was horrified at the scene that lay before him. The stench of burnt flesh permeated the chamber of the helicopter. Eight men laid before him, filthy from crawling through swampy areas of the jungle. They smelled like rotting vegetation. Flies covered the open wounds. There was a human foot sitting off to one side of the copter.

"Doc! Help my Buddy! Please!"

Mike moved quickly among the wounded, assessing the severity of the wounds. He immediately spotted the Marine whose right foot was missing. A medic or a friend had put a tourniquet around the stump of the leg to slow the bleeding. There were two belly wounds that needed immediate attention. One soldier was dead; a bullet had gone through his head. The corpsmen appeared and evacuated the wounded soldiers from the copter to the hospital. Mike stepped off the aircraft and immediately got sick. He was splattered with blood, shaking all over, and vomiting next to the copter when Phillip, one of the other doctors, came over to him.

"Is this your first week here?"

"Yeah, and my first day with casualties…" Mike suddenly felt very foolish. He was embarrassed at his reaction to the wounded men especially after all his training.

"You should have seen me on my first day here. I was shaking so bad that I had to miss my first day in the operating room. Come on and walk with me. We'll need you to help patch up these guys."

Mike seemed to feel better as he walked to the hospital tent with Phillip. His first patient had shrapnel wounds to his arms and legs, but Mike had seen similar wounds from explosions when he was working in the emergency room at Cook Country General in Chicago. Carefully he removed the bits of metal from the soldier, and set a broken arm on a third. His last patient was a small Vietnamese girl who had tripped a land mine and had to have her leg amputated.

"Good work, Mike." Phillip lay down on the cot across the tent. "Did you train in Emergency Medicine?"

"I did a rotation in Shock Trauma at Cook County General. It was probably the greatest learning experience of my medical career. The hustle-bustle of an emergency room really appealed to me. I found myself working in the trauma center on holidays and free nights. But it was nothing like this! The hustle-bustle of an emergency room quickly becomes chaos here!"

"Are you from Maryland?"

"Yes. I'm from an area called Deep Creek Lake. It's so different from this place. It is mountainous and cool with sweet smelling air. In the summer, the lake is filled with boaters, jet skis, and a few swimmers. In the winter, it is a skier's paradise. My folks still live near there, in a small town called Accident."

"Do you ski?"

"Everyone who lives near Deep Creek Lake can ski. We had some great times there when I was a kid. We had rubber tubes on the snow, sleds, ice skates for the ponds, and huge bonfires. It seems like such a long time ago."

Phillip continued to talk to Mike. He was the chief surgeon and was glad to know that Mike had completed a successful first day in the operating room. He was so pleased that Mike seemed to have left the horrors of war at the hospital.

"Elliott, let's go get a shower and grab some supper. I hear they are serving our main meal outside tonight, alfresco! We missed lunch, you know. You'll get accustomed to working through lunches and dinners. My record is a fifty-hour session with ten-minute breaks to rest my eyes or to grab a sandwich. Come on, Doc, move it!"

Mike pulled his exhausted body off the cot and dug in his duffel bag for clean clothes and toiletries. A shower would feel good and when he heard his stomach growl, he realized he hadn't eaten since breakfast!

After a few weeks, Mike fell into a routine. Many days there were no medical duties, so several doctors visited nearby villages, treating those who were sick or hurt. Other days, he was on duty in the hospital, and every day, at any moment, wounded men would come in, sometimes as many as twenty-five or thirty soldiers, needing treatment. Many of the wounds were horrible. Mike thought of the sacrifices those men were making and the demonstration against the war back in the United States in San Antonio. These antiwar gatherings were never mentioned at the camp.

After several months, Mike got a three-day pass and hitched a ride to Saigon on a helicopter. There he met Thom and the two of them discussed their experiences.

"Do you remember when we complained about a twenty-four-hour shift at a hospital? All those complainers should work my schedule for two weeks. They would never complain again." There was a long silence as Mike finished his beer.

"Is it bad out there?"

"It's overwhelming at times…the helicopters will bring dozens of wounded…you have to sort through them to find those that are the most critical. If you are seriously wounded, you go to the front of the operating schedule. I've seen five or six kids, who have been in an accident, come into the emergency room in Chicago, and we've had the staff to start treating all of them. No waiting. But to leave wounded soldiers sitting because there are too many of them or they are not hurt bad enough…and the helicopters keep coming."

"How about the noise?"

"The noise is deafening. Bombs are exploding in the distance, grenades detonating in the camp, the screams of the wounded, and the napalm-burned children shrieking for relief. I have never heard anything like it!"

"The whistling bombs near the boat bother me the most. We know the harbor is mined. Any time there is a loud thump near the boat, we're sure there will be an explosion soon to follow. Our staff is great, and it sure sounds better than a field hospital."

A smile came across Mike's face.

"Do you recall when the only sound that would alert us was the siren on an ambulance? Ah! The good old days."

Thom signaled the waiter and ordered two more beers. He was finally beginning to relax after two months of constant pressures.

"Have you heard anything from Casey?" Mike inquired.

"We got some casualties on the boat several weeks ago. One was a fellow who was shot near the kidneys. He needed to be on a dialysis machine for a while. I was hooking him up for a dialysis treatment when he saw my nametag and said to me, "Senor Rossi, your Amigo is Bueno!" He started laughing and told me that Dr. Casey said to say Hello. Casey did some great work on the kid's kidney; he's going to be OK. Now, enough war talk! How much time do we have in Saigon?"

"I have to catch my ride back tomorrow evening at four."

"That gives us twenty-four hours. Come on, my friends, let's see Saigon and forget the war."

An exhausted, but mentally refreshed Mike Elliott boarded the helicopter at four the following day for the ride back to the field hospital. For a brief moment, he had escaped the war.

The next few weeks, the war and its casualties dominated his life. The fighting had moved closer to De Nang. The doctors were on twenty-four-hour alert and no one was given a pass to go to Saigon. Wounded soldiers came in at all hours of the night and day.

It was after thirteen hours of working in the operating room that Mike finally got to rest in his tent. He had been asleep for only a few moments when he felt someone shaking him.

"Dr. Elliott! Dr. Elliott! Get up! Our sentries have reported enemy troops about a mile from the camp. You're to report to the hospital at once!"

"Are we expecting heavy casualties?" He asked, but the nurse was gone.

Mike hurriedly put on his boots and grabbed his shirt. He made a mad dash to the hospital.

"Dr. Elliott, we're moving all the patients to the bunker. Get all the medical supplies you'll need and HURRY!"

Phillip was rushing a wheel chair out the door as the nurses followed with the gurneys. Mike got crutches and started the ambulatory, wounded men toward the bunker. Mortars were exploding overhead causing an eerie glow over the camp. The noise became deafening. Nurses grabbed plasma, bandages, and blankets as the doctors gathered medicines and several surgical trays.

"There's no more time! Let's go!" Phillip was hurrying everyone into the bunker. You could now hear the screams and taunts of the Viet Cong as they approached through the jungle.

It was extremely crowded inside the bunker. The patients were made as comfortable as possible. Many of them were lying on the floor on blankets. Several had to have their stitches repaired as the sutures had torn in the move from the hospital.

Outside, the defense of the camp had begun. Smoke was everywhere as the flamethrowers were used to prevent the VC from emerging from the wooded area. The steady firing of the machine guns, combined with the exploding mortars and grenades, created an unbearable noise. Several nurses huddled together and cried uncontrollably. The chaplain led the group in prayers. A quiet pall had fallen over the crowded bunker.

"I didn't think the VC has ever read the Geneva Convention." Phillip was trying to ease the tension in the bunker.

Mike's body ached from lack of sleep, he was crouched in cramped quarters, and his mind was in complete chaos. "Is this where I'm going to die? Who will notify my folks? Do these people take prisoners? How will the enemy treat these women nurses? What will happen to the men who are wounded?" As Mike sat in the semidarkness of the bunker, his spirits sank. He had never felt so scared! But he had to control his fears so the others would not see the terror in his eyes. Fear could be contagious!

It was daybreak when an alarm sounded. They had spent over ten hours in the crowded bunker before a sergeant came and informed them that the fighting was over. Help from the battalion and Air Cover had come to repel the enemy. Cautiously, the doctors left the bunker to assess the damage. A section of the hospital was gone as was the entire mess tent. Small fires were everywhere. There was also the smell of burning flesh.

"You doctors look to see if there are any wounded that need our attention. We'll try to set up an operating tent! Some of you nurses get any surgical instruments you can find and sterilize them!" Phillip started barking out orders amid all the chaos. "We'll take our wounded first, and then we'll work on any of the Viet Cong that need attention. Let's move!"

Everyone scattered in an attempt to reorganize the hospital area. The operating room consisted of three gurneys out in the open air. It was the most sanitary place for surgery! Several corpsmen were folding tarps for a roof over the hospital ward. Still, others were putting out fires, and cooks were fixing food for the wounded, and anyone who had a few moments to stop and eat. Of course, the food was eaten outside, picnic style. Tents had to be set up for shelter, and the wounded were finally escorted from the bunker back to the make shift hospital. Mike and three other doctors worked steadily for twenty-three hours, stopping only for a fifteen-minute nap or to eat a sandwich. Strong coffee kept them awake.

After four days of operating, hiding in a bunker, and operating again, Mike finally lay down on his bed in the tent. He was too tired to take a shower or eat a decent meal. In the distance, he could hear the men bring up the dead Viet Cong for a body count to send to headquarters. Mike felt a sense of pride that he had been challenged and had performed as he had been trained. Through their efforts, many lives had been saved. However, he was still amazed at the destruction of the human body that another human being in war can inflict on a person. He was also surprised at the resilience of the men and women who are involved in this conflict and helped to repair their destruction. But he was disgusted with the dehumanizing of the human body with the daily body count of the dead enemy!

It took several weeks for the base camp to rebuild. Supplies came from headquarters and surprisingly, there were very few casualties during this time. Mike enjoyed the camaraderie with the other doctors, and he and the medical personnel became good friends. But it was Phillip that he most admired. He marveled at his surgical skills, but more than that, he was in awe of his management techniques. He made every doctor, nurse, orderly, stretcher carrier, and cook feel important and a vital part of the successful operation of the camp. His praise and guidance kept the hospital and the entire camp running smoothly. He and Thom talked on the phone several times, but Mike couldn't get a pass to go to Saigon and see his friend.

It was several months later when Mike experienced his worst moment in his Vietnam experience. The camp had been lulled into complacency after several seventy degrees days. The casualties had been light, and days were spent pitching horseshoes, playing softball and cards, and gathering with buddies for a few beers. It didn't seem possible that over one half of his tour to Vietnam was over. And nothing could have prepared him for the week ahead.

During the last few weeks, the shelling and artillery fire seemed to get louder and closer. On several occasions, the doctors had treated villagers from the surrounding area.

For several days, there had been rumors of infiltrators moving into the villages, taking control of them, and inflicting atrocities on them. Although the doctors talked to the villagers when treating them, no one would admit that these rumors were true. Fear can create a great deal of silence, but the rumors persisted.

The day started with heavy shelling several miles away. The camp put on alert as stray mortar shells sometimes fell near the hospital. Several small fires were extinguished and there were minor injuries from pieces of exploding shrapnel. At noon, huge clouds of smoke appeared to block the sun creating an ominous feeling throughout the camp.

"Boy...this is weird..."

"Yeah, it's like we're sitting here, waiting for something to happen."

"I haven't seen a villager for two days. Do you think all the villagers got healthy this week?" Mike finished his coffee as Phillip laughed at his remark.

"What is that smell?" Phillip walked to the door of the mess tent. "I'm glad it's outside and not the cook's food."

Mike moved to the door as the alarm sounded. There were unidentified people approaching the base. Everyone was on alert!

The camp stood in awe and silence at the scene that appeared before them. Hundreds of Vietnamese villagers emerged from the woods with the various degrees of burns or wounds on their bodies. Some were wearing clothing that was still smoking. Many had been beaten and then set afire. Others were shot as they tried to defend their families from the infiltrators. The smell of burning flesh permeated the air.

Phillip began to scream, "Litters! Get those litters over here NOW!"

"Miss, let me have your baby." Mike rushed over to a woman who was badly burned and extended his arms. He knew when he took the child that the baby was dead. Before he could assist her, the mother collapsed, dead, with her skin peeling off her body.

Again, it was Phillip who immediately started yelling orders and organizing the staff. "Mike, you and Jonesie take the gun shot wounds. Get your team into the hospital; we'll examine and send the victims to you. You two nurses check the children; try to evaluate the kids and send those we can save to John and Ralph!" He quickly selected two corpsmen. "You guys set up an area we can use as a Burn Center. Try to make it as sterile as possible. Ken and I will check out the adult burn victims. Let's go, folks! Jay, you get on some gloves and set up a morgue."

"Come on, Jonesie, let's go. We'll get as ready as we can. Heaven only knows how many wounded we'll have."

"I think this is going to be a long one!"

It was the most difficult operating session that Mike had encountered. Several children were passed over because of the severity of the burns; the doctors knew they could not save them. Many underwent surgery for gun shot wounds and then sent to the burn unit for treatment. Jonesie and Mike worked over two days steadily to treat the wounded and then did another six hours helping with the burn victims. The final total: fifty-seven gunshot patients, thirty-four burn victims, and forty-three dead, many of whom they worked feverishly trying to save. Others who were critical were treated and sent to Saigon as soon as possible.

"What happened out there?" a corpsman inquired. It was the first time since the nightmare began days ago that the men had a few moments to talk.

"An entire village was annihilated by a small group of renegade, North Vietnamese soldiers. They used flamethrowers at night, burning the huts while the villagers were asleep in them. As many people tried to escape, they were shot."

"It was just what we had heard that we thought were rumors."

"It's simple: several North Viet Cong come into a village looking for food, guns, or information. Most of the young men are in the army and gone from the area."

"So the old men and women are easy prey for them?"

"After a few weeks, these renegades had all the guns and food from the village, so they began shooting and turned several flamethrowers on the people. I would guess the village has been destroyed; it's been burnt to the ground." Phillip tried to explain the situation as best as he could.

"What will these people do?"

"Those that survive the bullets and burns will find relatives in other villages and get on with their lives. It is a completely different way of life than we know in the United States…very simple, very basic."

Mike sat quietly. "You never think of the other victims of war— the old men, women, and children. These people are tending crops or washing clothes and suddenly, they are in front of a flamethrower!" He immediately thought of the crowd of protesters in San Antonio. He wished those antiwar, sign carriers could experience the atrocities that they had seen this past week.

"These people have to be sick of war!"

"Suppose you had picked this week to visit your grandmother in the village?" Jonesie added.

Phillip spoke quietly, almost reverently. "I think that might have happened. I got a call from Graves Registration, seems there was an American in the village. I suspect he might have been a missionary. They bring supplies to the villages with the hopes of winning a few converts. There is no identification on him. The villagers were probably hiding him as long as they could. Jay put him in a body bag and his body is in our morgue. They are sending someone to pick him up."

"The missionaries are brave people. I'm not sure I'd go into some of these villages alone."

"The villages welcome the religious people. Most of the men are gone and the women eke out a living by farming or gathering plants and berries from the area. But there are no medical supplies, no clothes, or no spiritual guidance…and very little food. The villagers welcome anything the missionaries give to them."

"Could you tell if this guy had been tortured or shot?" Mike was tired, but he wanted to try to understand this strange country.

"I'm afraid he suffered quite a bit before he died. He had bruises on his wrists where he had been tied. There were welts on his back, arms, and chest where he was beaten. He was shot in the back of the head, gangland style. Several of the women brought his body here, hoping we could help him. But he was too far gone to help. We gave him a shot of morphine to help him with the pain. And he died a few minutes later. Poor guy…he was really treated horribly before he was shot. I'm not sure…"

Phillip was interrupted by a stranger who approached the table.

"Excuse me, Sirs. I'm from Graves Registration. Headquarters sent me to pick up an American who came in with the burnt Vietnamese villagers."

"He doesn't have any ID on him, not even a crucifix. The villagers don't seem to know his name or they don't trust us enough to tell us!"

"Just tell me where he is and I'll take him back to headquarters. We'll try to identify him there."

Mike rose from his seat. "I'm tired and I'm going to get some shut-eye. Come on; I'll take you over to the morgue. It's on my way."

The two men walked slowly across the compound.

"It's hard to believe that several hours ago this area was a Hell-Hole."

"Or that some Do-Gooder would go into a village alone in this area. These guys always want to save the world. And I have to risk my ass to come up here to pick up his body."

Mike became livid! "Don't ever let me hear you say anything like that again! These are brave men; you are just a delivery man!"

The two men entered the morgues and walked over to a body bag that he had been placed apart from the others.

"This place gives me the creeps. Unzip the guy and if it's our man, I'll put him in the back of my truck and be on my way."

"Why don't you just SHUT UP?" The young man's attitude was grating on Mike's patience.

Mike unzipped the bag and found himself staring at his redheaded friend Dr. Ed Casey.

"Oh, my God! It's Ed!"

Mike sank to his knees as the room began to spin…

When he finally became conscious, Mike found himself back in his own tent. At first, he thought the entire episode was a nightmare, but as he cleared the cobwebs from his head, the realization came upon him that his friend Casey was dead. Mike had felt compassion for the men he had treated and for those who had died. And he was especially sympathetic for the villagers who had to live in the total chaos of this war. But these were faces that passed before him. He had tried to stay detached from the war and persevere through these months, fulfilling his commitment to the United States and returning home to practice medicine. He wanted to leave Southeast Asia far behind him.

But Mike knew that he could never forget this war or the faces of the villagers. He would have nightmares of the people, burnt and screaming in agony. Imprinted on this memory was the face of every man and boy (yes, boy) on which he had operated, and especially he would recall the face of Ed Casey, who tried to help the local people and was rewarded with a bullet in the head. His thoughts drifted to Maureen and Ed's two little curly haired girls. His reverie was interrupted by a gentle shake of his hand.

"Welcome back! How are you doing, Buddy?" Jonesie and Phillip were sitting on the bed next to him.

"How long have I been here?"

"Three days. You were exhausted from treating the villagers and then you apparently recognized our dead American…the missionary?"

"He wasn't a missionary. He was my friend, Dr. Ed Casey. We met at Fort Sam Houston in San Antonio, got our military indoctrination there, and shipped over together. I haven't seem him for over a year. He was assigned to a field hospital near Hue. He was my friend."

"What do you think he was doing at the village?"

"Knowing Ed, I'm sure he was bringing supplies to the villagers and giving medical care to the children. One of the kids with a gunshot wound had splint on his arm had been broken and professionally set."

"Did he have a family?" Phillip quizzed Mike as he closely watched him. In the two years he had seen the chief surgeon at the hospital, he had seen three doctors who could no longer work in these conditions and were sent to Saigon for psychiatric help. Mike was a good surgeon, and Phillip didn't want to lose him.

"We called ourselves 'The Tall Texans.' Ed was our clown, always making jokes to boost our spirits…I've got to call Thom."

But as Mike started to get off the bed, his head began to spin and he almost fell into the table.

"Whoa, Partner! I don't think you should go anywhere. You need some rest. You have been drifting in and out of consciousness for three days, talking nonsense. Jonesie, sit here with Mike for a while. I'll call headquarters and inform them that our unknown American is Dr. Ed Casey stationed at Hue."

As Phillip walked from the area, his eyes told Jonesie not to leave his friend alone.

Several days later, Mike made his phone call to Thom, who already heard the news.

"We've been pretty busy here. As soon as I get some time off, I want to write a note to Ed's wife. He was really a pal. But I'm not telling my mother. I don't want her to worry."

"Did she know Maureen?"

"Mom and Dad came to San Antonio before we shipped out. They spent time with Maureen and the girls during the day, while we were at the base. They did all the tourist things together; you know, tour the Alamo, the River Walk, etc. They don't have any grandchildren and they really like those girls?"

"Does she still live with Ed's folks?"

"Yeah, on the West Coast…in Malibu, I think."

"I'm glad she's not alone."

There was a long pause before Thom continued. "Are YOU all right?"

"I'll be better after a few days rest. I hope I never have a shock like that again!"

"You've got to take care of yourself. You treat your patients better than yourself. Get a pass and come to Saigon. We'll spend some time getting reacquainted with the night life of the city."

Thom tried to lighten the mood of the conversation, but his jocularity only reminded them that Casey, the joker of the group, was gone. He could hear the sadness in his friend's voice.

"You might be right, but I think I need to get to work and keep busy at the hospital. I don't want a lot of time to think about what could happen."

"You're the doctor," Thom chuckled. "You know best. But let's keep in touch. Good buddies are hard to find."

"And in this war, good buddies are difficult to keep alive. I'll call you on the weekend." As he dropped the phone, Mike suddenly felt exhausted. Maybe he did need a few more days of rest before returning to duty in the hospital.

The remainder of the tour proved uneventful. He managed to get back to Saigon once and spent the entire time with Thom. He treated hundreds of wounded soldiers, but now he spent a few more minutes with each one, talking on a personal level. It was obvious that Mike's real talent was in the field of emergency medicine. He would stay calm when countless wounded soldiers, all screaming in pain, arrived at the camp. He fought death with every ounce of energy he had.

When his tour was finally over, Mike applied and was accepted at Cook County Hospital Emergency Room. He heard that Thom was back in New York, but the two friends had gone their separate ways after leaving Nam. They didn't even get to say good-bye before returning to the states. All reminders of the war—the horrors, the losses, the medical triumphs, and the friendships were left in Southeast Asia, *or so they thought!*

Mike Elliott was a natural in emergency medicine. The chaos of a major city trauma center was an easy transition for him. He was the newest member of a team of four physicians who worked the four to twelve o'clock shift at Cook County. This shift was the busiest: auto accidents, drive by shootings by the gangs, bar room brawls, and a large variety of street crimes and accidents dominated the time period.

It was a routine night in the middle of December when the incident occurred. Mike was examining a teenage boy who had been sledding in the park and hit a tree. He put in a call to an orthopedic surgeon to come in and set the badly broken leg. Things seemed quiet on a snowy, winter night. Crime injuries usually were down when there was a snowstorm.

At ten-thirty that evening, a call came into the emergency room. There had been an explosion at a high-rise apartment building. The police suspected a methamphetamine lab had been operating in the building and it had exploded. There were several ambulances due to arrive at Cook County Emergency Center in ten minutes.

The medical team shifted into action.

"We're going to be getting lot of burn victims. Let's get out plenty of burn gel, bandages, and oxygen. Let's move!"

"Get someone near the entrance to assess the patients. Send the more serious one to the right and the others to the exam rooms."

Mike froze as he gathered the bandages. His mind flashed back to Vietnam on that fateful day at the field hospital. Phillip's orders, as the villagers appeared, resounded over and over in his mind. "You check the children and send the ones we can save over here," echoed again and again. Mike could not move; he was locked in the past. He could see the faces of the villagers, screaming in agony, many of them dying.

"Dr. Elliott! Dr. Elliott! Mike! Are you OK?" The nurse's call seemed to bring Mike back to the present and focusing on the task.

"Just tired, I guess. Get that cart and help me with these boxes."

Susan Pascalleri pulled the cart into the supply room and together they loaded the bandages on it. They moved quickly, stocking each exam room with all sizes of gauze, and checking for other medications. The first ambulance arrived as they almost finished.

The smell of burning flesh began to permeate the emergency room. The first patient was a ten-month-old child, badly burnt.

"She had a pulse when we put her in the ambulance, but I can't get one now. It's hard to find a spot to touch her without her skin peeling away."

Mike rushed over to the paramedic and took the child from him. But to the shock of the staff, Mike just stood there, holding the child. The smell of the burning flesh and the sight of the charred child had triggered another flashback to the field hospital in Nam!

"Lady, let me have your baby," he mumbled. He stood there, holding the child and repeating the same words over and over. "Lady, let me have your baby..."

The entire emergency room became silent. Everyone stared at the doctor in disbelief as he stood there with the child. Suddenly, he passed the baby to the orderly and shouted, "The mother just collapsed. I think they're both dead! I'm going to the hospital and get scrubbed for gunshot wounds. Come on, Jonesie!"

Susan followed Mike as he moved back to the exam room. She found him standing there, staring at the wall...motionless.

"Dr. Elliott, why don't you come to the lounge and rest for a few moments? You've had a busy night."

Mike turned around quickly. "Nonsense, Susan. Let's get out there and help with these injured people."

For the next few hours, Mike Elliott worked furiously to save the fire victims. No one left when the shift ended, but at 3:00 AM, the last patient had been treated. Mike grabbed his coat and walked slowly to his car. He looked forward to a hot shower and some sleep. He was so tired that he didn't realize he was the only person in the parking lot. No one else was leaving the building.

Inside the staff lounge, he was the topic of conversation.

"What happened to Dr. Elliott in there?"

"He was hallucinating...he saw women who weren't there."

"I've heard these doctors from Vietnam are all hooked on drugs."

Dr. Stone, one of the surgical staff, shook his head. "I don't know what happened to Dr. Elliott tonight, but I know he doesn't take drugs. He's one of the best emergency room doctors I've ever seen. He makes the rest of us look like first-year residents. I've read that some Vets, who were in the harshest areas, have some problems when they return home. Sometimes, it's hard to forget all the atrocities they have witnessed."

"Should we report the incident to the hospital administration?"

Susan quickly jumped into the conversation. "I hate to report anyone unless it's absolutely necessary. A report goes into your file, regardless if the accusation is found meaningless. This 4–12 staff is one of the best, and I've worked with some good doctors."

"Once he started treating patients, he was the same excellent doctor that we expect he will be each time he is on duty."

"And it only happened this one time…"

Susan sat quietly, thinking about the incident in the supply room. She had decided not to mention the problem earlier in the evening.

"Let's keep an eye on him. If anything like this ever happens again, then we'll report it."

It was agreed that anyone working closely with Mike would look for odd behavior. Any problems would be reported to Dr. Stone and he could decide if the behavior needed to be reported to the chief of staff of the hospital.

The next few months passed without any problems. Several times, the emergency room was crowded, but everyone worked efficiently. After several days, the staff no longer felt it was necessary to closely observe Dr. Elliott as he practiced medicine.

It was an unusually warm June that year, and a very busy one for Mike. His desire to learn had returned; so during the days, Mike would observe operations, attend lectures, and sometimes sneak into specialized, closed conferences. He was at a discussion of knee replacements when someone put his hand on his shoulder. Mike was sure that he was going to be asked to leave the conference as he failed to secure permission to be there.

"Is this War Wounds 101?"

Mike spun around and stared into the eyes of Thom Rossi. The two men embraced, parted, and hugged again!

"Well, my Tall Texan, I never thought I would find such a hot shot emergency man learning about knees."

"And I never thought a big city bone man would come to Chicago, the stockyard capital of the world?"

Both men laughed and embraced again. "Let's get out of here. The knees can wait. We've got a lot of beer to drink and news to share. I'm off until tomorrow afternoon, at four o'clock. There's a local pub around the corner, cold beer, and hot BBQ ribs. Tell me, Thom, what is more important for us Tall Texans—knees or beer and ribs?"

It took only a few minutes for the two old friends to be seated on bar stools, eating peanuts and drinking a beer.

"How long has it been? Two years?" Mike could not believe his luck to see his war buddy again. "How is life in the Big Apple?"

"It's seems like after Vietnam, I could handle anything! I've worked in several New York hospitals, and I've just accepted a position as Chief of Orthopedics at Mass General in Boston. But the best news…I met a girl. I'm going to be married at Thanksgiving. You'll like Beth. How about you, Hot Shot?"

"I'm working in the emergency room at Cook County. It's a lot like Vietnam, only cleaner. The staff is something special; we have a good team."

"Is there a girl in your life?"

"Not yet. I'm still trying to decide if I want to go back to school for some specialized training. I can't seem to make up my mind anymore. But there's a cute nurse, Suzie Pascalleri, who I've dated a few times. I've not become a priest!" he laughed.

"Doesn't sound like you, Mike. Aren't you happy in emergency medicine?"

"Yeah, I guess so. We get busy I don't have much time to think about it. I guess it's good to keep busy."

Thom studied his friend's face for a few moments. "I got a call a few weeks ago from Maureen Casey, Ed's wife. She and the girls were going to be in New York for a few days and she wanted to meet me to talk about Ed. I called Beth, and we met her for dinner. She seems to have accepted Ed's death and is getting on with her own life. She teaches kindergarten in Malibu; both of the girls are in school. I think Ed's parents are glad she decided to stay in Malibu so they can see the girls and help her with them. You should see the younger one; she has a curly mop of hair and freckles. She looks like Ed if he had put on a red wig! She asked about your parents. She really liked them. I felt like an idiot that we hadn't been in touch for over two years."

Thom took a sip of beer. There was a moment of silence between the two friends. He continued to look deeply into Mike's eyes. "Do you ever think about it?"

Mike knew exactly what his friend referred to in his statement. "I try to stay busy in the emergency room and in my free time, I check out new procedures and a few lectures. And if I get a long weekend, I'll hop a flight to Baltimore and get back to Western Maryland to see my folks."

Tom lowered his head. "I guess Maureen stirred some unpleasant memories and made me revisit a place I thought I'd never think about again. I had never seriously talked to Beth about the years in Nam; I wanted to put the entire experience behind me. Ed must have written some graphic letters to Maureen, and of course, she saw the scars on Ed's body. I tried to emphasize the many good things that Ed accomplished while he was there. As we talked, it was Beth who was shocked at some of the atrocities that occurred. She didn't understand why soldiers would kill someone who was in a village helping sick kids. I told them your bunker incident and she was speechless. She was naive enough to think that hospitals and medical personnel were safe and off limits to the enemy. With the sentiment here in the states and the antiwar protests, the death of a doctor was not publicized in the newspaper. Maureen was glad that Ed had the Tall Texans with him; he was not alone. After all our time there, I still don't understand the country."

Mike quickly changed the topic. "Speaking of memories, remember the night we drank our way through Saigon? We must have had a drink in over one-half of the bars in the city! It's always been a mystery to me that bartenders didn't speak English, but they could understand the names of the drinks. We sure got 'loaded' that night!"

And they got "loaded" in Chicago.

Mike returned to work the following night. It had been good to see his old friend and he had promised to come to Boston over the Labor Day Weekend. He was anxious to meet Beth, the girl who had won the heart of Dr. Thom Rossi. He had also reluctantly agreed, in a weak moment, to be Thom's best man in his wedding. And…if she was still in Mike's dating scenario, he had even promised to bring Suzie to the festivities at thanksgiving. He felt better than he had felt in months.

The next night began as a quiet evening in the trauma center. An ambulance brought in a drowning victim, and the staff could not revive her. Several routine playground accidents (sprained ankles, broken arm, scrapes, and a concussion) were successfully treated.

An urgent call came from the police dispatch at 10:30. There had been a drive-by shooting at a popular downtown restaurant. A car had sprayed bullets into a crowd of late diners seated outside on the veranda. Fourteen people were injured and several ambulances were at the scene, eventually bringing the wounded to Cook County.

The emergency room staff went on high alert. The group divided into their respective teams, with Dr. Stone and Susan evaluating patients as they were brought in by the ambulances. Everything was ready as it could be.

A strange calm came over Mike, a feeling he had not experienced since he had been associated with the hospital. There was an inner peace and confidence that he could handle any emergency that would present itself. He remembered the fear he felt when he was forced to huddle in the bunker for hours, not knowing if the base camp would be overrun by the Viet Cong. Mike attributed his newfound inner strength to spending twenty-four hours with Thom, talking about their shared nightmare. It was good to talk about past experiences with an old friend who was there.

The first ambulance to arrive brought two small boys and their mother. They had been sitting in front of the window of the restaurant. The boys had cuts and bits of glass embedded in their skin. They were extremely bloody, but their wounds were considered superficial. The boy was immediately put into the care of a third year medical student, who could clean the cuts and determine if any sutures were needed. Mike's team took the mother, who was in shock and had a gunshot wound below her shoulder. The bullet had passed through her shoulder and exited out the back. The team treated her for shock, stopped the flow of blood, x-rayed her for damage, and stitched the area. They quickly moved her into a recovery room under the watchful eye of a critical care nurse.

The trauma center was now a blur of activity. Dr. Stone and Susan had deserted their post to treat a gunshot wound to the head. As a team finished their treatment of a patient, they would take the charge of the next ambulance with doctors moving from one area to another as needed.

The victims poured into the center. Mike worked furiously over a gentleman who had been shot over his heart. He split open his chest and stared at the man's aorta which had been grazed by a bullet causing a tear. Blood was seeping from a small opening into his chest cavity. Each time his heart would beat, blood would pump into his chest.

"Get me that needle and some gut," Mike barked to the nurse.

"Doctor, you haven't scrubbed!"

"And if I take the time to scrub, this man will die. Get me that needle! Stat!"

Mike jumped up on the stretcher and straddled the man. He lightly applied pressure to the tear, enough to stop most of the blood from filling the chest cavity, yet light enough to keep blood flowing to the other parts of the body.

"Get some suction! I need to see what I'm doing!"

"Suction, Doctor!" An intern put the suction tube into the chest cavity, drawing out some of the blood.

"Here's the needle!" The nurse passed the needle, threaded, to Mike.

Calmly, Mike made small sutures in the aorta, closing the tear. A small bit of blood seeped from one of the stitches, so Mike over the stitched area.

"Let's get him upstairs to surgery. This is just temporary; let the trained specialist do the fancy stitching!"

The intern rolled the stretcher toward the elevator.

"I've never seen that technique before," he called back to Mike.

"We saved a lot of soldiers in Nam with the 'Quick Sew' method. Has everyone who came in on the last ambulance been seen?"

Dr. Stone called out over the confusion. "There's one more ambulance coming in. There's a man with a gunshot wound to his arm and a little girl who was shot in the chest…Here comes the ambulance now!"

The ambulance backed up to the emergency room as paramedics jumped out. The back of the ambulance opened and the stretcher held a man, blood seeping down his arm, holding a small girl, with his bloody hand on her chest. It was rolled directly into the trauma center.

"Is Dr. Elliot on duty?" The man on the stretcher spoke quietly.

"Mike, come here!"

Mike came out of the exam room to stare at Dr. Thom Rossi, lying on the gurney.

"Mike, this little girl needs a 'Quick Sew' if she is going to make it!"

"Dr. Stone, this little girl has a hole in her aorta," Mike said with authority. "This is Dr. Thom Rossi. We served together in Vietnam."

"I'll take this little girl. You tend to your friend." He turned to Dr. Rossi and said, "I'll shake your hand later." Dr. Stone eased the child out of the man's arms and rushed her in for immediate surgery.

Mike rolled his friends back to the exam room. He carefully inspected the wound.

"How bad is it, Old Buddy? I'd like to have two hands when I operate!"

"I don't see any nerve damage. However, the bullet broke the humerus. I've got a call in to an orthopedic man, but you can't oversee the operation and give him directions. I'll clean the wound, and send you upstairs. My Buddy deserves the best! Good surgeons are hard to find."

Mike gave his friend a shot and then started to clean the wound.

"How many of these gunshot wounds in the arms do you think we treated in Nam?" Mike asked, trying to relax his friend.

Thom looked up at Mike. "Will you get my wallet out of my pants? Beth's phone number is in there. Give her a call and tell her that I picked the wrong restaurant again. I don't think I'll be on tomorrow's flight home…"

"Sleep well, my friend. We'll take care of you." Mike personally took his friend, Dr. Rossi, up to surgery.

At the end of the shift, Dr. Elliot walked into the lounge and sat down, exhausted. He just wanted to get home for a shower and a good night's sleep, but he had promised Thom that he would call Beth. He had waited until Thom was out of surgery with a good report on his arm. He carefully opened Thom's wallet to find a phone number. The first thing he saw was a photograph of the Tall Texans taken on the first day in Vietnam. He stared at the faces of Thom Rossi, Ed Casey, and Mike Elliot. And then something happened...

All this man could remember was waking up on a beach, with no memory of who he was or how he got to a place called Ocean Beach. And now he was on a bus going to Clarksville. Did he know someone in Clarksville? Did he have a family there? Was he Joe Smith? Did he know the little girl with curly hair?

A loud clap of thunder, followed by a flash of lightning, caused several people on the bus to awaken. The rain continued to dash against the windows.

And the bus rolled on...

CHAPTER 7

BEN SOMERS WATCHED AS THE MAN ACROSS the aisle stare at the little girl.

"Wow! What a space cadet!" he thought to himself. "There is nothing between his ears. He just seems to sit and stare into space. He doesn't even talk to his friend sitting next to him. He didn't even get off the bus for some dinner."

Ben sat quietly for a few moments, still observing the fellow seated opposite him on the bus. "Maybe the guy has a concussion or a brain tumor that caused his blank stare." He pondered these thoughts over and over in his mind.

Ben was always misjudging people and constantly ridiculing his friends and even strangers and playing practical jokes at the expense of others. Was it this attitude that got him into the trouble he had now? Was he still running from a need to grow up? Was he escaping from his responsibility by being on this bus to...? "Where in the *hell* was this bus going? Oh, yeah, some hick town named Clarksville. Well, at least no one will know me there. I can get a construction job or some other seasonal work for a few weeks until this mess blows over, or I can sort this out! After all, it was just an accident...and not really my fault..."

Ben Somers would have been called a spoiled child. He could never do any wrong in the eyes of his parents. He always had a reason to get excused from the simplest tasks. He was too tired to pick up his toys, and he couldn't finish his vegetables because he had a mysterious tummy ache. When he was four, he painted his cocker spaniel green, and as the vet was shaving his dog, Ben tearfully told everyone that since the leaves were turning green, Taffy should be green. He was such an adorable child, and it was such a cute story!

And the pranks didn't stop when he entered parochial school. Ben's grades were passing, but he found more pleasure entertaining his classmates. He was constantly in trouble, breaking all the rules. He wore a red shirt with his uniform, always ran in the halls, chewed gum and popped bubbles in class, threw paper wads, etc. Ben was a frequent visitor to the principal's office, but his parents had left strict instructions that Ben was a mischievous little boy and was not to be punished or disciplined in any way. Ben told the administrator that he was bored and thought the rules were stupid and dumb. When tested, his IQ was extremely high. It was very difficult for Ben to conform to class rules. Yet he seemed to know just how far to challenge authority. At the end of the school year, he was asked to transfer to another school, for the beginning of the fifth grade. If he couldn't follow school rules, he should look for another school.

Valentine's Day in the fifth grade was a special day at Grady Elementary School. The pupils had each decorated a shoe box for their classmates to deposit their valentines. Since it was an unusually warm day in February, Mrs. Riggin permitted the kids to stay on the playground an extra half hour after recess was over. Twenty-eight laughing students came off the playground to find their room resplendent with decorations for the holiday. Cokes were sitting on the desks, and the activity table was filled with cupcakes, brownies, a sheet cake, and a large assortment of candies, sent to the class the Room Mothers. Eleven-year-olds especially liked the small candy hearts with silly messages in them and the small cinnamon hearts.

"Get into your seats so we can start the party. Phil, you and Susan are our mailmen. You can start passing out the cards. Quickly, take your seats. We're not passing out any Valentines until everyone is in his seat, and the room is quiet."

The children rushed to get to their desks, giggling with anticipation. Ben was hungry; he had thrown away most of the nutritious lunch his mother had packed for him. He felt a pang of embarrassment because he hadn't bothered to get any Valentines for his classmates. After all, he was eleven years old and Valentines were for kids. With all the activity, no one would miss a valentine card from him.

Soon his desk was piled with cards from the other students. Karen brought him an empty paper plate, followed by a procession of classmates with food. His plate was filled with cakes, brownies, and several kinds of candy. He had enticed Brenda to give him extra valentine candles.

"This is cool!"

"Yeah! I wish we could have a party like this every day!"

Ben shoved a huge piece of chocolate cake in his mouth as he began to open his cards. His mother hadn't sent any treats; he hadn't bothered to tell her about the Room Mothers' Organization.

The party was interrupted by a knock on the door. Mrs. Riggin answered the door and took a note from a student.

"Class, I have a phone call in the office. I must answer it. Finish passing out the Valentines and the food, and when I return, we'll start the games."

Mrs. Riggin doubled as the fifth grade teacher and the principal of the elementary school. As she walked out the door, she turned to see that everyone was in his seat and only those who had jobs were walking about the room. She quickly eased out the door and walked toward the office. She had left the class many times to complete emergency principal's calls; she was very proud of the fifth grade and their behavior at these times.

Ben continued to stuff food into his mouth and open his cards. He began to read his card from Ted, the class bully.

"You're so Great
You're so Fine
Be Your Own
Valentine!"

Ben began to get angry. He and Ted were rivals on the playground and in all the games. Ted could kick the ball further in kick ball games, but Ben could run faster. Ted could dribble a basketball between his legs and win at "keep away," but Ben could really shoot the ball and was leading scorer in most of the games if Ted would pass him the ball. Ted was a hall monitor and Ben was the attendance runner. And now, Ted had sent Ben a nasty valentine. And Ben had not sent a card to him!

The mischievous boy looked about the room. Everyone was eating their treats and opening their cards. Cautiously, Ben picked up a red cinnamon heart from his desk and threw it across the classroom, striking Ted on the side of his head. The boy looked around, but could not distinguish who had thrown the missile. He immediately looked at Ben, who was busy eating a piece of cake. The class seemed intent on enjoying the food and the cards.

Ben had to keep from laughing. He wished he could look at Ted, but instead, he buried his head in his cards. After several moments, he raised his head, scanning all his classmates. He noticed that Ted was already engrossed in a conversation with the group around him. Feeling smug that he had already gone undetected, Ben selected another red cinnamon heart and let it fly across the room. This time, the candy skipped across Ted's desk and hit his chest. As he buried his head in his Valentines, he again fought back his urge to giggle. He did not dare raise his head and look at Ted, but he wanted to see the look on his face. Although he didn't see the questioning look on Ted's face, Ben's confidence in his prank was growing. In the next moments, he propelled several cinnamon candies across the room at Ted and his friends. The missiles had hit their targets!

However, Ben's luck had run out. Frank, one of Ted's buddies, saw Ben's last missile fly across the room.

"Ted! Ted! It's Ben! Let's get him!"

With that discovery, a barrage of candy flew across the room, striking Ben and several classmates sitting around him. The battle had begun! Candy hearts and red cinnamon candies became the bullets of the fifth grade war. Then someone threw a cupcake and the battle escalated! Party favors, candy, cake, hats, and spraying sodas were flying about the class when Mrs. Riggin appeared in the doorway.

"Stop it! Class, stop it!"

Everything quieted down in the room. There was a deathly silence.

"What are you doing? Look at this mess! What happened? Who started this?

The silence continued.

"We talked about our behavior at the beginning of the year and how we shouldn't do anything that wouldn't make our parents proud. Do you think our parents would be proud of us now? Look at this room!...And your clothes! Susan, you have a cake in your hair. Next year you'll be going to middle school; this is very childish behavior!"

There continued to be deadly silence in the class. Most children sat with their heads down, not raising their eyes. There were no giggles, smiles, or excuses—only silence.

"Whoever started this could step forward, take responsibility for his or her actions, and accept the punishment."

Again, no one moved. The silence continued.

"We were going to eliminate this type of behavior as we prepared for middle school. I need to see the hands of those individuals who broke that promise. Take responsibility for your actions."

Ben sat like a statue, keeping his head down. He wanted to glance across the room at Ted, but he dared not lift his head. Instead, he sat in silence, with the other classmates.

"Since the perpetrators are ashamed of their actions, and it appears that most of the class was involved, I think this will be our final party this year. We don't seem very appreciative of the efforts of our home-room mothers who brought us this delicious food. Frank, go down the hall and ask Mrs. Johnson, our custodian, for a large garbage barrel and a pack of paper towels for our cleanup. Connie, go to the bathroom and get some water in the pail. We'll all clean up this mess and maybe learn a valuable lesson. There are always consequences for our actions.

We don't seem to be able to behave ourselves to have a fun day. OK. Let's get busy!"

There was very little talking as the entire group began to pick up the candy from the floor. The room was scrubbed clean when the final announcements were made and the kids loaded their backpacks, leaving the room in a quiet, orderly manner.

"Hey, Stupid! You really got us in trouble this time."

Ben turned around to see Ted and his buddies walking up behind him.

"Yeah, but there was just as much candy on the floor on my side of the room as there was on your side! You guys have good arms."

The group walked along amicably, laughing over the events of the day. It was difficult for fifth graders to think ahead and realize that there would be no Easter party, play-day picnic, or final fifth grade graduation festival. There was no remorse on Ben's face as he walked with his pals.

His nonsensical attitude continued throughout the remainder of the year, and as the graduation ceremony neared, Ben decided to leave Grady Elementary School with a lasting impression of his one year there. The parents had pressured the principal to have a social activity after the fifth grade graduation as was the tradition. Mrs. Riggin said she would consider it.

"Well, tomorrow is our last day at this crummy school!" Ben and Ted were walking home from school, having turned in their books and all final assignments.

"Next year is really scary. We'll be the youngest kids at Piney Run Middle School and those big eighth graders will pick on us and all the girls will like them better than us. I heard those eighth graders make the sixth graders carry their books and everything. It's going to be HELL!"

Ted was swearing, pouring out his feelings to Ben as the two friends ambled their way toward home.

"Well, no one is going to make me carry his books! I ain't afraid of no eighth graders. Boy, I hate this graduation gig! Why can't they just give us our report cards and skip this dumb ceremony? I hate standing around with a bunch of parents all dressed up! Mr. Hodge asked if I could come in early and help set up the refreshment table. It's a surprise. Mrs. Riggin wanted to surprise the class with a small, dignified social. Who cares for punch and cookies at a dignified social?" Ben sneered and mocked the affair.

Ted left his friend when he came to his home and Ben continued on alone with his thoughts. Deep inside, he was also scared to go to the middle school. He liked being the oldest kid at a school—the top dog!

There was a note on the table informing him that his mother was at the market and would be home before five o'clock. Dinner would be at 5:30, and he was not to eat anything until then.

Ben got a snack and strolled through the house, drinking a soda. The idea came to him as he wandered into the den. He looked outside and when he knew that neither his mother's or father's car was in the driveway, he opened the music box and took out the key to the liquor cabinet. He quickly unlocked the cabinet, took out a bottle of vodka, and relocked the cabinet. The key was returned to the music box (where his parents thought it was safely hidden away) and the bottle of vodka was then tucked in the box containing his graduation robe.

Dinner was a celebration of Ben's elementary school graduation. There were two huge pepperoni pizzas with extra cheese, which was his favorite. It was a party atmosphere, with everyone laughing and telling stories about Ben's year at Grady Elementary. Time passed quickly, and soon the family was scurrying to get dressed and drive to the school. Ben put on his good clothes and picked up the box which contained his graduation robe. He carefully packed his robe around the bottle of vodka and ran to the car for the journey to school.

"Ben, glad you're here. Start setting up the chairs around the room while I get the refreshment tables." Mr. Hodge began giving directives to his helpers. He felt that the students could learn leadership skills if they were responsible for the organization of the reception. Several girls were waiting as their teacher set up the tables.

"Connie, put those paper table cloths on these tables and arrange the napkins. Susan, get the forks and cups. Ben, you and Ted get those punch bowls from the closet down the hall and then go to the cafeteria and see Mrs. Riggin for the punch from the cooler."

"Old Hodgie Podgie really likes to give orders, doesn't he? Come on, Ben. Let's go get the damn punch bowls!"

"Yeah, he really likes to give orders."

"Maybe he'll slip and fall in the punch bowl and drown." Ben laughed at Ted's suggestion as the two boys walked down the hall to the closet.

"After you put the punch bowls on the tables, go on down to the cafeteria, and pick up the bottle of fruit juices for the punch. You'll have to make several trips down there."

"You have to make several trips to the cafeteria!" Ted mimicked the teacher's instructions. "Why doesn't the Old Coot make several trips himself?"

"He should get off his fat ass and get the punch himself." As an eleven-year-old, Ben was proud of his swearing. The boys carried the two punch bowls to the reception area and left for the cafeteria.

"Hodge Podge is a fat ass! Hodge Podge is a fat ass!" Ted chanted his friend's words as the boys walked to the cafeteria.

Mrs. Riggin was waiting for them and gave each boy two containers of juice to carry upstairs.

"Tell Connie and Susan to open the bottles and dump the juice into the punch bowls. Put one container of pineapple and one cranberry into each bowl. You boys come back for some more containers."

Each boy took two containers and started back to the reception area.

"I wonder if she wants us to salute her when she gives orders like that. I don't think that she can carry two bottles of fruit juice. Her boobs are too big and would get in the way!" The boys doubled over with laughter.

"Why should she carry anything? She has slaves like us!"

The boys were proud of their mature attitude as they put the bottles of juice on the reception table, gave Connie her directions, and made their way back to the cafeteria. It took three more trips to get all the fruit juice to the reception area.

Connie and Susan had the cloths on the tables and the punch bowls filled with fruit juices. The napkins were arranged on the tables with large plates of cookies and cake, covered with plastic wrap and awaiting the proud parents and the graduates. Mr. Hodge looked at the tables with pride. The students had done a good job. Everything was ready.

"You students should be very pleased and proud of your work here. It looks very nice. You can go to Room 24 and put on your robes for the graduation. I'm going to the cafeteria to get some ice cream to put in the punch."

The four pupils and Mr. Hodge left the reception area in two different directions.

"Oops…I forgot my robe box…You go on, Ted, and I'll be right there."

Ben started back to the library as the others went to the assembly area. He found his robe box and quickly removed the carefully hidden bottle of vodka. He opened the bottle and methodically poured half of the vodka in each of the punch bowls. Then he left the area, walked slowly toward Room 24, depositing the empty bottle in a trash container under some papers.

The graduation ceremony was very brief and without any problems. Ben won the honor prizes for Science, Mathematics, and Athletics. Soon everyone gathered at the reception in the library. Connie and Susan began to dip cups of punch as the proud parents and graduates formed a line to get cake, cookies, and punch. Ben left his parents and kept himself busy setting up more chairs and rearranging some of the others.

"Mommy, I don't feel very good." Carol, one of the graduates, was approaching her mother. "I feel sick."

"This has been a very exciting night for you and your classmates. I'm sure you're just nervous leaving your old school and some of your younger friends and going to a new middle school where the work will be harder. But you will make new…"

Before Mr. Hodge could finish his encouragement speech, Carol threw up on the chairs.

"Ben, go find the custodian. Quickly!"

Ben dashed from the room, trying to suppress his laughter. When he returned with Mr. Johnson, the reception was in chaos. Several of the students were sick; their parents were running around hysterically, making accusations about the food. Connie was loudly sobbing, thinking that everyone was blaming her because she was serving the food. Mr. Hodge was trying to placate the crowd as several of the parents became ill.

"Someone call an ambulance! Call several ambulances! Don't eat any more of the food. Connie, settle down and give everyone another cup of punch to wash away the taste of the food. We need to all settle down and stay calm. Mrs. Mace, you don't look well. Please sit down over here and Ted will bring the waste basket over to you."

"I think there is some liquor in this punch!" A parent screamed. "This punch has been spiked! Someone has put liquor in the punch!"

"Don't drink the punch!"

The paramedics and EMTs soon arrived and transported several of the children and some of the parents to the hospital. The superintendent of schools, who was at the ceremony handing out report cards and certificates, called the police and demanded that the food and punch be tested for foreign substances. The evening was ruined.

The Somers family drove home in relative silence.

"I don't understand how this could have happened."

"Maybe Mr. Hodge put the booze in the punch," Ben chimed in.

"Don't be silly, Benjamin! Someone must have come into the school during the ceremony and added the liquor. It was probably vodka. I didn't smell anything. There were some older boys playing basketball in the school yard when we came in. Mr. Hodge should question those boys to find out the truth. One of those boys probably came into the building and put liquor in the punch." Mrs. Somers was using her best investigative reasoning to try to understand the chaotic evening. "I'll call the school tomorrow and talk with Mr. Hodge."

Ben sat in the back seat of the car, in the dark, with a smile on his face. No one would ever forget the last day that Ben Somers was enrolled at Grady Elementary School!

Piney Run Middle School was the next challenge for the irresponsible lad. Ben had no problem with the older boys or with the work being too difficult. He really excelled in the middle school athletic programs, and therefore, gained respect of the older boys. He now had physical education every day, instead of recess. Coach Frederick was amazed at the skills of a twelve-year-old boy, and soon Ben was starting quarterback on the middle school football team. He had the distinction of being the only sixth grader to make the basketball team, and after four games, he was starting guard. His prowess as a shortstop was unmatched by anyone who tried out for the baseball team and earned him a starting spot. Because of his math skills, Ben was elected treasurer of his sixth grade class.

But it was only a matter of time before the devilish side of Ben appeared. Piney Run Middle School had a policy that no one was to be excused from class unless there was an emergency. There would be no students roaming or loitering in the halls, getting into trouble.

It was two days before thanksgiving and the bell had just rung to begin sixth period class. Miss Parks had given the warm-up drill and the group had started checking the math homework. As several students stood at the blackboard solving problems, there was a loud explosion from the bathroom at the end of the hall. Work in the class-room came to a sudden halt!

"What was that? It sounded like something blew up!"

"Class, let's get those problems on the board! We can't let a little noise distract us." (Miss Parks was a very dedicated teacher!)

It was difficult for the class to settle down and do their work. The noise from the hall had broken the concentration of the students. Soon there was a knock on the door. Mr. Carl, the Vice Principal, stepped into the room. He held a writing pad and a pencil in his hand.

"Miss Parks, I would like the names of all students who left the room after the one o'clock bell rang."

"I don't excuse anyone from the room unless it is a dire emergency. Everyone was here, in their seats, before the bell rang, and no one was excused."

Mr. Carl scanned the room briefly, noticing several boys who had previously caused some problems in other schools. His eyes rested on a few boys, but everyone was working on the math problems. Susan turned around and continued to put some of the problems on the board. Mr. Carl quietly walked to the front of the class, turned his back to the students and spoke to Miss Parks in a muted voice.

"Someone set off a large firecracker in the boy's bathroom. It's caused quite a bit of damage."

"Well, no one left the room after the bell, but I'll listen to the children for rumors. Good luck with your search."

As the door closed, Ben looked up from his paper and smiled at Ted. It was difficult to keep from laughing aloud.

"The old bloodhound is on the trail," Ben smirked at Ted.

"Maybe he'll do tests on everyone's hands to see if there's powder…or call in the scent dogs."

"Boys! Let's get quiet and finish our math. All the problems you don't complete in class, you will have for homework."

It was difficult for Ben to continue his work; he just sat with his head down, stifling his laughter.

After what seemed like an endless amount of time, the bell rang and Ben packed up his books and quickly left the room. He dumped his books in his locker and ambled down the hall to basketball practice.

"Hey, Ben! Wait for me." Ted hurried up the hall to walk with his friend. "I don't know how you pulled off this one, but I can tell that you caused the explosion. How'd you do it? You were sitting next to me when we heard the big bang!"

"My friend," he said with bravado, "I am the master of confusion. It is my crazy mind that keeps old man Carl patrolling the halls. If you take an M-80 fire cracker and put the fuse in a little hole above the cigarette filter, and strike a match and light the opposite end of a cigarette, then you have plenty of time to get to class before the cigarette burns down and lights the fuse." Ben was laughing and boasting as he walked down the hall to the gym.

"Just keep your mouth shut. Let's hear how old man Carl explains this one to the principal."

Ben was so cocky that he found it difficult not to blab to the entire basketball team. He wanted to share how clever he had been and how he executed the explosion. But his superior IQ told him to keep his explanations to himself!

A year later, over the Christmas holidays, Ben found himself alone several days when his parents went to work. Three days he had basketball practice; Chuck's parents picked him up and brought him home after the workout was finished. The guys met at Ted's house for an afternoon of video games. But on Wednesday, there was nothing to do, so Ben wandered up to the attic and found some old shoeboxes filled with mementoes from his dad's high school days. He found his dad's varsity letter, a collection of trophies, old report cards, dance souvenirs, and an envelope filled with small eight-page booklets filled with the filthiest drawings and conversations that he had ever seen! The comic strip characters were in sexual positions and poses with explicit language. Ben was shocked that his dad had such material possession, but he was amused that his lawyer father was just a regular guy in high school. Carefully packing up the shoe boxes, he put them back in the trunk and the booklets were tucked in his pocket.

School was back in session on January 5, and of course, the booklets went to Piney Run Middle School with him. Ben shared them with his buddies after gym class and before basketball practice.

The following day, while in music class, Mr. Carl appeared, with his writing pad and pencil.

"It has come to my attention that there is some X-rated material circulating about the school in the seventh grade. We will not tolerate such filth at this school! I want you to give me the books immediately!"

The girls started giggling; although they had not seen the books, they had heard about them. The boys were mum. No one budged from his seat.

"Ladies, I see nothing amusing about this matter. I'm sure you don't wish to associate with those who possess this…this…trash!" I want those books now! No one will leave this room until I get them!"

The bell rang for the end of the fifth period and Vice Principal Carl told everyone to stay in their seats. The seventh grade would remain in music class until the books and their owner were revealed. The class just sat; no one spoke, Mr. Carl knew if the group left the room, the books and their owner would never be found. Soon it was time for dismissal.

Judy, one of the girls in the class, finally spoke up. "Mr. Carl, I have to go home on the bus and babysit my little brother who is in elementary school. You can look in my pocketbook and see that I don't have any books or anything bad. But I've got to go home or my little brother will be there alone." She was almost in tears.

Mr. Carl took a quick look in her purse and excused her from the room. She grabbed her jacket and ran to catch her bus! One by one the girls passed purse inspection and left.

Then it was just the boys and Mr. Carl. "Boys, we can all go home if someone will come forward and tell the truth. Because of your silence, you are punishing all the boys in this room—all of your friends. Why don't you just give me the books?"

Everyone just sat there in silence.

"Mr. Carl, I haven't seen the books you are looking for," Ben said with all sincerity. "I'll empty my pockets and you can search me and then let me go to basketball practice. Coach is going to be mad, really PISSED OFF!"

"Watch your language, young man. Come up here and empty your pockets. Raise up your shirt."

After Mr. Carl found nothing, Ben left for practice and one by one, the others emptied their pockets, were searched, and excused from the room.

Several minutes later, Chuck came up to Ben in the locker room as they both were changing clothes for practice.

"OK, Benny Boy, where are the books?"

"They exited the room in the hood of Judy's parka. She was sitting in front of me, so when old Carl went on the warpath, I put them in there! She was in such a hurry to catch her bus that she didn't put on her coat. I'll call her tonight. She's my buddy; I bet she had a good laugh. When she found them, she probably hid them in her book bag. Old Carl will go crazy after investigating and finding nothing. I'll tell Judy that she is guilty of aiding and abetting a criminal."

Ben finished Piney Run Middle School without ever being suspended, detained after school, or sent to the principal's office!

Been took his excellent grades and his athletic abilities to Northwood High School. He also took his talent for practical jokes, ridiculing people, and destructive behavior with him.

His personality again revealed itself in physical education class. During the fall, the class would run cross-country and after a few weeks, they would run the course and be timed. Hopefully, with practice, their stamina and endurance would improve and the amount of time that it took them to run the course would lessen.

Ben and his classmates quickly changed clothes and ran out on the cross-country course. They were to run from the school to the old church on Mariners Road and back to the school. It took only a few days for Ben to become bored with the cross-country workout. So one day, he happened to be the last runner out of the locker room. As he began to run, his motivation disappeared and he started to walk. But by coincidence, a friend of his dad's happen to drive by and saw Ben. He immediately stopped.

"Need a ride?"

Ben did not hesitate to hop in the pick-up truck.

"Where are you going?"

"Just to the church on Mariners Road."

"I'm going by there. I'll take you."

Ben rode silently down the road, bending down to tie his shoe laces when they drove by the class runners. After he got to the church, he started back and passed the runners going in the opposite directions. Naturally, his clock time was excellent! So Ben devised a plan; he wouldn't be the last one to leave the locker room, run until he was some distance away from the school and then relax under a tree in the yard of a vacant home. He carefully remained hidden from the road. When he heard the group returning, a rested Ben Somers jumped back on the course and ran back to the school.

Other days he would hitchhike and get a ride, at least for one section of the course. Naturally, his times were excellent! He was the fastest cross-country runner in his class!

And his pranks continued the following year.

The principal called an assembly for students in grades ten through twelve. The principal introduced FBI agent Harold Martin, who spoke to the group.

"Students, we have a problem. Several weeks ago, thirty-seven mailboxes were destroyed. This is not a matter that we, on the federal level, take lightly. Any one of you old enough to have a driver's license could be the responsible party. It seems this is a Halloween prank that has gotten out of hand. On October 30, thirty seven mailboxes were destroyed. Several dozen were uprooted and dragged down the road. Others were hit with a blunt object—a pipe or perhaps a baseball bat— and it knocked the boxes off their posts; they were damaged beyond repair."

There was a hushed murmur throughout the auditorium.

"I am here to tell you that destroying a mail box is a federal offense in the eyes of the law. Those found guilty of this act of destruction will be punished. If you know the names of these delinquents, it is your obligation to report the names to the proper authorities. I will be in the library, after lunch, for the remainder of the day. If you have heard rumors, or know who destroyed these mailboxes, stop in to see me. I will never reveal where I got the information. If you don't wish to speak to me and wish to remain anonymous, a box will be on the front table. Put in a note or just a list of names." (Donald Duck's name was submitted three times, and Goofy, the dog, was accused twice.)

A smile crossed Ben's face as he thought back to Halloween night. Tommy and Susan were coming out of the movies when Ben stopped at the red light.

"Hey! Where ya going?"

"We're just going to walk to Henry's for a coke. What's up?"

"Hop in. Let's see what's happening…"

"There's a costume party at the gym."

"We don't have any costumes," Susan added to the conversation. "We can't even go trick or treating without a mask."

It was one of those moments when Ben's devilish personality overruled his common sense.

"We won't get any treats, but I just thought of hell of a trick. Susan, you drive the truck. Come on, Tom; let's get into the bed of the truck and drive to the Constitution Park neighborhood. Come on, Susan, drive us to Miss Bern's house. Slow down when you get there, and if no other cars are coming, turn off the lights. If you see a car on the road, keep driving. We'll turn around and come back!"

Like robots, Susan jumped into the cab of the truck as Tom hopped up on the bumper and into the bed of the truck. He and Ben settled down with their backs against the cab. Susan hurriedly drove away. They rode in silence until they turned on Saxis Road and neared

Miss Bern's home. The road was deserted, so Susan slowed the truck and turned off the lights.

Ben moved quickly; he took a rope that was lying in the bed of his truck and tied a loop at one end.

"Susan, stop the truck by Old Bern's mailbox and when I bang on the top of the cab, get the hell out of here!"

Susan stopped the truck beside the mailbox and Ben draped the rope around it. He banged his fist on the top of the cab and Susan mashed her foot on the accelerator. The truck lurched forward, and the mailbox, with the post attached, uprooted from the ground and clanged down the road behind the truck. After about 500 yards, Susan stopped the truck, Tommy jumped out and freed the rope. He hopped back into the truck, rope in hand, and Susan raced away. A shout came from the Halloween cowboys who had lassoed a mailbox.

"Let's go over to Miss Parks's house. I've got a baseball bat here in the truck. We can hit a home run or at least hit a mailbox off a pole! Onward!"

Not thinking of the consequences, or the cost of replacing the mailboxes, the final count was twenty-four lassoed mailboxes and thirteen boxes pounded with the bat and ruined. Ben, Tommy, and Susan swore to silence, and it wasn't until later that year, when Agent Martin appeared that Ben even thought of the consequences of their actions. No one knew the perpetrators of the mailbox caper, and as long as Tom and Susan were quiet, it would remain a mystery.

But later that same year, Ben's life changed.

It was one of those nights when everything for a high school teenager was perfect. Ben was a sophomore on the varsity basketball team, consisting mainly of his classmates. They had just upset the Indians, a rival basketball team, in the districts playoffs. Spirits on the bus were high; cheerleaders were chanting and clapping, team members were boarding the bus and screaming celebratory yells, and everyone was trading seats to sit with their favorite cheerleader or basketball player. Ben found himself sitting with Patty, one of the cheerleaders who lived in his neighborhood, and had been like a buddy to him for years.

"I can't believe we won! We beat the Indians! Who will we play on Friday?" Patty was so excited that she threw her arms around Ben's neck and hugged him.

Suddenly, the platonic feeling that Ben had for Patty over the years disappeared. He liked the feeling of Patty's arms around him.

"We play the Crompton Warriors on Friday, and when we win, I expect you to sit with me on the way home. This is your reserved seat for the playoffs."

And instead of releasing her, Ben kissed her, a long passionate kiss, and Patty melted in his arms. They sat very quietly for the remainder of the trip home.

Friday's victory over the Warriors was easier. The Shoremen won by ten points and the mood in the bus was ecstatic. Patty waited on the bus as the players showered and dressed.

"Is this seat taken?" Ben smiled as he looked at Patty.

"Only if you have a reservation."

Ben quickly sat down as the bus erupted with a victory celebration. Cheerleaders were chanting and singing fight songs. Victory yells came from some of the players as they boarded the bus. Seats were traded, once again, for the players and their favorite gals to sit together. The scene was wonderfully chaotic!

"OK…Let's get settled! Everybody take a seat and quiet down. Anyone not here on the bus?" Coach Gray turned to the bus driver. "We're all here. I counted heads. Let's go!"

As the bus pulled out the parking lot, the lights went out, and Ben quickly took Patty in his arms and kissed her. The adrenalin rush from the victory and the kiss stirred feelings in Ben that he had never known before. He was on top of the world.

"I can't believe we won again." Pat murmured, never leaving Ben's arms. "One more win and we'll be going to states. Who do we play next?"

"The Northwest Panthers, next Saturday night. Are you going to save me a seat?"

"Do you have a reservation?"

"I'd like to make a reservation for the movies tomorrow night...
for two...can I pick you up at 6:30?" Ben found himself very nervous
as he asked his old pal for a date.

"Sounds great! You know where I live...You've been there enough
times to see my brothers...It's just down the street from your house."

It was the beginning of a teenage love affair that lasted for two
years. They were inseparable! She cheered for him at football games,
and as was the custom at that time, she waited in the gym for him after
the games as he showered and dressed. Friday and Saturday were date
nights—the movies, cokes at Henry's, sock hops at the high school,
pep rallies, Friday night parties—cheap dates, but they were together.

When Ben was with Patty, he was a completely different person.
Coach Gray was pleased that the two were dating. Ben never broke a
curfew, his grades were excellent, and he stayed out of trouble when
they were together.

On Saturday afternoon, the football team had a beaten rival Clayton, and Ben picked up Patty at eight that evening.

"Do you want to go to the sock hop at the gym?"

Patty was still excited about the game. "I don't care. I could dance
down Main Street! How can you be so calm? You scored two touch-
downs today! We beat Clayton! Let's go to the dance and celebrate with
the rest of the team. But let's not stay too long...I want to snuggle with
my favorite guy."

She reached across the front seat of Ben's old pickup truck and
kissed him.

The dance was crazy! The music was loud and the beat was fast.
Ben and Patty circulated about the room, reliving moments from the
game. Suddenly the song "Fascination" began to play and couples quietly went to the dance floor. Ben led Patty to the floor, held her close,
and they began to dance. He put both arms around her waist and she
put her hands around his neck. They moved slowly around the floor...
"and Fascination turned to love..." The song wafted throughout the
gym as Ben held Patty closer as they finished the dance.

"Let's get out of here."

They held hands and walked quietly out of the gym, each caught
in a trance in a magical moment. It was a special time when everything

that was important in the universe was good and the world revolved around two teenagers who left a dance, holding hands. They quickly drove to their private "lovers" lane spot.

Ben lovingly took Pat in his arms.

"Patty, I love you...I want you to always be my girl...We belong together...We're good together...I've never felt this way before..."

He kissed her passionately over and over again, and soon his hands were moving to Patty's breast. His hands moved stealthily to the buttons on her blouse, unbuttoning them as he kept kissing her.

"Oh, Patty, I love you so much. I want to make love to you."

Ben continued to unbutton Patty's blouse as he held her tightly and continued to kiss her.

"Ben, please stop."

"Patty, we belong together. You are my girl, forever. You know I love you, but you never tell me how you feel. Prove to me that you love me." His hands moved deftly over her pulsating breasts.

"Oh, Ben," she moaned.

His hands moved from her breast to her knees and then up her legs. He slowly stroked her thighs and moved to unbutton her jeans. His hand rubbed the wetness of her silk panties.

Patty suddenly broke away from Ben's arms and moved to the other side of the truck.

"Ben, you'd better take me home."

"Patty...I..."

"Ben, take me home. Please!"

Ben silently moved under the wheel of the truck and turned the key. Patty straightened her clothes, buttoned her jeans and blouse as they rode home in silence. They stopped in front of her home and she jumped out and ran from the truck to the front door. She disappeared inside; she didn't even say good-bye. Ben sat in silence for a few moments and then slowly drove away. He knew he should have gone after her, but he didn't.

Instead he drove to Center Street, where he had gone several times before tonight. He stopped at June's house and blew the horn. He waited for a few minutes and then blew the horn again. June appeared at the door and Ben whistled!

"Come on, let's celebrate! We beat Clayton! Let's get a six-pack of beer and have some fun! Hop in!"

"I'm ready to have some fun…Let's get some beer!" She grabbed his jacket, pulled him to her and gave him a long kiss. "Just a preview of things to come." She moved across the cab and sat snuggly against Ben and put her hands between his legs. She knew how they were going to celebrate!

It took only a few minutes to get to Percy's, a sleezy bodega that had a reputation for selling beer to minors. He parked the truck, kept the motor running and went into the store. Several minutes later, he jumped back into his truck with a six-pack of beer and some condoms. He popped the caps of a couple of beers and sped out of the parking lot. He was going to celebrate the victory!

Ben parked his truck behind the junior high school and tossed out his empty beer can.

"June, get me another beer; we don't want them to get hot!"

"But I don't want you get cold." She laughed as she again slid her hand between Ben's legs.

"No danger of that, when I'm with you." Ben kissed June as he laid her down on the front seat and had sex with her. He had celebrated the victory!

For the remainder of the weekend, Ben was miserable. He wanted to call Patty, or see her, but he couldn't. He didn't know what to say. He had acted like an *ass*! Should he act as though nothing has happened? Should he apologize? Should he beg her to forgive him? He finally decided to talk to her at school on Monday.

He was at school at 7:30, and sat in the parking lot in his truck waiting for Patty to come up the sidewalk. He tried to organize his thoughts and even practiced what he would say.

Soon Patty and Ruth walked up to the school, and Ben immediately jumped out of the truck and hurriedly approached the girls.

"Hi, Ruth. Hi, Patty."

"You really had a great game on Saturday," Ruth said. "Do you think you can beat Frederick next week?"

Ben ignored Ruth and took Patty by the arm. "I need to talk to you," he whispered to Patty.

"I don't have time to talk now. I have to get to homeroom to collect cans for the food drive."

"How about at lunch?"

"Some of us are taking our lunches to Coach's office to look at the samples of the new field hockey uniforms, and I have a hockey practice after school."

"Can I come over tonight?"

"You know my dad doesn't let me have friends over on school nights. I can't even talk on the phone."

"Patty, I'm sorry about Saturday night. I've been miserable all weekend. I need to talk to you!"

"I have to go." Patty walked quickly into school, hoping Ben did not see the tears in her eyes. She dashed into the bathroom and splashed cold water on her face. Patty also had been miserable all weekend.

She and Ben had been going steady for over a year, and she always liked the feeling she had when they were together. But she was not ready to take the next step in their relationship. Many of her friends were having sex with their steadies, but she wasn't sure she was ready. However, last Friday night, when she was with Ben, she felt she was ready. But later, she had conflicting thoughts. Patty dried her face and dashed into homeroom.

Ben ambled into homeroom, feeling dejected. He wanted to talk to Patty and make up with her. Was she purposely avoiding him? He didn't want to think of her not being his girl. Had she really dumped him?

Patty and Ben were friendly throughout the week, but they had no chance to really talk. Football practice, field hockey practice and games, food drive, homecoming communities, and pep rally plans kept the two teenagers very busy. They spoke in the halls and sometimes walked to class together, but the conversation never approached that last night in the truck. The bonfire on Friday night finally provided an opportunity to really have a good talk.

The fire was blazing as the football players took the sledgehammer to the old car that had been painted with slogans to defeat Frederick. The cheerleaders were chanting as the cocaptain of the team took his place on top of the car with the sledgehammer in his hand.

"Are we going to beat Frederick tomorrow?"

"Yes!" The crowd screamed.

"I can't hear you."

"YES!" The crowd screamed even louder as Dennis brought the sledgehammer down hard on the car. After another whack on the windshield, Dennis jumped down and Ben grabbed the hammer. He let out yell and hopped up on the car. He slammed the hammer on the car.

"That hit was for my girl, Patty! And this is how hard we're going to be hitting the cadets tomorrow!" He hit the car again.

As he slid off the car, Patty walked over and took Ben's hand. They quietly wandered away from the bonfire and disappeared into a grove of the trees. The crisp October air sent a shiver of excitement into the twosome.

"Patty, I'm sorry about last Friday night. I was so excited that we won the game; I guess my emotions took over…"

"Ben, you know how I feel about you. I've been miserable all week. I don't want to lose you…You are very special to me. But… (there was a long pause) I don't think I'm ready."

"I was foolish to try to rush you into doing something you don't want to do. But I do want to hold you close and be with you. Patty, I want you to always be my girl."

Ben slipped his newly purchased class ring off his finger and gave it to her. "Will you wear this? Will you be my girl? I love you."

"Oh, Ben." Patty took his ring, stood on her tiptoes and kissed Ben long and passionately.

They were a couple again; they threw themselves into the activities of their senior year.

The field hockey team was undefeated that year. Patty's play in the backfield earned her all state honors and a chance for a scholarship to play field hockey in college. She was invited to the University of Delaware for a weekend tryout with the Delaware team.

Ben was lost that Friday without Patty. He went to football practice, but his parents were at a dinner/dance and he was alone for the remainder of the evening. He approached Tom in the locker room before practice.

"Tom' let's go out tonight after practice; your folks are at the same banquet/dance as mine. We'll get some burgers and beer from Percy's and toast the fact that we are undefeated, with three more games to go. Come on, Buddy." Ben laughed.

"You know Coach might call your house tonight. He expects everyone home by nine o'clock. He called my house before the North Hampton game to check on me."

"We'll be home by 9:00. How long does it take to drink a six-pack and eat a burger?"

"I'll meet you at your truck after practice," Tom said enthusiastically.

It was six-thirty before practice ended and the boys left the school. They woofed down several burgers and then paid a wino to get them some beer. Ben dropped Tom off at his home at eight forty-five, and Tom was to pick him up the next morning to catch the team bus to the game.

But Ben was restless. He wasn't ready to go home. He still had eight beers left. His folks were at the gala with friends and wouldn't be home until late. So he drove to his favorite spot behind the middle-school in his old truck and popped the tab on a beer. He just wanted to relax. He was the starting quarterback on the football team and tomorrow was a big game!

After drinking three of the beers, Ben felt light-headed. It was best if he quit drinking for a while and go home. He drove on the back roads until he reached his home safely. The place was dark. Ben parked his truck, grabbed the beer, and went to his room. He finished off two more beers and was asleep when his parents came home.

Saturday morning, Ben was still very shaky. He dressed and carefully avoided his parents.

"Ben, you've got to eat some breakfast," his mother called to him.

Ben ducked into the bathroom; he felt sick! After throwing up, he washed his face with cold water and waited.

"Are you all right?" His mother called to him from the kitchen.

"Just nervous, Mom. I've got to go…Can you put some bread in the toaster for me?"

Ben waited until his mother went upstairs. He came out of the bathroom, grabbed the toast, and his duffle bag and ran to his truck.

He was still sitting in his truck when he got sick again and had to open the truck door and throw up. The smell of the toast was nauseating and he threw it out the window. Tommy picked him up a few minutes later.

When they arrived at school, he waited until Coach was busy talking to Chuck's dad to get out of Tommy's car and get on the bus.

"You look like SHIT!"

"Thanks, Buddy. I feel like SHIT!"

"What time did you get home?"

"I had to finish up some of the beer."

"You smell like it. Sit down here and pretend you are asleep. Coach won't bother you."

Ben sat down, put his coat against the window of the bus, and rested his head on it. He was tired and his stomach was still churning. Putting his earphones on, he nestled down to get a nap as the bus left the school for Millsboro. The team became quiet; all thoughts were on the big game. Ben began to doze as the rhythm of the bus lulled him into a fitful sleep. He thought he would feel better after a nap.

However, a few miles into the trip, his stomach continued to churn. He woke up, knowing he had to throw up. Ben fought the nauseated feeling as long as he could. He lowered the window, hoping the cold air would help relieve the queasiness.

"Tom, I've got to throw up."

"Oh, SHIT! Coach is sitting two rows in front of us."

"I don't care. I'm going to throw up."

"Hey, Coach! Ben don't feel so good."

"What's the matter, Somers?" Coach Gray left his seat and walked to the back of the bus. It was almost simultaneous: as soon as Coach got to the seat to check on him, Ben threw up again. He grabbed Tom's towel and held it over his mouth. The sickening smell of beer permeated the bus.

"Tom," Coach said sternly, "take a seat at the front of the bus. I need to sit here for a few minutes."

Tom quickly moved to an empty seat next to a teammate as Coach Gray took his seat.

"Ben…Do you have something to tell me?" There was a long moment of silence; Coach put his hand on Ben's shoulder. He repeated his request to Ben. "Son, do you have something to tell me?"

"I don't feel so good." Ben kept his head down, avoiding Coach's stare.

"How much beer did you drink?"

"I don't know, but I've got to throw up again."

"Pass that trash container back here."

The guys at the front of the bus had been riding in silence, listening to the dialog in the back of the bus. Tom grabbed the wastebasket and they quickly passed it back to Coach, who immediately gave it to Ben.

"When we get to Millsboro High School, stay on the bus. We'll talk later about this incident."

Ben was suspended from the athletics for six weeks. After losing their quarterback, the football team lost their last three games. I was the longest six weeks of Ben's life. Did they blame him for their losses?

Patty was really disappointed in Ben's behavior. He had let down his teammates who had depended on his skill as a quarterback. But it was Patty's parents that were very upset. They didn't like the idea that Patty was dating someone who would drink and be suspended. However, she convinced her folks that it was a one-time mistake, and Ben would not do anything so stupid again! Because they were good friend's with Ben's Parents and with Patty's coaxing, they continued to let Patty date Ben.

Ben's suspension was completed during the first week of basketball season, and he immediately joined the team. He and Patty continued to date and participate in senior activities. She waited for him in the gym after basketball games. They danced the entire night at the Christmas Ball. When the freezing weather arrived, they skated together on the lake. And…Patty was cheering when the boys basketball team went to College Park and won the state championship. Ben's final year at shortstop saw the baseball team win the county title, and lose by one run in the state semifinals. The prom was a magical night; they danced every dance in Candy Land. They were a couple, enjoying their senior year.

It was graduation night—the end of twelve carefree years. Patty earned a scholarship to college at the University of Delaware. Ben had an appointment to the United states Naval Academy. Both students won awards at the graduation ceremony.

It was at the graduation party that the realization of their time together as a couple was over. Patty was leaving Saturday to spend summer at the beach, waitressing at a popular restaurant. Ben reported to the academy on the first day of July. Tonight was their final night together; no more school events for the couple.

Patty slipped Ben's class ring off her finger.

"I guess you'll want this back."

"Please keep it. I'll try to get down to the beach a few times before I go to Annapolis. Patty, you are my special girl. I don't want to date anyone else. Do you want to date other people? I'll be home for Thanksgiving and maybe Christmas. We'll write to each other."

"Four years is a long time to make a promise." Patty held the ring in her hand. She had an exceptional feeling for Ben and didn't want it to end. He was special to her. However, she knew of his visits to June on Center Street and his reckless behavior. But she put the ring back on her finger and kissed Ben, holding him close to her.

"Let's go back inside and enjoy the party. We're out of high school and we'll go our separate ways soon enough." She took his hand and together they walked back into the party. The following day Patty and Lynn began their jobs at the beach.

Summer passed slowly; Ben drove to the beach several times and he also visited Center Street on several occasions. He entered the Naval Academy in July, and successfully completed the plebe indoctrination. Regular classes began and he adapted to the strict regiment of military life. At the end of summer, Patty only had a few days at home before she was to leave for freshman orientation at the University of Delaware on September 4. The promised letters kept the teenagers informed of the activities at their schools and their feelings for each other.

It was Thanksgiving before Patty and Ben saw each other again. The months of separation melted away as though they had never been apart. A full course load of freshman classes and a college JV hockey schedule and practice had kept Patty busy. It was her first time home since she began her freshman year at Delaware. Ben explained the strict regiment of academy life in Annapolis—classes, military training, rigid discipline, etc. It was all very time consuming; however, he forgot to mention the Saturday night passes to Annapolis or the weekend cruises to Chestertown and the dances with the Washington College girls. They went to the "Turkey Day" football game and later had dinner with their respective parents. After stuffing themselves, they went out together, in Ben's old truck, to Henry's to see their high school friends who were home from college.

Later in the evening, they found themselves alone in their favorite spot.

"I had fun at Henry's tonight," he remarked when things were quiet.

"I miss the old high school crowd—Susan, Tom, Chuck, Roy, Ruth…We had some good times together; there's always a special spot for high school friends," she remarked. She nestled down in his arms.

"It didn't seem as hard or as difficult in high school as it is at the academy, and school keeps me busy every minute of the day…and night, too. At least there is no time to get in trouble…And I miss my girl."

Ben pulled Patty close to him and began kissing her. "God, I've missed you!" His hands move to her blouse and in a few moments, it was unbuttoned and her bra was off.

"You are beautiful!" Ben continued to kiss her as he slowly laid her down on the front seat. Patty seemed unable to fight her desire, and she continued to kiss Ben as she unbuckled his belt and slipped off his shirt.

"Oh, Patty, make love to me. I love you so much. "And with the tenderness and the pent-up desires of teenagers, Ben and Patty made love.

Afterward, Patty was very quiet as she got dressed. Tears were streaming down her face.

Ben took her in his arms and held her close.

"Patty, I love you…You are my girl…You will always…be my girl…I love you so much."

"I don't know when we'll be home and together again. Basketball season has started. I landed a spot on the Junior Varsity; our schedule is brutal. I hope to get one or two days at Christmas," she explained.

"It will probably be Easter before I get time off. If I got home for Thanksgiving, I can't get off for Christmas. I'll be on a Navy cruiser over the Easter holiday. But we have some dances and socials that our girls can come down to Annapolis for a weekend. I'll send you some dates…I can get you a room if you can get to Annapolis. But this has been a very special night for me. These memories will stay with me until we both get home again."

Patty pulled closer to Ben. "I'll try to get down; one of my college friends has a car." This desire of Ben to see her seemed to reinforce that he really loved her. They parted with promises to see each other soon.

When Patty came home for Christmas, she suspected she might be pregnant. The desire for each other had been so strong that no one thought of protection. She had hoped that Ben's schedule might have changed and he would get home, but he didn't. She knew he was busy; she only had two brief letters from him. So on the pretense of shopping, Patty went to Salisbury to a clinic for a pregnancy test. She had the results sent to college.

At the end of the Christmas holiday, Patty returned to college with a sense of dread. She was almost positive that the pregnancy test would confirm her suspicions. She would then have to make some decisions. She had received only two notes from Ben since Thanksgiving, and she had heard nothing from him over the Christmas vacation—no contact, no letters, no phone calls or any gifts, not even a Christmas card.

Trish, her roommate, was already in the dorm when Patty piled her suitcases on the bed.

"Wow, roomie…You must have had a great Christmas. Look at all the goodies!" Trish grabbed a cookie from one of the tins on the bed. "Did you see Ben?"

Patty continued to hang her clothes in the closet. "No, I didn't see Ben. He was home at Thanksgiving and couldn't get away from the academy and come home for Christmas. I really miss him. I saw some friends, but spent most of my time with my family. How about you?"

"Dad took our whole tribe to Bermuda. We spent the entire holiday on the beach—no white Christmas. I met some really cute guys, and Marcie's family was there for the last week."

Patty continued to unpack her suitcases, listening to Trish and saying very little. She was envious of Trish's vacation. "Is there any mail?"

"I cleaned out the mailbox just before you came in. I put your stuff on your bed; it's probably buried under your suitcases. Just a bunch of junk. Are you OK? You seem awfully quiet."

Patty continued to empty the suitcases and when finished, she took them down to the storage room. Walking back to the room gave her time to collect her thoughts. When she got back, several girls had stopped to share their holiday experiences. She walked over to the bed, picked up the mail, and dropped it into her desk drawer.

"Did you see Ben? Did he get away from the academy?" Marcy then grabbed Patty's left hand. "Did you get a ring?"

Sally immediately chipped in. "Don't be silly. We're freshmen. You can't get engaged when you are a freshman. There's too much fun to have in college when you are a freshman. Upper classmen like to look us over, take us out, and check out the prospects in the freshman class. It's great!"

"Ben and Patty have been dating for three years. They know each other well. She could get a ring anytime," Trish chimed in!

It was difficult for Patty to concentrate on the jovial conversation. Her thoughts were on the envelope that was in the desk drawer.

"Ben didn't get home for the holidays. He was stuck in Annapolis." She failed to mention that she heard nothing from Ben, not even a Christmas card. She tried to laugh…"No ring this year!" Patty hurriedly grabbed the cookie tin. "Who wants some leftovers from my mom's kitchen?"

"Sally, go get some cookies. If you go to Bermuda, you don't get to chow down on Christmas cookies, not homemade ones! And Patty's mom is such a good cook." Trish organized the group for a party.

"I've got some brownies," Marcie said as she disappeared to her room.

"I brought my appetite!" Trish was always the clown.

The remainder of the evening was spent eating, laughing, and of course *boys*!

Later, when the dorm was quiet, and she was lying on her bed in the dark, Patty thought of the letter in the drawer. Trish had an early class; after breakfast, she would have an hour to herself. This was the time to return to the room and check the mail. Tears streamed down from her eyes. The thought of breakfast made her sick. She always excused herself to the bathroom, and to her knowledge, no one suspected that she was throwing up. What was she going to do if the test was positive? Who could she trust? She must see Ben! Would they have to drop out of school? What would my family do? And Ben's family? Patty continued to lay quietly in the dark, crying herself to sleep.

The first day of classes after the Christmas break was hectic. The girls raced to breakfast, gobbled down some cereal and donuts, and parted—Trish went to Freshman English and Patty ran to the bathroom. She threw up her breakfast, washed and splashed cold water on her face, and walked slowly to her dorm room. She wanted to know the results, but she didn't want to know the results. Maybe she had a stomach virus; some of them were very difficult to cure.

Patty was pregnant. Her plans and dreams were now in limbo. She thought back to that Thanksgiving night with Ben. It was a magical night, but they had been careless. She knew about Ben's visits to Center Street and June. A large number of the basketball team and the football team had visited on Center Street. But she always thought Ben loved and respected her.

She was sitting on the bed, dumbfounded, when Trish returned from class.

"Well, are you pregnant?" Trish crossed the room and sat on the bed next to Patty. "I saw the return address on the envelope and unless you like to visit hospitals in your spared time, I suspected what it might be." Trish tried to keep a sense of humor as she put her arm around her friend. "What are WE going to do?"

Patty was sobbing uncontrollably now. "How could I have done something so stupid? Or been so careless?"

"Does Ben know?"

"I haven't heard from him in weeks."

"Well, I think the first part of the solution to this problem is a trip to Annapolis. You have to tell Ben, don't you?"

There was some hesitancy in Patty's movies. "I really don't think he cares about me anymore."

"Do you have his phone number? Call him and make up some excuses that you are going to be in Annapolis for a day. Tell him it's a conference, or a basketball clinic, or a symposium. Don't go for a weekend…Just a day for a few hours, and you are free for dinner. You just need to talk with him face to face. After your chitchat, you'll know when your next step."

"Oh, Trish, I didn't know what to do, but I think you are right. I'm going to call him now…No, I can't call now; he has a class. I'll call tonight."

Her mood seemed to change; she had a plan. She grabbed her books and dried her tears. She dashed out the door as she yelled, "Professor Williams is waiting."

Later that evening, Patty nervously dialed Ben's room in Annapolis. Brandon, Ben's bunkmate, answered the phone.

"Hello."

"Hi, Brandon. It's Patty. Can I speak to Ben, please?"

"Oh, hi, Patty. Ben's not here. He went down the hall to get some help in calculus. Can I get him to call you when he comes back, if it's not too late? Sometimes, these study sessions go until after midnight."

"Just give him a message…I've been picked to attend a field hockey clinic in Annapolis on Saturday. I'll be busy all day, but I'll be at the Steak & Ale Restaurant at seven for dinner. If he can't get away from the academy on Saturday, tell him to call me, or I'll see him on Saturday. Thanks, Brandon. Good night."

"Good night, Patty. I'll tell him."

Patty was shaking as she hung up the phone. Sally would loan her a car (she thought it was romantic that Patty and her plebe were having a rendezvous in Annapolis), and the couple could meet and decide what to do. When she didn't receive a phone call, she became excited that she would see Ben. Patty arrived in Annapolis on Saturday and waited three hours at the Steak and Ale Restaurant, but Ben never came. She drove back to the college in silence.

Trish would not allow Patty to dwell on her problems. So after lunch on Sunday, the two girls took a long walk around campus.

"I feel like such a fool. I thought he really cared about me. He gave me his ring!" She rubbed the ring on her finger.

"Well, we know that he won't figure in your plans. I was just thinking; what are your options? You could drop out of school and have your baby. You know you won't keep your scholarship if they find out you are pregnant and cannot play sports. Do you want this baby?"

"NO!"

"Finals are the first of May. With a few loose blouses, we might keep this a secret until then. Come home with me and spend summer at my house on Cape Cod. You can have the baby and put it up for adoption. My mom would be glad to help you, and she is good at keeping secrets. We could tell your folks that we have summer jobs there. Or the next weekend, I'll go with you when you go home and tell your parents. Just think about what *you* want to do. This is your decision and your life. But you know I am your friend and I will respect and support your decision."

Patty gave Trish a bug hug. "I don't know what I would do without you."

"Come on. Let's get back to the dorm. I'm freezing my buns off!" Trish grabbed Patty's hand and they hurriedly walked to their room.

In the middle of February, Ben got a note from his parents telling him that Patty had slipped and fallen down the steps at her dorm and was hospitalized with a concussion. It had been snowing and there was ice on the stairs. He didn't see her that summer; he was on a ship in the Mediterranean Sea and she worked in Cape Cod. Ben was seldom home for holidays and after graduation, he was stationed in Europe and in Hawaii. He knew that he had put his hometown behind him; he might visit his folks on holidays, but he would never live there again.

After his commitment to the navy was fulfilled, he got a job in a lab in the Chicago area; with his training, he soon became the chief lab tech and the manager there.

Chicago Testing Services had the contract for all testing done at the Mayo Clinic. Through Ben's expertise, the lab landed a large contract to do testing for the Chicago Police Department and several of the local, smaller hospitals. Chicago Testing Services, under the management of Ben Somers, was very successful.

In the mid 1980s, AIDS testing was rampant. The laboratory was extremely busy and very successful.

John Samuels was HIV positive. He was also an irresponsible playboy, who disregarded the dangers of his behavior. He cruise bars at night, with ecstasy, his date/rape drug of choice. He raped as many girls as he could, saying he was "getting even" with society for the nasty diagnosis that had been dealt to him. Finally, laws were passed to punish this behavior. John Samuels was arrested and removed from society.

After his conviction appeared in the newspapers, doctors and prosecutors encouraged all victims of John Samuels, or if you suspected that you had been with the convicted rapist, to be tested for the virus.

Four girls arrived at the reception desk of the City Emergency Center almost simultaneously on a Friday afternoon.

"I want to be test for the virus!"

"I beg your pardon," the receptionist was confused. "Do you all need to see a doctor?"

"I think I was raped by John Samuels," one of the girls whispered. She was ashamed to tell the receptionist her plight.

"I was sitting at the bar, talking to this good looking guy…and when I woke up the next morning, I was in a motel room and had been raped. I don't know how I got to the motel, or I don't even know the man's name!"

"The prosecutor strongly urged us to get tested."

Another girl was crying. The receptionist passed her a tissue and gave each girl a clipboard. "Fill out this form and I'll call down to the lab and tell them that you need to be tested in the Samuel's case. We'll then send it downstairs to the lab for analysis and give you a call when the results are done. It will take about two weeks, but we'll try to rush it. All results are confidential. We'll give you a number; no one will know your name."

Chicago Testing Services received the specimens with a note to please rush the testing and the results. Ben decided to handle the project himself. He completed the analysis in less than two weeks and was concerned that indeed, one of the girls tested positive for AIDS! He organized the results, putting the diagnosis in each folder. He typed the labels to be attached to the folders. The folders were identified only by number to assure complete confidentiality.

"What are you doing here? It's late…I thought you had a hot date," one of the lab techs was teasing his boss.

"I do. I just have to attach those labels to the envelopes."

"It's hot in here. Let's turn on the fan." As then fan began to rotate, the labels flew across the room.

An eerie feeling began to overtake Ben. In his haste, he had forgotten to type the number on each label to match with the folder. Instead he had put them in a pile in order. Now they were scattered across the room. What label should go with that envelope? He would have to retest each of the four specimens, and it would take another two weeks! What a mess!

It was then that Ben made a reckless decision. He picked up the labels and affixed a label to each envelope; he then put the envelopes in a folder, with number matching, and put them in the outgoing mail basket. He had no idea if the diagnosis matched the correct envelope. He had a hot date! He hurriedly grabbed his coat and rushed out the door.

"Turn out the lights and lock up," he called to his assistant. See you on Monday, bright and early."

The incident disappeared from his thoughts until an article appeared in the newspaper. A young woman who had been sexually assaulted by John Samuels had committed suicide after discovering she was HIV positive. However, an autopsy revealed that the girl was not infected with the virus. Her parents were considering legal action against the hospital. Ben read the article several times. Could this be one of the girls whose test he had done? Was it possible that she was the envelope that he had haphazardly put on the label that indicated the subject had tested positive? Was there a woman who was unknowingly infecting her sexual partners? Why didn't the girl insist on a second test instead of resorting to suicide?

There was something about this article that Ben couldn't get out of his mind. Was he responsible for a woman's death? He immediately walked out of his office and stated that he was leaving for a two-week vacation. He rushed home, packed a bag, and soon found himself at Ocean Beach. For the first time that he could remember, his conscience kept him awake at night. Was he a murderer?

Ben woke up in a sweat. His mind was churning. Why was he now recalling people from his past who he had forgotten or harmed? He was trying to solve his problems and find solutions, but he was arriving at no solutions. He found that he could not go back to sleep.

And the bus rolled on…

CHAPTER 8

A MUTED SILENCE CAME OVER THE BUS AS nightfall encompassed it. The laughter and friendly exchanges between passengers gave way to hushed murmurs. Sami had settled down in a seat next to Debbie and had quickly fallen asleep. Her dad watched her quietly, knowing the events of the day and the subsequent glee during the bus ride had exhausted her. He studied the girl who had offered her lap as a pillow for Sami's head. The couple behind him talked in muffled tones as they held hands. No one noticed that the warm October had turned cold. The monotonous rhythm of the wheels had lulled the passengers into a hypnotic silence.

"Miss…Miss…" whispered John Webster in the darkness. "If she is bothering you, I'll bring her over here with me."

"Let her stay here. She looks so peaceful."

"Perhaps I'd better bring her over here by me; she'll wake up and be scared." He quietly rose up from his seat and lovingly gathered Sami in his arms. She immediately woke up and settled in a seat next to her dad.

The bus turned off Route 68 and continued west. A light rain had been falling steadily as the mountains loomed before them. The weather conditions had made the roads slippery. Traffic slowed down to a crawl. The movement of the bus seemed to lull its passengers into a quiet acceptance that many had successfully escaped from the beach. Several people listened to their radios using their earphones for privacy.

Jim Sterling wrapped his jacket into a ball and put it behind his head, hoping to catch a nap. He really needed to sort out his feelings for his job, his family, and especially his brother. But he needed to put some distance between himself and his dilemma. Should he betray his job and parents for his brother? He watched as the little girl had run down the aisle of the bus, attempting to share her M&M's with the college girl who sat alone. He had wondered about the teen since they had boarded the bus. She didn't seem to be going to college; she only had one small bag, which she clutched tightly. Was she running from something? Was she scared of something? Or someone? The analytical mind which made him a good policeman tended to examine people who were in situations that he couldn't comprehend. And why did the mysterious guy who he had befriended ignore everyone and pretend to be asleep? There were some really unique people on this bus; his trooper training had analyzed them all.

Mr. Joe Smith shifted in his seat. He had stayed on the bus during the supper stop and pretended to be asleep. His new friend had brought him some food. This new friend had a gun! He was having some flashes of events in an emergency room. This area of the hospital seemed to stir some feelings in him, but why? He seemed relaxed as he had these flashbacks; he almost seemed to be comfortable there. So why did he go to the ocean? Had he served in Vietnam? Was he a doctor or a medic? In his mind, he saw pictures of jungles, camps, dead bodies, and a trio of men that made his smile. It was the first time he had thought about his training. He had glimpses of being a doctor in an emergency room.

Just thinking about this caused his hands to begin to shake. He was glad it was dark, so no one would notice that he could not stop his hands from trembling. He had no idea where he was going or what he was going to do. And what was his real name? His friend had called him "Joe Smith." Perhaps he should go to a Veterans Hospital and seek help. "The doctor needs a Doctor!" He mused to himself. A doctor, especially an emergency room physical, had to be prepared to work in extraordinary circumstances, make quick diagnosis, handle several critical patients at one time and treat all types of injuries. He couldn't do these things now! Did something happen to him in an emergency room? Was he hurt? Why were his hands shaking?

Debbie Pierce sat quietly in the dark bus. She was glad she was getting away from what she thought was an impossible situation. There should be a way to notify her parents that she hadn't been kidnapped or she wasn't hurt. Until she had a solution to her problem, there would be no contact with them. Debbie also wondered about the guy sitting across the aisle from her. He didn't get off the bus for the dinner stop; he just sat there, pretending to be asleep. He ignored the little girl who tried to share her candies with everyone. She envied the carefree lives that most of the others on the bus were leading, especially the couple who sat quietly, holding hands and whispering to each other. It was easy to tell that they were in love. Her mother and father were like that. They were still very close after being married all these years. What would be her parents' reactions to her secret? She had once tried to tell her mother, but she had dismissed her accusations. If they believed her, it would destroy her father's medical practice. Many of his colleagues would never believe that Dr. Fredericks would be capable of such actions. Debbie settled back in her seat, pondering her predicament as the bus rolled along.

Kate sat quietly in the dark, holding hands with Clint, and just reveling in the fact that they had this time together. She watched as the little girl (Did she hear that her name was Sami?) roamed up and down the aisle, offering everyone a candy. She was so cute...I wonder where they are going? You seldom see a man traveling with a small child, especially a little girl. Maybe they are going to see the girl's grandmother; she talked about a grannie. I wonder where the mother is...Maybe she died…He still has on his wedding band. I'd like to have a little girl like her some day. She snuggled down and put her head on Clint's shoulder. Maybe we should have gotten married before I went home. Then no one could try to convince me to marry Jay and not Clint. No, I'm not ready to get married. I just want to be loved and enjoy life. I'm sure my mother will be so upset; she thinks that Jay and I should be together. But it never felt so right as when I'm with Clint. The summer was one of the best I've ever spent. I've found out things about myself that I never knew! I can't imagine burying myself in a museum after spending a summer at the ocean. I wish this bus was carrying me back to Ocean Beach and not to Omaha. She closed her eyes, and reminisced about the summer and meeting Clint. She was a different person from the girl who had packed up her dorm room, sent her college belongings home with her fiancé, Jay, and went to Ocean Beach for a vacation. There was nothing her folks could say to make her change her mind. She was *not* going to marry Jay! Gifts must be returned, cancellations of the church and the reception hall, and extensive talks with her parents concerning her decisions. But Kate felt she could accomplish these things as long as Clint was with her. She smiled, closed her eyes, and was more relaxed as the bus rolled westward.

Sami Webster sat quietly in the seat next to her dad. John was pleased with his daughter's behavior on the bus and at Ocean Beach. She seemed very happy and had never mentioned her grandparents. He still had not formulated a plan to counter the efforts of the Stevens firm. He just wanted to get to Clarksville, change buses, and go south to Louisiana. Had he been a coward to run? When he was away from the influence of Janice's parents and the prestigious law firm, he felt no court would remove a child from her parent. He looked down and saw that Sami had gone to sleep again; so he closed his eyes, hoping to get a nap.

Ben watched his fellow travelers from the back seat of the bus. Throughout his life, he had acted carelessly and with total disregard for his friends. But usually he walked away from problems, laughing. He envied others on the bus who were going to an appointed destination, not running from an impossible situation. His reputation in the medical community was impeccable; the blame would be placed on one of his assistants, and he would be fired. The insurance company would offer the family a settlement and his life would go on. But why did this incident bother him so much?

And why were other friends, who he had discarded and ignored, now on his mind?

He wondered where Tom and Susan are today and what they are doing? They were partners in the mailbox caper; their silence perpetuated the story and the escaped from the feds. They were probably just a high school romance…And then his mind wandered to his teammates, that group of guys who had highlighted their senior year in high school by capturing the state basketball championship. This group of guys brought a sense of pride and elation to the town. For a few years, while they were in school, they were inseparable! They had covered for him when he bounced the basketball in the locker room and broke the light. (They smuggled the broken pieces of glass out in their gym bags and Chuck sat on Toby's shoulders to replace the light.) No one squealed on him concerning the cross country/hitch hiking caper. And during the senior week, he had come to school smelling of alcohol and set off the fire alarm. It was Roy who pulled him into the bathroom and saved him from suspension. This group of guys had marveled at his hubcap collection, stolen as a Halloween prank.

"I think Toby played basketball in college," he mused to himself. I heard he married, moved to Baltimore, and had a son that played college basketball. Chuck became a state trooper and married the prettiest girl in town. Roy moved to Baltimore…I think he was our class president…I don't know what happened to Tom; he was the devilish on of the group. Did I hear that he went to California? Or did I hear he was now living on his yacht in a marina somewhere? He blamed his estrangement from this group of guys on the academy. He didn't get home for the holidays or the fifth-year reunion. (Of course, Ben never blames himself or his attitude toward his hometown as the reason for the distance between his friends!) Then his thoughts drifted to Patty; he had tried to put her out of his mind. Why did she keep reappearing in his imagination? He had heard that she graduated with honors from the University of Delaware. He didn't want anyone to know that he was thinking of her, so he never asked his parents or inquired about her. "Boy, we were crazy in those days." He thought to himself. As he tried to sleep, the friends of his youth kept materializing in his dreams.

A light drizzle of rain had begun to fall. The monotonous sound of the windshield wipers added to the background of murmurs of the passengers on the bus. Route 40 was a winding, very curvy road, slowing down the progress of the trip.

It happened in an instant. As the bus negotiated a curve, three deer appeared, startled by the headlights. They froze in the middle of the road as if paralyzed by the lights that were shining in their eyes. Quickly, the driver put his foot on the brakes, but the bus did not respond. It began to skid on the wet pavement, striking the deer as they attempted to run into the woods next to the road. The bus continued to slide on the wet highway. It continued its sideway path, moving out of control on the loose gravel. The driver struggled to gain control, but the bus slipped off the side, flipping over, and came to rest upside down in a shallow ravine. The wheels were still spinning, and the rain continued to fall. A small whiff of smoke began to rise from the back of the bus. One of the deer lay shrieking, unable to stand due to a broken leg. His two companions lay dead on the road above. An eerie silence fell on the scene as the wheels of the bus soon stopped turning aimlessly. A foggy mist engulfed the area, making the bus impossible to see from the road. The deer soon succumbed to his injuries, and the smoke and mist blanketed the accident.

Ben found himself lying in the aisle of the bus. But this wasn't the aisle. The vehicle was lying upside down, on its top, with the wheels in the air. He was on the ceiling of the bus. What had happened? Ben sat there for a few moments, trying to orient himself with his surroundings. The seats were on the ceiling, and personal debris was everywhere. He was sitting on someone's shoes, with newspapers covering much of the area. Because of the darkness, it was difficult to access the chaos which was apparent around him. He just sat there, not realizing he had had a concussion from the fall. He tried to clear his head, but it continued to throb. For a few minutes, he did not move, mentally checking his body parts to see if anything was broken. There was a large gash on one side of his forehead as blood trickled down his face. He could move both arms although one arm was aching and bloody. Then he tried to stand, but found one of his legs was caught on something. But his eyes had not adjusted to the darkness to discover his captor. A few moments later, he lost consciousness…

John did not know how long he was unconscious, but it took several moments after he was alert to remember where he was. He still did not know how the bus came to be upside down. After his eyes became adjusted to the darkness, he saw his foot was trapped under a metal bar which had penetrated his shoe. He willed his body to try to sit up, but some metal was across his chest, pinning him at his present location. And where was Sami? Before he could call for help, he lost consciousness again.

Debbie Pierce heard a low mean as she struggled to sit up. A blanket of chipped glass covered most of her body. She scanned the dark environment for something to wrap around her hands as she attempted to wipe off the shattered chips.

"Is everyone OK?" She called to her fellow passengers, hoping someone would answer. For the longest time, there was no reply.

"I'm here, but I can't move my legs. Something is on them."

Debbie slowly tried to stand up. Struggling, she yelled, "Where are you? It's Debbie Pierce…I can't see you, but when I can, I'll try to follow your voice!"

Mike Elliott was completely alert. His left arm was broken, but he had already made a sling from his jacket and had his arm resting close to his side. It was as if his life had become a flashback to the chaos in Vietnam. He thought of the Three Tall Texans. The smell of diesel fuel filled the bus and the fumes caused an eerie mist, making it more difficult to gain one's bearings…He deftly began to move to the door of the bus, inching along as he felt his way over the debris.

"Ouch!"

Mike stopped moving, listening for another cry…He heard nothing.

"Hey! Does anyone need help?"

The first voice he had heard in the darkness was from behind him. He slowly turned around and listened carefully…The silence was deafening…

"Hey! I'm Mike…Where are you? Let me help you get out of here. Do you need help?"

"Ouch!" The voice whimpered again. "You stepped on me."

Mike froze where he stood. He immediately lowered himself to the floor, which was the ceiling of the bus. He began to feel around in the darkness.

"Where are you?"

"I'm here," answered a soft voice, fighting to hold back some tears. A small hand reached up and grabbed Mike's shirt.

Mike slowly began to lift suitcases, various shoes and clothing, newspapers, and other debris from the area with his one good hand. After raising a bus seat from the vicinity, two small arms encircled his neck, clinging tightly. He immediately felt her arms and legs for any broken bones. His medical skills and memory had returned!

"Where's my daddy?" Sami was in tears, but she would not let go of Mike's neck. "Where's my daddy?"

"I'm going to get you off the bus and then I'll look for your daddy." Mike's eyes had adjusted somewhat to the darkness and he thought he could tell that he was facing the front of the bus. "You keep holding on to me and we'll get out. He slowly inched his way to the front of the bus. As he approached entrance, he passed the driver, lying across the steering wheel with a large shard of glass in his chest. Mike rolled on his back with Sami still tightly clinging to him and began kicking the door. Although it seemed like an eternity, after a few minutes, the door became ajar. Mike slid out of the bus, with Sami's hands still tightly clasped about his neck.

The rain had stopped; Mike inched on his back to a log which had fallen on the ground in a flat area of the ravine. He gently pulled the child from around his neck and set her down next to the log. It was muddy, but Mike didn't care. They were safely out of the bus.

"I want you to stay here while I go back to the bus and find your daddy. I want you to be a brave little girl. Do you know any songs?"

"I can sing my ABCs."

"You sit here near the log and sing your ABC song. I will know where to find you and where everyone can meet when they get off the bus. Can you do that for me?"

Dr. Mike Elliott slowly got to his feet. His arm was throbbing, but for the first time in months, he felt alive! He attempted to make an imaginary list, in his mind, of the passengers on the bus that night. There was this little girl and her father, a pair of lovebirds sitting in the back, the cute coed in the front, the kook who slept on the backseat, the two elderly people who boarded the bus at the restaurant, a fellow who Mike thought had a gun, and the bus driver. Did a young fellow with a backpack also get on the bus at the restaurant? Like his platoon, he had to account for everyone. He tried to visualize where everyone was sitting, to better know where to look for them, although a wreck like this would scatter the passengers throughout the vehicle. He also smelled the diesel fuel and there was smoke wafting from the bus. The Dr. Mike Elliott who disappeared from the emergency room six weeks ago no longer existed. He was totally in control of the situation—a doctor with a broken arm and sore from head to toe.

"You aren't singing very loud," he called to the little girl. "I want to hear you."

Mike boarded the bus and was immediately confronted with the bus driver. Although the position of the glass in the man's chest told the doctor that it was hopeless, he nevertheless found a man's neck and felt for a pulse. As he suspected, there was none. A sweater was lying over the next seat. Mike eased the sweater over the dead man's face. There should be some dignity in death. Behind the driver sat the couple who boarded the bus at the restaurant. They were both dead, having been crushed by the impact of the seat in front of them as it separated from its position.

"Blondie, you aren't singing very loud," Mike called out the door. "How will I know where to find you?"

Suddenly a voice resonated from the inky atmosphere. "If you come to help me, I'll sing as loud as you want me to sing."

A sense of relief came over Mike. Others had survived the crash. But he first turned his attention to the little girl who sat alone in the dark, trying to fight back her fears and the tears streaming down her face.

"Blondie, I don't hear those ABCs…I want to hear your loudest voice…I'll be back there in a few minutes."

Instead of the refrain of an elementary tune, Mike heard the scared voice of a terrified little girl, sitting alone in the dark.

"Where's my daddy?"

"If you don't keep singing, he won't know where to find you. Now, let's hear those ABCs!"

Once again the silence of the night was interrupted with the familiar tune.

"A B C D E F G..."

Mike redirected his attention to the crumpled mess in the bus. Although the rain had stopped, it was still impossible to see anything in the bus as it sat in the ravine. The footing was treacherous; the area was strewn with items from the overhead compartment, contents from destroyed suitcases, twisted metal, and crushed glass. Mike's arm ached as he felt the flooring for a spot to step.

"Hey...I can't see a thing...Keep talking and I'll try to find you."

A woman's voice answered. "I'm stuck...I was sitting three rows behind the driver...I don't know where I am now. There is something heavy in my lap. I think it's a piece of glass...And it's also sticking in my leg. I can't lift it. If you can find me, maybe the two of us can..."

Her voice trailed off. It sounded like she was going into shock. Mike couldn't hear her, only some deep throated moans. He moved toward the sounds, using his night-maneuver instincts from Vietnam to guide him. Something caught the fabric on his pants leg as he carefully maneuvered toward the moans. As he flailed in the darkness, his hand touched an arm.

"Hey...Hey...Are you all right?"

"My leg hurts. There's something sticking in my leg." Her voice was low, and barely audible. "It hurts...It hurts..."

Mike stealthily felt her leg and discovered a huge piece of glass that was embedded in her thigh. As he felt the entry point, he knew that it might have cut an artery. He had to find something to use as a tourniquet if he was to get her off the bus. As he groped in the darkness, his hands felt the body of an elderly gentleman he had found earlier. He thought he recalled that he was wearing a suit and tie. He remembered the many times he had removed dog tags from dead soldiers as he loosened the tie and slipped it over the man's head.

"Sorry, Sir," he murmured to himself, "this young lady and her doctor need this tie more than you do."

He returned to the injured girl and deftly tied the necktie above the shard of glass. As he pulled the tie tightly, the girl uttered a low moan.

"Ah…You're coming back to us. What is your name?" He did not want her to slip back into unconsciousness.

"Debbie." She was barely audible. "My name is Debbie. Am I going to lose my leg?"

"Now where did you get an idea like that?" Mike kept her talking; he didn't want her to go into shock. "Where were you going? To college? I'm a doctor, Debbie, and I don't like it when my patients ask those questions."

"My dad's a doctor."

"Debbie, this is going to hurt. I'm going to pull this piece of glass out of your leg and I must tighten the tourniquet. Then we'll get you off this bus. Did you ever watch those old western movies? Now is the time to bite the bullet. Are you ready?

Debbie grabbed his broken arm and sent waves of pain throughout his body. He carefully maneuvered the glass and luckily, there were no jagged edges. He then swiftly pulled the glass from her leg and placed it behind him. Tightening the tie on her leg, he got her up from the seat and dragged her over the rubble and out the door of the bus. Sami ran over to them.

"Is that my daddy?"

"No, this is Debbie. She is going to stay here with you while I go back to find your daddy. I want you both to sit over there by the log."

He walked back to the bus, grabbed a suitcase, and brought it outside. The crash had torn the case open and Mike took out a blouse and wrapped it around the gash in Debbie's leg.

"Thank you for rescuing me. I was afraid that the bus would catch on fire and I couldn't get out." She tightly grabbed his arm.

"I'm going to cover you with some towels I found in the suitcases. Put on this jacket. Debbie, this is Blondie. I want you two girls to wait here near the log while I go back into the bus. Talk to each other. Blondie, you can sing to her if she gets quiet. I also found some chocolate bars in the suitcase. If you get hungry, have some candy. Debbie, keep that bandage tight on your leg."

Debbie put on the man's jacket and sat down next to the log, with Sami beside her.

Mike cautiously walked back to the bus. He watched her move closer to the little girl, who welcomed her new friend and snuggled up against her.

"I want my daddy! I want my daddy!" The little girl began to cry.

"Our friend is going back to the bus to look for your daddy. It's very dark in there, and really hard to find your way out. Let's sing a song...A B C D E..."

Mike smiled as he reentered the bus. He paused a few moments, waiting for his eyes to adjust to the darkness again. The smell of diesel fuel seemed stronger. He carefully moved toward the back of the bus.

"Anyone needs help?" he shouted in the darkness. He remained still, listening for any sound or movement. The silence seemed endless. Finally, the stillness was broken with a weak voice.

"I'm back here...There's something heavy across my legs."

"Keep talking. I'll try to follow your voice and get you out of here. Tell me about yourself. Are you married?" Mike asked the first thing that came to him mind. The voice sounded weak and Mike just wanted to keep him talking. His movements to the back of the bus were slow. Suitcases had fallen from the overhead bins; twisted metals dangerously littered the walkway and the seats were dangling at various angles.

"Hey, Buddy. Are you married?"

"No, I'm not married. I was sitting in the back of the bus, but I'm not sure where I am now...What happened? My leg is pinned down by a piece of metal, and I think it's broken. It hurts like *hell*! I feel real sleepy."

"Don't go to sleep on me, Man! Keep talking and I'll try to free you. What is your name?"

Mike adjusted the sling on his broken arm; it throbbed each time it struck a piece of debris that was in the aisle. There was a long pause; the only sound was a dripping noise, presumably fuel. The smell was sickening.

Finally a weak voice penetrated the darkness.

"Ben. My name is Ben. You sound so far away…" The voice faded away, followed by the darkened silence…

"Ben! Ben! Don't go to sleep on me, Man. It you don't keep talking, I'm going to have to sing the ABCs to you, like my little friend. If you're not married, Ben, tell me about your girlfriend, or is it girl-friends? Keep talking to me, Man. What do you do when you are not lying on the ceiling of an upside down bus? Talk to me, Man." Mike knew that Ben could be going into shock and he wanted to keep him talking.

"Are you bleeding, Ben? Talk to me! Help me find you."

"I can't feel my legs…But you sound close."

"Wave your arms…I think I see you."

Mike lifted a suitcase and set it to the side. As it fell, there was a soft moan.

"Did I hit you with the case?"

"No. I heard a strange voice, too."

It was then that Ben's arm hit Mike's broken arm. He flinched as the pain radiated throughout his body.

"Hi, Ben. I'm Mike. I'm an emergency room physician who hap-pened to be a passenger on this bus. I'm going to put my hand on your head and feel over your body for the extent of your injuries. I've never groped a patient in the dark. Just let me know if I hit a spot that is especially sensitive and hurts more than the rest of your body."

"OK."

Mike put his right hand on Ben's head and stealthily moved over it. There was a large bump on the back of his head, but no blood. It was large enough to cause a concussion. His hand then went over Ben's shoulders and down to one hand, over the shoulders and down to the other hand. Nothing seemed broken and he felt no blood. He eased his hand down over the hip area, but a bus seat, torn loose in the crash, was lying across his hips. Mike knew it would be impossible for him to lift the seat with the use of only one hand.

"Ben, we have a problem. The seat you were sitting on is now sit-ting on your legs. Can you wiggle your toes? Ben, don't go to sleep on me now! Wiggle your toes for me…Come on, Ben!"

After what seemed like an eternity, Ben's toes slowly began to move.

"Atta boy, Ben…Ben, the only way I can move this seat is to push it with my feet. It's going to hurt like HELL!"

Mike felt the seat and determined that if he shifted himself to the left about two feet, he could push the seat off Ben's legs without hurting his feet. He carefully eased his body to the left and braced his feet against the seat.

"Are you ready, Ben?" Before he could answer, Mike thrust his legs hard against the seat and it tumbled off Ben's legs into the darkness. Mike immediately felt Ben's leg for blood; there was none. His legs didn't seem to be broken. However, the silence was deafening…

"Ben! Ben! Are you OK? Ben! Ben! Answer me, Man! Are you OK?"

Mike moved back to Ben's side and felt for a pulse. A low moan was a welcomed relief for a doctor administering to his patient in the dark.

"Ben, we've got to get out of here. Button or zipper your jacket. I'm going to grab the back of your coat and pull you as hard as I can. But you've got to help me, Man. When I start to pull, I want you to scoot along on your ASS! Don't try to stand; you've had a hard blow to your legs and might have trouble getting on your feet and walking through this debris. Go easy, Man."

Mike grabbed the back of Ben's coat with his one good hand and gave a tug. He was relieved when he felt Ben's body shift with his effort.

"Atta boy, Ben. We'll be out of here in no time. Let's go again." Slowly, inch by inch, the two men made their way to the doorway.

"Debbie, I need some help. Can you come to the door of the bus? This guy is going to be coming out backward on his butt. I want you to help me drag him out of the bus. Don't worry about the mud. His legs are hurt and he might have a concussion. Help me get him out of here. That diesel fuel smell is getting stronger."

Debbie checked her bandage and moved to the other door of the bus, after instructing Sami to stay on the log. She carefully put her hands under Ben's arms and gently helped Mike lower him from the bus. The two of them carried his body over to the logs.

"Sorry, girls. I'm going to cover him with the towels! We need to keep him warm. He might go into SHOCK!"

"I found the bus driver's coat. Put this over him."

"Did you find my daddy? I want my daddy?" Sami's lip began to quiver and tears rolled down her cheeks. "I want my daddy!"

"I'm going back into the bus to look for your daddy. But I want you to stay here and help Debbie. Can you do that?"

"I'm a good helper." Sami sniffled and moved closer to Debbie.

Debbie rested her hand on the little girl's shoulder. "You are a good helper. And we know a new song…the Itsy Bitsy Spider. We can sing that together and it will help keep him awake. Do you know his name?"

"This is Ben. He was sitting in the back of the bus. Keep singing and talking to him. You know about treating possible concussions; have you had some medical training?"

"My dad is a doctor. I guess you pick up some information by being around his apprentice."

"Were you off to college to pursue a medical career?"

"That's a long story. Go ahead and look for others. We'll be OK out here." She carefully tucked the jacket tightly around Ben. And… there suddenly was a hint of coincidence and self-assurance in her voice that Mike had not noticed before now.

"Come here, Blondie; let's sing our new song for Ben. Maybe he will sing with us."

Mike carefully adjusted the makeshift sling that he held his throbbing arm. When he kicked the bus seat off Ben's legs, he thought he had heard a moan from the left side of the bus. He again tried to imagine the seating arrangement on the bus. Among the missing, as he remembered them, were the love birds, Blondie's father, the guy with the gun, and a hiker guy with a backpack. Was there anyone else? The young girl, Blondie, and Ben from the backseat were outside. The driver and the older couple were dead. There were five more people to get from the bus and the diesel smell was getting stronger. He took a deep breath and returned to the dark confines the bus.

"Hey. Does anyone need some help? We need to get everyone off the bus. I smell some fuel and if a fire should start…"

Mike stood in silence, listening for any sound of movement on the bus. After a few moments, Mike moved to the area where he had found Ben. He then bent down to his knees, moves to the left where he thought he had heard the sound, and began to move around. He gently moved the bus seat which he had kicked off Ben's legs. Groping through a pile of wreckage, Mike found an arm. He grabbed it firmly, but there was no movement. As he slid his hand down the arm to the wrist, hoping to get a pulse, he felt a slight movement in the fingers.

"Hold on, Buddy. I'll get you out of here..."

He stealthily moved his hand over the wreckage; it seemed to be twisted together. He then backed on his knees to the door.

"Debbie, come here. I need you. I found someone who is not alert. There is a pile of wreckage on him, and I can't move it with one hand. How are things out here?"

"Ben is awake. I'll ask him to watch Sami until I come out. I'll ask her to hold Ben's hand."

Debbie returned to the door of the bus. It was difficult to see anything in the darkness. She checked the bandage on her leg and slowly went inside.

"I can't see a thing!"

"Grab my belt and just follow me."

Slowly the two rescuers crept into the bus. Mike felt his way back to where he had discovered another passenger. A twisted pile of wreckage loomed over the prone figure. Carefully, he groped in the darkness up a leg and finally grabbed an arm. Although there was no movement, Mike found a steady pulse.

"Did you find him?"

"Yes, but he is buried under a twisted pile of metal. I'm going to check to see what we have to do to get him out of here."

"I've got some matches. Do you want me to light one so you can see?"

"No! We don't dare strike a match! Too much diesel fuel! If I can, I'm going to put my back under the rubble and try to lift it up. You grab his legs and pull him toward you."

"Should we move him? Dad said that you shouldn't move an injured person; you could make his wounds worse."

"We've got to get him out of here. There might be a fire. Do you have a grip on his legs? Are you ready to pull?"

Debbie eased over, putting her hands around the victim's ankles. Mike shifter his weight and moved to put his back under the heap of wreckage.

"Ready? On three...One, two, three!"

Mike pushed up and slowly raised the scrap a few inches. His left arm and shoulder were screaming with pain! Debbie slowly pulled the young man toward her as the pile of wreckage came down.

"If you can raise the pile one more time, I think I can pull him free."

With one last exhausted push, the stack of debris shifted again. Debbie pulled the body a bit to the right and freed him from the pile.

"Got him!"

Mike eased down the pile and collapsed against it. But he immediately revived when he heard a weak moan. Debbie was slowly pulling the unconscious man toward the door. Mike followed behind, cradling the man's head in his hands.

As they eased the body out of the bus, Mike was relieved to see Ben sitting up with his back resting against the log. Once they had exited, he collapsed on the ground, completely exhausted. But his medical training alerted him to his responsibilities. He pulled himself to his knees and carefully began to examine the passenger. The first thing that he discovered was the man had a gun! Mike quickly removed the gun out of the shoulder holster and stuffed it into his jacket pocket. As he brushed over the man's torso, there was a low moan.

"Possibly broken ribs...Could be a crushed sternum..." His hands expertly continued their path over the torso and down his legs. There was a bone protruding near his ankle. Mike searched about for something to use to stabilize the ankle and found a piece of a seat, dangling apart from the cushion.

"Debbie, bring me one of those towels."

"I'm wearing a belt you could use. Debbie, just pulled it out of my pants." Ben called from the log.

Debbie quickly maneuvered around the log and gently leaned Ben forward. She unbuckled his belt and eased it from his waist. She watched intently as Mike methodically splinted the man's leg, using the belt to strap the bars on each side of the broken area. He then slid the man over to the log, next to Ben. He was exhausted; his arm was throbbing.

"Ben, my man, have you had some medical training? You volunteered that belt really fast and knew exactly what to do with it."

"Four years at the Naval Academy and manager of a pathology lab. Not a doctor, very little medical knowledge, but lots of practical instincts."

"Is my daddy still on the bus?"

"Doctor, we should get EVERYONE off the bus, in case there is a fire." Debbie stressed the word everyone; she also wanted to remove the dead bodies, but would not say the obvious in front of the little girl.

"There are four more people who are on the bus that we haven't found. There are three deceased in the front. How does your leg feel? Are you ready to go back in the darkness?"

Debbie adjusted her shirt bandage on her leg, reached inside herself for some courage, and moved toward the bus.

"Was our last guy one of the lovebirds?"

"I don't think so. He was tall, blond and muscular, with a good tan. And you are right. We should get those bodies off the bus, but let's hope that we can find the others alive." He lowered his voice…"I think I saw one of the lovebirds with a cell phone. If we can find it…"

Slowly the twosome moved past the deceased bus driver and the elderly couple to the back of the bus. They found themselves reaching side to side, hoping to touch a human. It was a slow process, but Mike and Debbie felt that there was no one alive in the front of the bus.

"Where are you?" Debbie called. "If you can hear me, call out or make some noise. We're here to help you get off the bus."

Just as she became quiet, her hand touched some human hair.

"Doctor, I think I found someone. Over here!"

Mike moved quickly to the left of the bus. He followed Debbie's arm to the side and then to the head of a man. He was buried under debris. Slowly they lifted or twisted the wreckage off the passenger. Mike felt for a sign of life, but he found none. As he was reaching to check for a heartbeat, he discovered a sharp piece of metal imbedded in the man's chest. Death was instantaneous! From the size of the man's chest, Mike believed this was the young fellow who had boarded the bus with the elderly couple at the restaurant. He appeared to be a hiker with a backpack. Mike had thought, at that time, that he was a loner, speaking to no one.

"There's nothing we can do for him. Let's mark him, somehow, and we will recover his body later. Keep looking for the others. There are three more."

Debbie removed a scrunch from her hair and wrapped it around the stake as Mike pulled the backpack off his body. He searched it for a cell phone or any other device to call for help. There was none! However, he found a wallet which he put in his pocket for later identification.

"*Shh*...I thought I heard something. If you can hear me, make some noise. We can't see you in the dark!"

CLANK! CLANK!

"We hear you! We hear you! We're coming...Make some more noise!"

CLANK! CLANK! CLANK!

A hoarse, raspy voice struggled to be heard in the darkness.

"Here...Over here..."

CLANK! CLANK! CLANK!

"We hear you, Buddy. We're coming. Keep making the noise."

CLANK! CLANK!

The noise continued as the two moved through the darkness. Mike reached the man first.

"We've got you, Pal. Can you tell me where you are hurt?"

"My foot. I caught under something. I think I'm bleeding into my boot! I moved several pieces of metal that were across my chest and throat. I'm sore, but I don't think anything is broken. My throat hurts like HELL! Did you find my little girl? Did you find Sami?"

"If she has blond, curly hair and knows how to sing her ABCs, we've got her. She's a cutie; she's entertaining everyone."

Mike tried to calm the man as he probed the man's leg and foot. There was a piece of bar, from the side of a seat, which had gone through the man's shoe and possibly his foot. His hand was drenched in blood as he tried to evaluate the wound. He could tell that several of his toes had been severed. He had to get the man out of the bus to treat his foot. He could not remove his shoe until he could stop the bleeding. Mike needed to see how much damage had been done and the shoe, although it had a gash across the top of it, served as a cast and bandage on the injured foot.

"We need to get you out of here. I've only got one good hand, but my assistant is here. Debbie, come here and get behind this gentleman. What is your name? Blondie's father?"

"I'm John Webster. Samantha is my daughter. You are sure she's OK?"

"She is a very brave little girl," Debbie chimed into the conversation. "She is entertaining the others out by the log. I'm going to take hold of your belt and pull. Try to push back with your good foot."

Slowly, the twosome backed their way, inch by inch, to the front of the bus. Mike tried to steady the man's head so he would not bump it on any of the loose debris.

"That fellow knew what he was doing. Is he a doctor?"

"I think so. He is trying to get everyone off the bus, in case there's a fire. He has a bad arm, but he is doing the best he can…"

"Just a little further; We're almost to the door. I'll get off and help you down."

Debbie jumped off the bus. But before John attempted to leave, he caught Mike's good arm, and in his hoarse voice, whispered to him.

"There was a couple sitting behind me before the accident. I called for them, but got no answer. If you are trying to find everyone, go back to where you found me and check to the right. How about the hiker who boarded at the restaurant? He was in front of us."

"We found him. Watch out now. Try to turn around and ease out of the bus on your good leg. I'll be right behind you to look at that foot!"

"Daddy! Daddy!" Sami was near the door of the bus and spotted her dad as he started to slide out.

John eased out of the bus and he and Sami clung to each other. Using Debbie as a crutch, he hobbled over to the log. Sami grabbed her dad's shirt and followed along. Debbie helped John to sit down next to Ben, who was awake and trying to help keep the wounded passenger next to him covered with some towels.

"Go back and look for the others. I'm not going anywhere with this foot. And it's not going to get any worse until you come back."

Debbie immediately moved to the door of the bus and followed Mike back into the wreckage. John pulled his daughter close to him as he introduced himself to Ben. The two men talked quietly while closely watching the unconscious man lying next to them.

Inside the bus, the diesel fuel odor was more pungent. Smoke was beginning to fill the inside area. The two rescuers moved stealthily through the coach, inching along over the debris-filled aisle. After advancing a few feet, they paused to listen for any movement.

"John said there were two people sitting behind him on the bus. With the roll, they should be on the right side. Have we passed the hiker yet?"

"Keep going. We just passed him."

Debbie felt the scrunchy she had wrapped on the piece of metal. Something stirred inside her; the dead young man was about her age, and she had forced herself to ignore him. It didn't seem the right thing to do, but it was more important to look for survivors. Debbie shelved her feelings and kept moving toward the back.

"Did you find anyone?" she asked.

Mike continued to grope in the darkness. "Be quiet...I think I hear something."

Silence fell on the bus. There was no movement or sound, only the dripping of the diesel fuel. "Keep looking they should be in this area."

A shriek echoed through the coach!

"Debbie, what's wrong?"

"I found a hand...and just a hand!" Her voice trembled as she held the detached limb in her hand. "It's just a hand...a hand...nothing else."

"Stay there; I'm coming back to you!"

Moving as quickly as he could, Mike backed himself to Debbie's voice. It was a slow process; his injured arm kept bumping into the wreckage, causing the throbbing pain to intensify. His mind wandered back to Vietnam and the marathon sessions in the makeshift operating room. He had done "field surgery," operating on men to stabilize them so they could get to the operating room for proper care. He had amputated legs, arms, and hands to save a life. He remembered Thom Rossi and the bullet wound to his arm. Could he still use his hand? He had left the emergency room before…The diesel smell was terrible…He had to concentrate and get to Debbie…She was holding a human hand. What could a teenager be thinking? She had put her wounded leg out of her mind and was working to help others…She was quite a kid!

"Almost there…"

Debbie sat in the dark, her body paralyzed and in shock. She could not move. She just sat motionless, holding the severed hand. She had never experienced anything like this, having been raised in a very protective family. She had been to the hospital many times and seen her father tending patients, but she had never helped or witnessed anything other than minor injuries or illnesses. Could a person still be alive without a hand? Would a person bleed to death?

"Debbie, say something!"

"I'm here."

Mike slowly crawled his way back to her voice. His knees were bleeding from moving on the broken clutter on the bus. It seemed like he traveled for miles before he finally touched Debbie's hair.

"Debbie, where did you pick up the hand? Take my hand and direct me to where you were searching!"

He gently took the severed hand from her and set it aside. His military training had taught him to concentrate on helping the living and not dwelling on those victims who were dead.

A shaking hand sharply grabbed his hand and guided him to the left of where they sat in the dark. They followed a pool of blood to a lifeless body lying under a pile of wreckage. Mike desperately searched for a sign of life on the body when he discovered that there were two people lying together with their hands intertwined.

"The lovebirds," he thought. He immediately shifted his concentration to the second person, who was a muscular male. He moved his hands to the man's chest, his wrist, and his throat. However, when he tried to get a pulse in the man's neck, he soon discovered that a piece of glass from the window had almost decapitated the young man. He probably died instantly. Returning to the young girl, he again searched for any sign of life, but there was none. One of the seats had become loose and crushed her chest.

"Is it the lovebirds?"

"Yes, but they're gone."

"Can you find her pocket book? I think she was talking on a cell phone; if we can find it, we could call for help."

There was no response and Debbie was panicked.

"Doctor! Mike! Are you OK?"

It seemed an eternity before Debbie finally heard a low moan.

"Mike, are you OK?"

"Guess my mind wandered a bit." He thought he had fainted, but he did not want to scare her. Or perhaps the finding of two dead bodies took him back to the carnage of the war. "Just give me a moment to collect myself!"

"Did you find the cell phone? It could be in her pocketbook or maybe in one of her pockets."

Mike groped around in the dark and finally found a large purse. After a brief search, he discovered a phone.

"Let's get out of here. I've got the phone; we can call 911 and get some help."

The two started the slow journey to get off the bus. When they reached the front, they carefully lowered the bodies of the driver and the elderly couple from the bus. Mike made the call, requesting help. His accident report listed six dead and six survivors who needed medical attention. A light drizzle had begun again, and Debbie looked for something to cover the bodies, but could find nothing. The twosome returned to the bus and extricated the three remaining victims, carefully including the severed hand. They placed them away from the log, away from the little girl's view. It was not something they wanted her to see. She had talked to all the passengers, offering them candy.

After the retrieval was complete, Mike sat down next to the log and slipped into unconsciousness. The smoldering flame on the bus came brighter as sirens screamed in the darkness.

CHAPTER 9

THE LOBBY OF THE WESTERN MARYLAND MEDICAL Center was very quiet at 2:00 AM. The lights had been dimmed and the atmosphere was austere and sleepy. An insomniac volunteer sat behind the information desk, leafing through a magazine, when the door opened and a very harried couple rushed in.

"Excuse me...I'm Dr. Robert Pierce and this is my wife Ellen. We got a call yesterday that there had been a bus accident and my daughter was hurt! She was brought here."

The volunteer jumped to his feet and came from behind the desk.

"Follow me. They brought the bus survivors here last evening. The emergency room is this way."

Ellen Pierce gasped when she heard the word "survivor." She and Bob and been frantic when Debbie wasn't at home or on her way to Stanford when they returned from the seminar in Baltimore. After a few days of inquiry, they had notified the police and had eventually hired a private investigator in an attempt to find her. But they had heard nothing for months and then to get a call tonight that there had been a bus accident in Maryland and their daughter had been injured. She was so thankful that Deborah was alive. She didn't even complain when Bob raced the car at eighty miles per hour to get here from Centerville.

The group moved quickly down the hall to a waiting area outside the emergency room, a young girl with curly blond hair was asleep across several chairs as a young candy striper sat beside her.

"I'm a physician. Could I see…"

Before he could finish, Dr. Butler appeared in the waiting room.

"Are you Dr. Pierce?"

"Yes," Dr. Pierce answered as he extended his hand. "And this is my wife, Ellen. How is our daughter, Deborah?"

"I'm Dr. Butler. She has an injury to her thigh, but with some rest and therapy, she will be fine. Come on back and see her; I understand she was quite a heroine."

Tears of relief streamed down the cheeks of Ellen Pierce as she took her husband's arm and the proceeded through the double doors. They were passed by a gentleman on crutches. His foot was in a cast; anyone could see that he had lost his toes.

"Dr. Butler, do you know where the girl took my daughter?"

"Were you on the bus?" Ellen Pierce blurted out to the passing stranger.

"Yes. I was. I'm John Webster. Please excuse me; I must find my daughter." He hurriedly disappeared to the nurses' station, hobbling on his crutches. He wanted to find Sami, hoping the emergency room staff had already examined her for any injuries.

"Have you seen my daughter?" He inquired. "She's a five-year-old with blond curly hair and a quick smile. She is missing a front tooth."

A nurse quickly rushed to John's side, put her arms around him and guided him to a chair. He was weak and he had become pale.

"Mr. Webster, you must sit down. Samantha is fine. She has just a few minor cuts and bruises. She's been entertaining the nurses at the station with stories about the accident and singing for us. She told us about her Pop Pop, her grannie, a puppy, and the beach. Mr. Webster, do you want us to call some family members for you?"

John sat quietly for a few moments. He had survived a bus crash and somehow felt stronger for it—both mentally and physically. He decided to rest for an evening and call his father-in-law in the morning. The accident had given him the courage to confront the Stevens family. He had loved Janice, and he treasured every moment with his daughter. If the Stevenses wanted to be a part of Sami's life, they would have to have some rules and an understanding between the grandparents and the Websters. They would talk tomorrow. He and Sami would continue on their journey to New Orleans for a holiday and then decide where they would settle down and live. Before he could speak, Sami ran up, and jumped in his lap.

"If they found our suitcases on the bus, before it burned, I think we will spend a few days at a hotel here in town. We'll decide when to continue on to New Orleans. I thought I heard in the emergency room that AMTRACK stopped here!"

"Just tell me when you are ready and I'll make those phone calls for you."

It was then that Dr. Mike Elliott appeared. His left arm was in a cast, but he had taken a shower and his cuts had been treated. His bloody shirt had been replaced with a scrub top, on loan from the hospital.

"How's my patient doing?"

Mike looked down at the bandaged foot, knowing it was missing the toes. He only hoped that John Webster didn't have a job that depended entirely on his ability to stand on his feet for long periods of time or depended on constant walking.

"And there's my favorite girlfriend! Can you sing you ABCs for me?"

Sami giggled as she jumped off her dad's lap and ran to Mike.

"You have a Boo-Boo," as she pointed to Mike's arm. "My daddy's got a boo boo on his foot!"

"We might not be sitting here if it was not for you. How can we ever thank you?" John Webster slowly stood up, leaning heavily on his crutches. Sami immediately ran back to him.

"Did the bus go BOOM?"

"No, I don't think so, but it was really burning when we left."

"Did you get everyone out?"

"Yes. The rescue squad took those who we couldn't help and probably brought them here." Mike didn't want to discuss the dead people in front of Sami. He was upset that some of their fellow travelers were already dead when he tried to help everyone. But like Vietnam, many were beyond help before a medic could reach them. He was pleasantly pleased that he did not get a horrible headache or experience a flashback when faced with a scene of total chaos.

"But I can't take all the kudos for saving everyone. The surgeon said if you hadn't kept the severely injured passenger quiet and stationary, he could have punctured his lung or suffered more damage. And we all liked how this young lady entertained us." He smiled at Sami as she clung to her dad's leg, still giggling. Mike was please to see the little girl seemed happy and not traumatized by the accident.

"How are the others?"

"The unconscious gentleman is still in surgery. He was pretty badly banged up. And…I know moving him was not the best thing to do, but we had to get him off the bus. The doctors are very optimistic; it will take a while, but he should be OK. He's probably facing months of rehab and hospitalization. The hospital is keeping Ben, your partner on the other side of our wounded man, for a day or so. He really took a blow to the head; he has a major concussion. I talked to him earlier and he seemed coherent as he asked for the condition of the other passengers. He has quite a headache. The staff is keeping the room dark and really limiting his visitors. He might have to wear dark glasses for a while when he's around bright lights or in the sun. But the good news…He has severe hematomas on his legs, and few deep gashes, but no broken bones and no permanent damage. As soon as his head clears a bit, the staff will get him on his feet for a few steps. You should try to see him before you leave. The two of you might have saved a man's life."

As the two men continued to talk, a couple of strangers approached.

"Have either of you seen Dr. Butler? We are looking for our daughter. She was in the bus accident and was brought here. We talked to Dr. Butler earlier, but we still haven't seen Deborah. I'm Dr. Pierce, Deborah's father, and this is her mother…"

His introduction was interrupted by Dr. Elliott and John Webster.

"Are you Debbie's parents? You have quite a daughter! I'm Dr. Michael Elliott and this is John Webster. We were also on the bus when it overturned." And the two men revealed, to a set of stunned parents, how their daughter, although injured, had teamed with Dr. Mike to rescue the injured from the bus. The parents stood in awe as the two men detailed Debbie's efforts.

"I assumed that Debbie had a medical background, but there was no time to question her. She just worked with me, crawling in a bus that was in shambles, filthy with diesel fuel, and assisting with any medical or removal procedures that were necessary. Is she in college, training to be a nurse or a physician? Or some other medical career?"

It was Ellen Pierce who spoke up, still puzzled at the scenario that was being presented to her.

"Debbie graduated from high school in June and was preparing to go to Stanford. She had spent much of the summer in Virginia at a special riding camp. Her main desire was to qualify for the Olympic trials, with her horse. Deborah has never expressed any desire to pursue any type of career in medicine. We were at a seminar in Baltimore when we got a call from Stanford explaining that Debbie had not matriculated. Dr. Fredericks was to accompany her to Stanford, but our Deborah was gone. Neither the local police nor a private investigator could find her. And then, we get a call yesterday that our daughter was in a bus accident and being treated in a hospital near Cumberland, Maryland. We are anxious to see our Deborah. We want to know what happened that she disappeared from home. Was she kidnapped?"

"You should be very proud of her," John added. "She worked with the doctor until all survivors were off the bus and then helped remove the others. As we were being loaded in the ambulances, she aided the EMTs with the deceased passengers, giving them as much information as you can gather about fellow travelers. Debbie's efforts helped to get everyone off that bus before it was totally in flames. And…she kept my daughter, who is a very active five-year-old…"

His voice drifted off as the swinging doors flew open and an aide appeared, pushing a wheelchair. Although her leg was heavily bandaged, Deborah Pierce was in good spirits and broke into smile when she saw her mom and dad.

'Mom! Dad! What are you? How did you?..."

John and Mike stood back as a set of thankful parents rushed to their daughter's side. As second nature, Dr. Pierce deftly felt the bandage on his daughter's leg and expertly examined the cuts on her face. Ellen Pierce, in tears, fell to her knees and hugged Debbie, being careful not to squeeze her too tightly.

"How are you feeling? Are you in pain?"

"How did you get here? Is Daddy mad?"

"Daddy is not mad," Dr. Pierce said with a smile. "We're just glad that we are here with you. The hospital found our address and phone number in your personal belongings and gave us a call. The Maryland State police insisted that we be notified. We have been looking for you for months!"

Dr. Mike interrupted as the Pierces huddled around their daughter.

"Come on, John, let's go get a cup of coffee. I think Sami needs an ice cream. We'll let these people talk. (Mike had noticed that Debbie had not called her parents; they had found her.) Debbie, if you need us, or if you get a sudden urge to crawl back into a filthy, smoking bus, we'll be up in the cafeteria. Samantha might sing for you!"

"If I never hear my ABCs again..."

Deborah laughed, as tears ran down her cheeks.

"Please don't leave. I need you here."

The two men paused, questioning expressions on their faces. Debbie seemed glad to see her parents, but she didn't want to be alone with them. Something was terribly wrong here.

"Mom. Dad. I'm not going home with you. When I'm well enough to leave the hospital, I'm going to take a bus across country to Stanford. I'll get an apartment and work on rehabbing my leg. You can send my things after I send you my address. Mom! Dad! LISTEN! I never intend to be alone with Uncle Fred...EVER AGAIN! I have come home scratched and bruised from fights with that 'Slime Ball' for the last time! He's a pervert and shouldn't be around young girls.

I've tried to tell you many times. I know he's a colleague of Dad's and they are partners in their medical practice, but I've had enough! If I can crawl up and down in a wrecked, burning bus, I can tell you the truth about Uncle Fred. He's sick!"

Tears streamed down Ellen Pierce's face. She was shocked at the words that spewed from her daughter's mouth. She remembered an occasion when Deborah made some accusations about her Uncle Fred and she had dismissed them as a teenager's vivid imagination. And now she was amazed at Debbie's determination and her resolve. This was not the same carefree teenager who had graduated from high school in June, or had she missed the signs of abuse? She had heard rumors that Stanley Fredericks had been accused of lewd behavior by several of the female nurses on the staff, and a few lawsuits had been filed against him for inappropriate behavior, but she didn't want to believe that Stanley, their friend and business partner, would abuse their daughter, his godchild. She had ignored the whispers, but she couldn't ignore the determined tone in her daughter's voice. It was difficult to equate a naive high school senior with the girl who had risked her own life crawling in and out of an overturned, burning bus to save lives. Had a tragic accident caused a transformation in their daughter?

John Webster and Dr. Mike Elliott stood transfixed as the teenager who had been so vital in the rescue of the passengers declared her independence. She had mustered her courage to crawl back into the bus to help others and now to confront her abuser.

John Webster began to contemplate his own situation. Since his wife's death, he felt that his father-in-law was attempting to wrestle custody of his daughter from him. Why had he taken Sami and run? He had cowered away from Joseph Stevens instead of directly confronting him. He had witnessed an eighteen-year-old girl with more courage than he had demonstrated. She had informed her parents, not of suspicions, but of personal knowledge of the sexual exploits of their closest friend and colleague. She also had a plan to go on to college and avoid the situation at home. He didn't have a plan to attack his problem.

Ben appeared through the double doors, wheeling his chair into the crowd, over the objections of a nurse's aide.

"Is this a private party or can any wounded bus passenger join the group? I couldn't stay in that bed one more minute! I've got a slight headache and the doctors suggest that I wear these dark glasses. I'm not going to go to Hollywood!"

Debbie wheeled her chair to greet Ben as the two men hobbled over to his chair.

"Mom. Dad. This is Ben. He was on the bus with us, as you can tell."

Dr. Pierce, Debbie's father said, "How are you feeling, son? I hear your legs are not broken, just deep hematomas. You certainly have a number of contusions and bruises on your body! How is that bump on your head?"

"I'm fine, Sir, thanks to the good doctor here and your daughter. I call them 'The Dynamic Dou' and they saved my life."

"Ah! Another traveler! Ben Somers, I believe," and he offered his hand. "I'm John Webster. We met by the log near the bus…and you know my daughter, Sami. I didn't know if you would remember us, with your concussion!"

"She's quite a singer. Has anyone heard from…" It took several moments for Ben to recall a name. "I think his name is James. Yes, it is Jim Sterling, but I'm not sure. I met him on the beach." His memory kept drifting as his head continued to spin. "He was the injured guy that John and I tried to keep quiet and warm."

Mike immediately interjected into the conversation. "The guy had a gun. I gave it to the trooper who came with the ambulance crew. I hated to move him," and he looked over Debbie, sitting quietly in her wheel chair. "But we had to get him out of the bus."

"He's not going to be joining us tonight." Dr. Pierce chimed into the discussion. "I talked to Dr. Pasquelle, the orthopedic surgeon who has spent the last few hours putting some of your back together. James is in satisfactory condition—a broken pelvis, ribs, and leg—and more bumps and bruises than any of you. And you boys who kept him from going into SHOCK! Dr. Pasquelle highly praised how everyone was moved from the bus with no damage or further injuries. Son," he turned to Mike, "Where did you get your medical training? I'll assume it was emergency medicine."

"Sir, I graduated from the University of Chicago in general surgery, but I got my real training in emergency medicine in a field hospital in Vietnam. However, Sir, my arm was broken. Your daughter deserves much of the thanks. She's the real heroine."

"Where are you practicing now?" Dr. Pierce inquired.

There was a long hesitation before Mike answered. "I'm a member of an emergency medical team at Chicago's Cook County Hospital, at least I was until a few months ago. I sort of went AWOL. As soon as I'm feeling better and discharged from here, I'll go back with some explanations and hope I still have a job!"

Before he could elaborate on his explanation, two Maryland State Policemen joined the travelers.

"We have a group of people out here who are inquiring about the wreck. We know that three deers were involved in your crash; possibly they were the cause. There were also some sharp curves in the road, and the pavement was wet. Can anyone give us any information on the deceased? Most of the personal items were lost in the fire."

It was John Webster who started the discussion. "We had a fellow passenger who has come out of surgery. We're concerned because he had a gun!"

"That's Sergeant James Sterling of the New Jersey State Police. He's pretty banged up, but he'll be all right, in time. There were two couples who were killed. Any information on them?"

"The elderly couple got on the bus when we stopped at a diner for our dinner. I think they were local folks; they seemed to know the waitresses at the diner. The young fellow got on the bus at that stop too," John continued. "I have his wallet; it was with my belongings when I came in the hospital. I think the people at the diner in Hancock could probably give you more information about those people than we can. They weren't on the bus that long before the accident."

The trooper wrote down the information and then quizzed the group again. It was obvious most of the personal belongings of the deceased had been lost in the fire.

"There is a gentleman from Nebraska in the lobby who professes to be the husband-to-be of one of the dead women. But the first information that we got was that she was on the bus with her fiancé. No one has come forward to identify the fellow with her. Both were very tan, so I assumed they had been at the shore for some time."

"They got on the bus in Ocean Beach. They were definitely together on the beach. She didn't act like she had another boyfriend. Debbie, did you keep her pocketbook after we found her cell phone?" Mike quickly added to the conversation.

"I had it with me when I came in...Check my room...It's bright red with a sailboat on the side."

Mike was secretly pleased that he could remember some of the people sitting on the beach at the ocean. So much of the past months were a blur to him, but today, his training and skills thankfully returned to him. There had been flashbacks of his tour of duty in Vietnam, and his work at Cook County had been coming back to him, one memory at a time. He thought of Thom Rossi and their experiences in the war. He also thought of Dr. Ed Casey, his medical colleague that he could not help. There were still some blank spots—incidents in medical school, family events, and especially the last few months, but the memories were returning. What had happened when that bus overturned? His reverie was interrupted, as he was brought back to reality by the sound of Ben's voice.

"The young couple sat in front of me, and I could hear them talking. I think they were engaged. They were making plans to return to Ocean Beach. I think the fellow's family has a business there, but I also heard talk of business in Boston and living here. Boy, I feel like a real eavesdropper, but the bus had quieted down after dark and the entertainment (he looked over and saw Sami asleep in the big chair) was bedded down for the evening, so I could hear some of their conversation. I don't know if I would mention her traveling companion to this fiancé from Nebraska."

The state policemen left to confront Jay Coleman. Perhaps he could make a positive identification of one of the deceased. The troopers also decided to call city hall at Ocean Beach to try to get an identification of the young man who had been killed. They had notified Sergeant Sterling's family that he had been in a bus accident in Maryland when the accident occurred. They had also made the call that reunited Dr. and Mrs. Pierce with their daughter, Deborah. In both cases, they realized there was some disconnect in the two families. And the three men in the waiting room had not contacted anyone. They had called no family, no friends, or no coworkers. Yet the three of them...No... He had to include the girl, too...the four of them seemed to have formed a bond that united them. Was it survivors' guilt?

It was Debbie who broke the silence. "We're leaving to go back to Centerville as soon as I'm discharged. Dad has convinced me that he would be a good rehab facilitator. When I feel I can, I'll be going on to school in California. I feel I've known you guys for ages, and I hate to say good-bye." Debbie confessed her plans and her feelings to the group.

Dr. Pierce just stared in amazement at his daughter. She was so confident and determined to live life on her own terms. It was difficult for him to think of his daughter crawling around in a stinking, wrecked bus with a serious injury to her leg. He was so proud of the eighteen-year-old who sat in the wheel chair with a bandaged leg.

"I left Chicago rather abruptly, and I've got to return and try to explain. I have a large group of people who deserve an explanation for my behavior, if I can explain PTSD and get some counseling. I'm not sure I still have a job at Cook County." Mike lowered his head, ashamed of his actions, but glad to unburden himself.

"Young man, if you need a reference or an explanation of your actions, please call me." Dr. Pierce stepped forward and put his hand on Debbie's shoulder. "I will gladly explain to your superiors your heroics in getting all living wounded of the bus and subsequent medical treatment. And this isn't your only amazing feat; we cannot explain the positive change in our little girl. We are so grateful for your medical treatment of Debbie and your influence on her."

Mike slowly rose to his feet, walked over to Dr. Pierce and shook his hand. "Thank you, Sir, for that praise, but much of the thanks should go to Debbie. We were quite a pair: Debbie had two good hands and one good leg, and I had two good legs and one good hand! And as for medical treatment, our blouse bandage certainly will not be included in the newest copy of the medical journal." He took his one good hand and ruffled her hair as she sat in the chair, listening to the praise.

"And…if for some reason your superiors do not reinstate you, come to Centerville. There's always an opening for a good emergency man."

John Webster slowly rose to his feet, balancing on his crutches. His foot was throbbing, as he inched his way to the group.

"No one gained as much as I did, thanks to Dr. Mike and Debbie. You got Sami off the bus and assured her that everything would be OK and not to be scared. Your care and expertise saved most of my foot. As I lay trapped on the bus, I watched the two of you work together. You ignored dangers and crawled through rubble and diesel fuel to get everyone of the bus, without causing any further damage. You didn't consider the harm that you could do to your own wounds. When I got on this bus, I was running from a cross roads in my life. After watching you two, I've decided to make some phone calls. Sami and I are going home to New Orleans and decide where we are now going to live. We've been stagnant since her mother died, and it's time we get on with our lives. Sami will be going to school in the fall and we need to establish a permanent home."

Just as he finished his statement, a volunteer appeared with a highly emotional couple, searching for Dr. Butler. But the doctor wasn't in this group of people.

"Maybe you would like to meet these people," the volunteer said. "They were on the bus with your son. This is Mr. and Mrs. Sterling."

Mike immediately stepped forward and grabbed Mr. Sterling's hand. "I'm Dr. Elliott. I…No…We were on the bus with Sergeant Sterling and this is…"

Before he could introduce the band of wounded travelers, Mrs. Sterling rushed up and threw her arms around him. "The nurses here told me that you saved our son's life…Where is that nurse that helped you?"

The group laughed as Mike pointed Debbie, a teenager sitting with her a bandaged leg propped up in her wheel chair. She blushed at all the attention that was directed to her.

"Dr. Butler told us that Sergeant Sterling was pretty banged up, but he would make a complete recovery. Have you seen him yet?"

"We went to his room, but the nurse with him said he was resting. She told us how you pulled everyone from the wrecked bus. We still don't understand what happened. Several months ago, James completed his shift, and seemed to vanish. Neither his police colleagues or any of our family knew where he was…and then we got a phone call from Cumberland, Maryland, that he is here, in the hospital, having been in a bus accident. The nurse told us that his condition has been upgraded to satisfactory. We are so grateful to those who got him off the bus."

"Ma'am, this is the Dynamic Duo," Ben grinned as he stepped up to greet them. "This is Dr. Mike Elliott and his trusty second in command, Miss Debbie! Please excuse me; I've got to sit down. My head is beginning to spin."

Mike quickly stepped forward to help Ben back to his wheelchair.

But Mrs. Sterling was so thankful that she threw her arms around Mike again and gave him a hug as tears streamed down her face. She then moved over to the wheelchair and bent down, giving Debbie a kiss on her cheek.

Mike added, "We also have to give credit to these two wounded gentlemen who kept him warn and immobile to avoid further injury."

"We just buried our younger son after his car veered off the road and hit a telephone pole. No one knows any details of the accident. Why was he speeding? Where he was going? Why did the car leave the road? And when we heard that Jimmy had been in an accident…" She couldn't continue as she was overcome with tears. Ellen Pierce put her arms around Mrs. Sterling and guided her to a seat. But before she would sit down, Mrs. Sterling had to also hug Ben and John.

Ben's mind had cleared somewhat and he continued to try to lighten the mood. "We thought your son was running from the law. He had a gun. Instead, he *is* the law! Glad to hear that he is going to be OK."

"There is a young man in the waiting room with us who was very upset. He thinks his fiancée was on the bus. The police tried to calm him down, but he is very demanding. Mr. Coleman insisted that he be taken to the morgue. He says one of the deceased is his fiancée;

his address was in her wallet. He said she was returning home from a vacation and they were to be married. The staff tried to explain to him that they had been so busy that, after an examination, the deceased were covered and put in a cold room. I'm sure they wanted to clean up the bodies before they let people see them. You know, give them some dignity." Mr. Sterling added.

"She certainly seemed to really like the fellow she was sitting next on the bus," Debbie said. "I thought they were engaged or newlyweds. They definitely were together. I saw them on the beach in Ocean View. I'm glad I don't have to be with him. Her purse and cell phone are in my room unless the police took them. We used her phone to call for help!"

Mr. Sterling was the first to notice that the sun had come up. It had been less than twenty-four hours since five-thirty bus had left Ocean View, but so much had happened since that time.

"Let's go up to the cafeteria and get some breakfast," Dr. Pierce suggested to the group.

"Good idea," John answered as he gently nudged his daughter who was asleep in her chair. "This little girl needs to get some breakfast and we probably should get on our way, if I am discharged."

The group quietly moved up to the cafeteria, pushing wheelchairs and struggling on crutches, and one by one, they filled their trays. Dr. Pierce insisted on paying for the breakfast, and since the men did not have their wallets returned to them, they welcomed the kind gesture. After a brief period, he spoke to the travelers.

"I know Deborah's plans. She has agreed to come home with us and then, when sufficiently healed, we will take her to California to begin her college life in Stanford. How about the rest of you? What are your immediate plans?"

"I think you know my plans. I have to return to Chicago and Cook County General. If I still have a job, I plan to try to redeem myself with my colleagues. But I also know that I need some counseling. I can't explain what happened to me in the emergency room several months ago, but I don't want it to happen again. It took an accident to jolt my memory and return my medical skills. I got my life back; now I need to get it in order! I also need to recall the last several months; they are returning to me in small flashes. And…I must call an old friend, Thom Rossi!"

"My offer of a job still stands. If Cook County is so shortsighted that they dismiss one of the best emergency men that I've seen, our hospital in Centerville wants you! I have learned, from eyewitnesses (and he smiled as he looked around the room), the way you handled yourself and the injured. You have my full recommendation!"

"How about you, John? Are you and your daughter doing back to New York? Stevens, Stevens, and Associates have called the hospital several times inquiring about your condition. Is that your law firm? Very prestigious! Excellent reputation!"

"I'm not sure who notified them that we were here, but Samantha and I are going to New Orleans to visit our aunt Hattie. I've decided to resign from Stevens & Stevens and either join a smaller firm or open my own office. This episode on the five-thirty bus to Clarksville reminded us that we want a slower pace of life! We'll be leaving as soon as the doctor says this foot is ready for travel. I'm going to submit my resignation, and we'll get on our way. I can't say that a bus accident was a good thing, but it certainly made me think about what is important for my daughter and me." His foot was throbbing, so he spoke from his chair.

Mr. Sterling quietly rose to his feet. "We are calling our lawyer and explaining Jimmy's condition. He was scheduled to testify in an accident where two other troopers were murdered. That trial must be postponed until our son is well enough to attend. There have been suggestions that our deceased son, Martin, was involved in those murders and it probably cost him his life. Pending when he will be discharged, we'll be spending time here in Cumberland. When he is better and discharged, Mrs. Sterling and I will drive him home. We lost one son in a questionable auto accident and we're so thankful for Dr. Mike and all of our new friends for saving Jim's life."

Mike walked over to the Sterlings and wrapped his arms around the two of them as Debbie rolled her wheelchair to their table. "We all have a lot to be thankful for. I only wish we could have saved the others."

"I guess it's my turn," Ben said, as he wheeled his chair away from the table. "I've made a mess of my life. I never cared about friendships or the feelings of others. Life was like a big game to me; I have wronged a lot of people. My first obligation is to find an old friend and see if I screwed up her life…And then, John, I might need your legal services for some other messes I've created. I'll be in this chair for several weeks, and it might take that long for my head to clear. Progress in 'righting my wrongs' will be slow, but it must be done! I was the one of the last survivors pulled from the fated bus to Clarksville, and lying there in the diesel fuel, horrific smells, and smoke, I thought I was going to die! The couple or lovebirds who sat behind me and the older folks didn't make it! It's time I do something right with my life."

"I hope John might represent all of you in a class lawsuit against the bus company. I know I want him to represent Deborah, both against the bus company and our doctor friend. And someone must step up for the two deceased couples and the young man who was killed. John, do you handle this type of litigation?"

John Webster smiled as he continued to eat his breakfast and encourage his daughter to also eat. He felt he would be seeing a great deal of this group of people in the future.

Debbie, who had been sitting quietly in her wheelchair finally spoke to her fellow travelers. "I feel I've known you people all my life. We shared something terrible and WE SURVIVED!"

And then Debbie, the innocent teenager, reappeared. "I'm so sorry for the people who we couldn't help. But I'd like to think the couples would have been glad they were together—and the girl's cell phone helped to save us. The entire time we were trying to get people off the bus, not one car passed the accident site. The cell phone was a lifeline."

"I want everyone's address so I can write to you and see how everyone is recovering. I'll give you my home address in Centerville, and later I'll send you my address at Stanford."

Her teenage wishes echoed throughout the group including the Sterlings. Although she had risked her own life to save others, Debbie was now a typical teenager, organizing a group of pen pals.

A quiet aura fell over the entire group. The long ordeal was over! Fate placed these six people, who were each facing a crisis in his personal life, on the *5:30 Bus To Clarksville*. What had happened to this band of travelers, who by chance, had innocently boarded the bus that day and survived a fateful accident? What had caused Dr. Elliott to regain his memory and his medical skills to be able to save others? How had an eighteen-year-old girl shelved a severe wound and aided others who were injured? What had given her the strength to pull grown men through rubble and get them safely off the bus? Why had two influential men deferred treatment to care for a severely wounded man and free the rescuers to look for other passengers? Why did a young college graduate perish in the crash, yet supple the phone to save the others? Why had a state trooper survived a horrific accident when his brother was killed? Had the travelers cheated on death and been given a chance to redeem themselves? Decisions had been made that had evaded this group of people for many months—decisions that would affect the rest of their lives. Only the paths that they have chosen would determine the answer!

ABOUT THE AUTHOR

Growing up in Crisfield, Maryland, a small fishing town on the Chesapeake Bay, was idyllic for Polly Ward McVicker. Her father was a waterman, harvesting crabs, clams, oysters and fish in season, and she would join him on the boat whenever possible. Graduating Crisfield High School in 1957, she considers herself fortunate to have had teachers and mentors who inspired the class to "reach for the stars." The author continued her education at Washington College, Maryland, graduating in 1961, and then began a teaching career which spanned over 30 years. Much of this career was spent in Carroll County, Maryland.

After retiring, she had time to go on many adventures. Some of those adventures included a hunting safari in Africa, swimming on the Great Barrier Reef, walking on the Great Wall of China, fishing in Alaska, and touring 48 out of the 50 states in the United States. She finally had time to pursue her dream and write a novel "5:30 Bus to Clarksville."

Married for 45 years, the McVickers reside in Cumberland, Maryland, while escaping to the beach at Ocean City, Maryland for the summer. She continues to enjoy travel and activities with friends.